Photo by Jude Dillon

About the Author

Brian Brennan is an award-winning Alberta author who specializes in books about the people and the social history of Western Canada. His recent titles include *Boondoggles, Bonanzas, and Other Alberta Stories* (Fifth House, 2003) and *Scoundrels and Scallywags: Characters from Alberta's Past* (Fifth House, 2002), which was a finalist for the 2003 Grant MacEwan Author's Award, one of the richest literary prizes in Canada. He is also the author of *Máire Bhuí Ní Laoire: A Poet of her People* (The Collins Press), which was nominated for the Irish Times Literature Prize in 2001. He is the first winner of the Dave Greber Freelance Writers Award, presented in 2004, and is featured regularly as a guest on CBC Radio's *Daybreak Alberta*.

website: www.brian-brennan.com

Cover and interior design by Cheryl Peddie/Emerge Creative

Cover illustrations courtesy (clockwise from top left) Whyte Museum of the Canadian Rockies V439/PS-6; Glenbow Archives NA-4348-3; Jupiter Images; Whyte Museum of the Canadian Rockies V439/LC accession 2769; Whyte Museum of the Canadian Rockies NA66-1673

Copyedited by Terry McIntyre

Proofread by Geri Rowlatt

Scans by St. Solo Computer Graphics

The publisher gratefully acknowledges the support of The Canada Council for the Arts and the Department of Canadian Heritage.

Canada Council   Conseil des Arts
for the Arts   du Canada

We acknowledge the financial support of the Government of Canada through the Book Publishing Industry Development Program for our publishing activities.

The author gratefully acknowledges the support of the Alberta Foundation for the Arts.

Printed in Canada by Friesens

05 06 07 08 09/ 5 4 3 2 1

First published in the United States in 2005 by
Fitzhenry & Whiteside
121 Harvard Avenue, Suite 2
Allston, MA 02134

Library and Archives Canada Cataloguing in Publication

Brennan, Brian, 1943-

    Romancing the Rockies : mountaineers, missionaries, Marilyn, and more / Brian Brennan.

Includes bibliographical references and index.

ISBN 1-894856-40-6

    1. Rocky Mountains, Canadian (B.C. and Alta.)—Biography—Anecdotes. 2. Rocky Mountains, Canadian (B.C. and Alta.)—History—Anecdotes. I. Title.

FC219.B73 2005   971.1'009'9   C2004-906449-5

Fifth House Ltd.
A Fitzhenry & Whiteside Company
1511, 1800-4 St. SW
Calgary, Alberta T2S 2S5
1-800-387-9776
www.fitzhenry.ca

Romancing the Rockies:
MOUNTAINEERS, MISSIONARIES, MARILYN, AND MORE

BRIAN BRENNAN

DEDICATED TO THE MEMORY OF MARY GILCHRIST
AND GORDON LEGGE

Contents

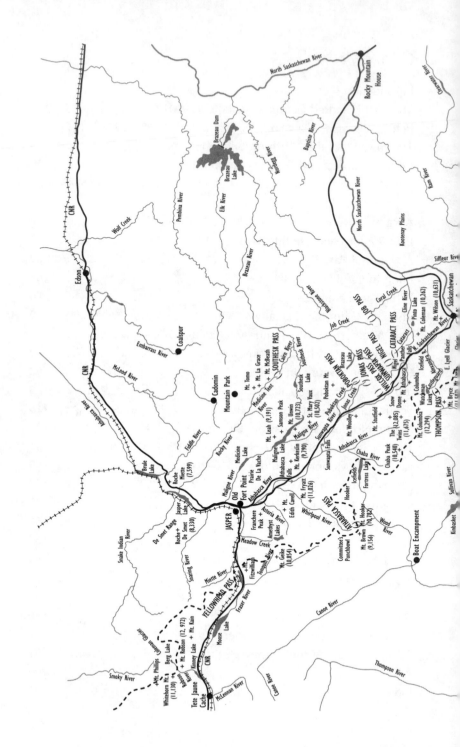

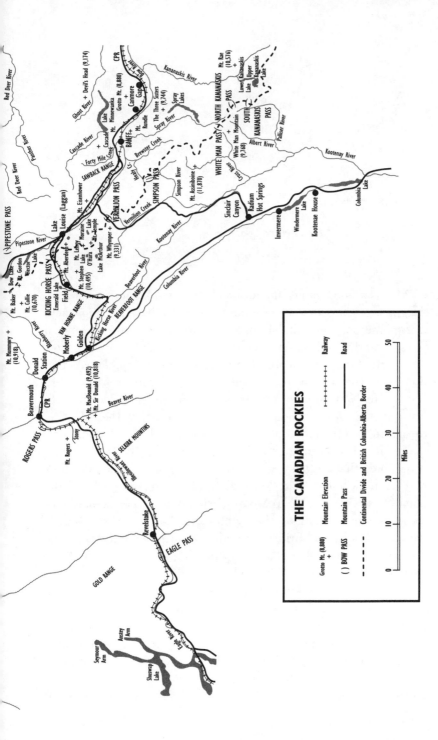

THE CANADIAN ROCKIES

Grotto Mt. (8,880) +   Mountain Elevation   +-+-+-+-+ Railway
( ) BOW PASS   Mountain Pass   ———————— Road
                        – – – – Continental Divide and British Columbia-Alberta Border

Miles
0   10   20   30   40   50

Introduction

This is a book about human journeys, a book about what happens when people meet mountains. Some have been journeys of exploration, some of pilgrimage, some of adventure, some of physical endeavour, some of cultural achievement. All were journeys to the Rocky Mountains, those magnificent sentinel peaks that dominate the North American landscape from northwestern Canada to New Mexico and draw humans to them like bees to honeysuckles. All were journeys by people drawn by the romance, the allure, and the mystique of these ancient and fabled mountains.

The first European tourists likened the Rockies to the Alps, and proclaimed that certain peaks were as impressive as the ones they had left back home. "The Matterhorn of North America" was the name these visitors gave to Mount Assiniboine, a spectacular limestone pyramid straddling the Continental Divide on the border between Alberta and British Columbia. But this comparison, while doubtless intended as a compliment, served to diminish Assiniboine because—as a climbing challenge, for example—it stood aloof and unconquered for more than thirty-five years after the Matterhorn had been scaled by Edward Whymper's British party in 1865. And even after a British clergyman named James Outram had reached the top of Assiniboine in 1901, it remained remote and inaccessible to all but the most determined climbers. The Matterhorn, on the other hand, became a popular three-day ascent for accomplished weekend alpinists who brought ropes and crampons with them and were also prudent enough to make their climbs accompanied by experienced alpine guides.

Climbing is just one type of journey covered in this book of Rocky Mountain odysseys. It came relatively late in the day as a mountain pastime, not becoming a significant part of Rocky Mountain life until the railway penetrated the wilderness in the 1880s and Victorian dreamers and adventurers—who included hunters, scientists, skiers, writers, photographers, and painters as well as climbers—flocked to this mountain playground to tarry awhile and leave their markings upon the rocks. For more than a century before that, journeys to the Rockies were mainly about business—fur trading, gold seeking, mapmaking, Christianizing, scientific exploring, policing, treaty making, railway building, and land settling.

My goal when I started writing this book was to trace the footprints of humans in the Rockies from the silent tread of the earliest travellers to the noisy tramp of the contemporary day-trippers. But, like all books about the human history of North America, the story had to start toward the end, with the arrival of the European fur traders in the 1750s, because the only knowledge we have of the people who lived in this region for perhaps eleven thousand years beforehand comes from the discoveries of archeologists and the legends of Native peoples. I have included a few references to legends drawn from Stoney oral tradition, but mostly this is a book derived from written records, beginning with the eighteenth-century journals of the fur traders and explorers.

This book, then, is fundamentally a historical miscellany, dealing with many of the different types of individuals who have visited or settled in the Rockies during the past 250 years. The goal of the fur traders, the original white and Métis explorers, was to push the trade westward across the continent to the Pacific, and what a great adventure it was for them. Because their stories are well covered in other books, it suffices here just to briefly acknowledge the achievements of Alexander Mackenzie, David Thompson, and Simon Fraser, three of the great explorers in Canadian history, who took on the challenge of finding a way across the mountains when it became obvious that the geography of Canada changed dramatically once you left the Plains behind.

Mackenzie wrote his name into the history books when he achieved the first known crossing by a white man of the Continental Divide. Thompson opened up navigable water routes to the Pacific with his discovery of two mountain passes, the Howse and the Athabasca, that functioned as gateways for the fur trade for more than fifty years. Fraser established the first permanent white settlement west of the Canadian Rockies at what is now McLeod Lake, British Columbia, and also established other important white footholds on the western side of the Continental Divide.

Once the trade routes were established, it became possible for pioneering missionaries such as Robert Rundle and George McDougall to pursue their goal of converting the first peoples to Christianity, and for nineteenth-century botanists such as David Douglas and John Macoun and painters such as Paul Kane and Henry James Warre to travel to wilderness regions previously inaccessible. Then came the Palliser expeditioners, assigned to investigate the agricultural potential of the Canadian Northwest. They were followed by the North West Mounted Police and then the treaty makers, who paved the way for future white settlement.

The builders of the Canadian Pacific Railway made it possible for settlement to occur on a grand scale. The empty spaces quickly filled up with homesteaders, land speculators, entrepreneurs, shopkeepers, and tourists. The tourists eventually came to be viewed as a necessary evil by the year-round residents who—if they had not relied on tourism for their daily bread—would have preferred to keep the place to themselves. Jimmy Simpson, a Banff guide and outfitter, compared the tourists to Columbus: "When they leave home, they don't know where they're going; when they get there, they don't know where they are; and when they get back home, they don't know where they've been." Banff author Jon Whyte could sympathize with Simpson's comments: "How would you react if your turf was invaded every year by so many people you had difficulty locating a crony on the street?"

The stories of Simpson and Whyte are included in this book. So are the stories of such one-time Rocky Mountain residents as Byron Harmon, the first professional photographer to make his home in the Rockies; Carl Rungius, the first significant artist to live and paint in the Rockies; Chief Robert Smallboy, who led his

Cree band into the Rocky Mountain wilderness to find peace and harmony; Norman Sanson, the weatherman for all seasons who climbed Sulphur Mountain a thousand times over a thirty-six-year period to check meteorological data; and Jim and Bill Brewster, the enterprising brothers who built a small livery service into the largest privately owned sightseeing company in the world. And, of course, there are the tourists—the climbers, trail riders, hunters, and movie stars—whose dollars made it possible for the residents to be residents. Marilyn Monroe was one such tourist. Fifty years after the fact, people are still talking about the time she came to the Rockies to make a movie called *River of No Return*. You'll be hard-pressed to find the movie in your local Blockbuster store, and you likely won't see it playing very often on the movie channel, but you will find people in Jasper and Banff who can tell you all about this film and its doomed, beautiful star.

This book has been an interesting project for me because I don't climb, scramble, ski, canoe, or spend any more time in the outdoors than it takes for me to carry home a chai tea latte from Central Blends. But I do have a passion for storytelling and the mountains are full of stories. Some are found in the writings of Jon Whyte, some in the songs of Wilf Carter, and some in the wildlife paintings of Carl Rungius. All demand to be told. The hot chocolate may run out and the sleeping bag may beckon but we must remain by the fire till the tale is told and we reach the harbour at world's end.

My journey to the Rockies has been more spiritual than physical, so I thank all the explorers, adventurers, artists, and climbers who blazed the trails to make my storytelling possible. Aside from the writers acknowledged at the end of this volume, I want to thank author Dave Birrell, whose constantly updated PeakFinder Web site (www.peakfinder.com) is by far the best on-line source of information on the Canadian Rockies. Whenever I needed to check the height of a particular mountain or discover who named it, I turned to PeakFinder and found the answer. I'm also grateful, as always, to the history librarians and archivists at the Whyte Museum of the Canadian Rockies, Glenbow Museum, Calgary Public Library, and University of Calgary, who all help to make possible this work of mine. I also want to thank my friend and fellow scribe Bob Bott, an outdoors enthusiast and scramble climber who actually goes up the mountains that I just write about, and who acted as my safety net (or perhaps my virtual rope partner) on this project, gently correcting my errors of fact and suggesting pertinent data that I might include. And, finally, I would like to thank both the Alberta Foundation for the Arts and the Alberta Historical Resources Foundation, which came to my doorstep at the eleventh hour with welcome funding for my research.

Brian Brennan
December 2004

The First Hundred Centuries— 9000 BC-AD 1759

STONEY LEGENDS AND THE WESTERN EXPLORATIONS OF ANTHONY HENDAY

You hike uphill for three hours on a summer afternoon, step from shadowed greenery into sunlight, and then see it heave into view—two shimmering mountain waterfalls of ageless beauty. Here stands mighty Twin Falls, high in British Columbia's rugged Yoho National Park, far away from cellphones and traffic noise, in a mountain range where the air feels not just clean but bright, like the backdrop for a toothpaste commercial.

Meltwaters from *Glacier des Poilus* crash over a lip of limestone, divide into two volatile streams, and cascade down to the rocks eighty metres below. The twin streams sing and shout as they gambol, jitterbug, and then join forces as one, whirling past a grove of old firs blasted by lightning and avalanches. At the end of their downhill journey the waters slow and sink into the meandering Yoho River. Five miles meandering with a mazy motion, the poet said. You stand at the base of these silver waterfalls, beyond the reach of their spray but not of their roar that, paradoxically, has a soothing, steadying effect on city-battered nerves. You watch them for an hour, and then you know why people have been drawn to this place, to this landscape of stony heights and others like it in the Rockies, for dozens and perhaps hundreds of centuries.

We know virtually nothing about the prehistoric people who

*Author Brian
Brennan at the foot
of Twin Falls in July
1989: "You know
why people have
been drawn to this
place."* (Tom Walker)

first travelled past
these stunning
waterfalls, by these
lofty crags, across
the bumpiest ver-
tebrae of our conti-
nent's backbone.
Were they tracking
wild animals?
Archeologists have
uncovered rem-
nants of ancient
subterranean pit
houses in the
Vermilion Lakes
area west of Banff
and speculate that
nomadic hunters
and food gatherers from the western side of the Continental Divide
used them as temporary dwellings while venturing to and from big
game hunts on the Plains. Early twenty-first-century discoveries of
ancient bison skulls near Banff suggest that some of these hunts
could also have occurred in the mountain valleys of the Rockies.
Radiocarbon-dated readings of their hunting tools (they used
stone-tipped spears before the advent of the bow) suggest they
entered the Rockies toward the end of the last glacial epoch, at
least six thousand years before the Egyptians left their records in
tombs and pyramids. The Canadian novelist Rudy Wiebe has written in an elegant afterword to Robert Kroetsch's travel book
Alberta that when these wanderers gathered around their fires
eating giant bison and bighorn sheep they surely must have been

impressed by the "magnificence of these mountains, these rounded opening valleys, these rivers hidden in the trees, these brilliant lakes shifting colour at every brush of wind. It is a land to make any human heart sing."

You wish there were more than just the archeological evidence of their existence. These prehistoric pioneers spoke languages long forgotten, never written. Who were they and where did they come from? Scientific arguments abound. One theory suggests they came perhaps twenty-five thousand years ago from Asia, across the land bridge of the Bering Strait (which later disappeared under water) to Alaska. Then they moved southward, seeking warmth and food, in a trek lasting thousands of years that took them across the great land mass of the Americas. Another theory suggests they came to North America by boat, via the Pacific Ocean. A third theory, propounded by North American Natives, argues that the first peoples of this continent were here from the very beginning. As George Bowering has written in *Stone Country*, his witty and ironic history of Canada, "if some Darwinian accident could make humans in Africa, why couldn't a similar thing happen in North America?" (An American Native chief named Little Turtle came to a similar conclusion in 1798 when he met five Tartars in Philadelphia and noticed that he shared certain physiognomic characteristics with them. "Isn't it possible that the Tartars, who resemble us so closely, came from here?" he asked. "Why shouldn't we have been born of this soil?")

The details of the Native history are shrouded in mist and speculation, in myth and fable. We have no contemporaneous written records, but we do have the lore and the legends—like the legends of ancient Ireland and the legends of ancient Greece—passed down through the Native families that became the keepers of the stories. Some of these stories are included in the book *These Mountains Are Our Sacred Places*, published in 1977 by a Stoney (Nakoda Sioux) chief named John Snow. Drawing on Native oral tradition affirming that his ancestors "have always lived here," Snow writes that the Rocky Mountains are "our temples, our sanctuaries, and our resting places. They are a place of hope, a place of vision, a place of refuge, a very special place where the Great Spirit speaks with us. Therefore, these mountains are our sacred places."

3

Chief Snow writes that the Great Spirit, the Creator, spoke to the Stoney (so named because they used hot stones to cook their meat) through their prophets and teachers. The most celebrated of these was a medicine man named Iktûmnî whose name is still invoked whenever medicine bundles are opened and healing herbs dispensed. "He communicated and talked with the spirits of the mountains, who revealed ancient truth, philosophies and prophecies to him. In turn, he taught these things to the Stoney people."

Inspired by Iktûmnî, successive generations of Stoney ascended the mountains and prayed that their hunt would always be bountiful. "In our long history there was never a story of a Stoney atheist, and none of the animals hunted ever became extinct," Snow writes. The recognition of the Great Spirit in all of life was essential for his people's survival. They shared and lived as one big family with "human kindness imprinted in our hearts" until the first white explorers, missionaries, and settlers arrived with their trade goods, bibles, firewater, and land aspirations.

Who was the first white visitor to see and write about the Rockies? Reports vary. Some historians say it was an English-born Hudson's Bay Company net-mender named Anthony Henday who came to what is now Alberta in the fall of 1754, "stood silent upon a peak" near present-day Innisfail, looked toward the west, and wrote in his journal that he had seen what the local Natives called the "shining mountains." Others say it was Jacques Legardeur de Saint-Pierre, a Montreal-born military officer and explorer whose men supposedly reached the Rockies in May 1751 while looking for a mythical "western sea" that would provide the French fur trade with a navigable northern water route to the Orient.

The Saint-Pierre claim is based on a report that he sent to his boss, the Marquis de Vaudreuil, governor general of New France, in October 1753, after he had spent three years supervising the construction of trading posts west of Lake Winnipeg. In the report, Saint-Pierre said he ordered his men to establish a post "three hundred leagues" (1,250 kilometres) west of an existing fort at today's The Pas, Manitoba, and that they travelled up the Paskoya (Saskatchewan) River as far as the "Rock Mountain" (*la Montagne de Roche*) where "they built a good fort, which I named Fort La Jonquière." However, there is no evidence to suggest that his men actually travelled three hundred leagues to build the fort. Most contemporary scholars, including Antoine Champagne, Donald Chaput, and Marcel Trudel, have pinpointed the fort's location near today's Nipawin, Saskatchewan, which is 250 kilometres northeast of Saskatoon and much too far away from the Rockies to be within sighting distance. The "Rock Mountain," say these scholars, could have referred to a height of land along the Saskatchewan River that local Natives used as a lookout.

Englishman Henday travelled farther west than the French explorers. He came with a directive from his boss, James Isham, the chief factor at Fort York (York Factory), the Bay's tidewater headquarters on the Hayes River in what is now northeast Manitoba, to try and convince the Native trappers of the Plains to bring their goods all the way to the company posts on the shores of Hudson Bay—rather than give their business to the French traders working in the hinterland. "If a proper person were sent a great way up onto the country with presents to the Indians, it may be a way of drawing down many of the Natives to trade," Isham said.

If Isham had known of Henday's background, it's doubtful he would have considered him a "proper person" to undertake the expedition. Born in the Isle of Wight, Henday had worked as a fisherman and been outlawed for rum smuggling before joining the Honourable Company of Adventurers of England Trading into Hudson's Bay (to give the Bay its full title) as a net-mender and labourer. However, the Bay officials were unaware of his smuggling history when they hired Henday, and they seem to have regarded him as a responsible employee. They described him as "a bold and good servant."

Henday journeyed for a year, first hunched in a canoe with a group of eleven Cree heading toward their ancestral hunting grounds, and then slogging on foot across rolling parkland, after which he recorded the details of his odyssey in a journal that has, unfortunately, not survived. There are four texts in the Bay's Winnipeg archives that were transcribed from the original Henday journal, but these are considered unreliable because they contain serious inaccuracies and contradictions. A Bay employee named Andrew Graham transcribed them between 1755 and 1782 and, for reasons best known to himself, made each text different from the other three! The differences range from alternative spellings to varying word choices and contradictory statements on distances travelled and locations reached.

In two versions of the journal, Henday is reported as saying that on 24 December 1754 he climbed to the top of a hill somewhere near today's Innisfail, seventy kilometres southeast of the future trading post of Rocky Mountain House, and had a good view of "Arsinie Watchie" off in the far distance. One Canadian historian, Arthur Morton, has interpreted this to mean that Henday saw the Rocky Mountains and identified them by their Cree name. A second historian, James MacGregor, asserts that Henday thus became the first white man to see the mountains: "His cup was full. His throat was full, and his eyes too." However, Henday's journal is curiously silent on his reaction to such a dramatic sighting. He even raises doubt about the possibility of the sighting when, in another part of his journal, he translates Arsinie Watchie as "Dry Country." His copyist, Andrew Graham, also raises doubt about such a sighting when he says, in a memoir that he composed while transcribing the Henday journal, that no mountains were ever discovered by Bay employees "who have travelled far inland to the distance of 1,200 miles WSW from York Fort."

So did Henday actually see the Rockies? The simple answer is that nobody knows for sure. Many historians have attempted to chart his trip from the information contained in the different versions of his journal, and several maps have been drawn of the areas he may have traversed, but all involve considerable guesswork. Scholar Barbara Belyea, who has edited and published the four texts of the Henday journal in a book entitled *A Year Inland: The Journal of a Hudson's Bay Winterer*, concludes that any historical and anthropological studies that use the journal as factual evidence "have built on a dubious and elusive foundation." While one cannot entirely rule out the possibility that Henday saw the Rockies, Belyea says, "it is just as likely that 'Arsinie Watchie' referred to stony hills of quite different proportions. For Bay men used to the flat shores of Hudson Bay, any height of land was impressive."

Besides, like every other explorer of his day, Henday hoped to discover a western ocean, not a huge rock barrier. This could account for the fact that in another part of his journal he wrote that the water tasted "very salt, smells like brine." Historian Glyndwr Williams has argued convincingly that Henday, who received a £20 bonus from the Bay for his exploration efforts, tried to present his achievements in a "dishonestly optimistic light."

Henday made a second trip west in 1759, but again was unsuccessful in his efforts to persuade the Native trappers of the Plains to bring their goods to Fort York. He resigned from the Hudson's Bay Company in 1762 because he had not received the recognition and rewards he felt his journeys had earned him. In 1954, two hundred years after Henday first arrived in Alberta, a 2,682-metre peak in Jasper National Park was named in his memory.

With Henday's 1754 Rocky Mountain sighting thus in doubt, we have to jump forward thirty-three years to 1787 for a more reliable sighting. That's when a seventeen-year-old Welsh-born Bay clerk named David Thompson travelled west with a party of five traders on a mission similar to that of Henday. They carried orders to make friendly contact with the Natives of the Plains, learn their languages, and persuade them to bring their furs to the HBC trading posts. Crossing into what is now Alberta they journeyed south and then westward by canoe along the Bow River toward the Rockies.

When he approached the Rockies, Thompson became the first known chronicler to refer to them by name in his journal. Sitting at his campfire, balancing his leather-covered journal on his knees, and using a quill pen that had to be dipped into an inkwell for every other word, he wrote: "At length the Rocky Mountains came in sight like shining white clouds in the horizon. As we proceeded they rose in height, their immense masses of snow appeared above the clouds and formed an impassible barrier, even to the eagle."

Peter Fidler: Canada's Forgotten Explorer—1769-1822

THE FIRST WHITE VISITOR TO THE ROCKIES

The maps of the Pacific Northwest in the late 1700s contained many blank spaces and invisible question marks. Where was the fabled Northwest Passage that would link the Atlantic to the Pacific through the Canadian Arctic by sea? The explorations of Sir Francis Drake, Captain James Cook, and other mariners had failed to uncover any sign. How about a transcontinental inland water route running from east to west? No sign of that either. But the fur traders who had made their way by canoe from the shores of Hudson Bay to the foot of the Rocky Mountains remained convinced—based on what they had learned from the Natives along the way—that a "Great River of the West" existed that would take them from the mountains to the Pacific. If such a river could be found, the fur men said, it would not only provide them with a transcontinental passage and a western port, but also open up a lucrative trade route to China and Russia.

In the summer of 1790, a twenty-year-old Hudson's Bay Company (HBC) journal writer named Peter Fidler was given a rare opportunity to chronicle the search for a Northwest Passage, though he did not appreciate the wider implications of the expedition at the time. Born in Derbyshire, England, and trained as an astronomer and mapmaker with renowned HBC surveyor Philip Turnor, Fidler got his chance to join the expedition to the fur-rich Lake Athabasca region when another Turnor student, David

Thompson, fractured his leg in a dogsled accident and then lost the sight in his right eye because of an infection. The real purpose of the Turnor expedition was to survey the extent of the North West Company's (NWC's) hold on the fur trade of the Athabasca country, and to determine if, in fact, there was a great river linking east to west. However, Fidler seems to have been under the impression that the sole motive for the expedition was to correct some mapping errors by NWC explorer Peter Pond, who had long harboured a dream of discovering a Northwest Passage and had grossly underestimated the distance from Lake Athabasca to the Pacific, placing the lake some one thousand kilometres west of its true position. Turnor's more accurate astronomical observations did place Lake Athabasca closer to Hudson Bay, but his search for the fabled "Great River of the West" proved unsuccessful.

While the 1790 Athabasca expedition was a disappointment for Turnor and the HBC, it did give Fidler an opportunity to improve his surveying and mapmaking skills to such an extent that Turnor was moved to describe him as "a likely person to succeed me." The trip also gave Fidler a chance to learn Native language and customs. A sojourn with the Chipewyans of the Athabasca country resulted in an invitation to spend the winter of 1791–92 with them in the area of Great Slave Lake. After a further stay with the Chipewyans in the spring of 1792, Fidler reported proudly that he had acquired "a sufficiency of their language to transact any business with them."

In the winter of 1792–93, Fidler wrote his name into the annals of the Rockies by becoming the first known European to enter the mountains, name one of the peaks, and scale another peak. He came on a trading and surveying trip to what is now southern Alberta in November 1792, and when he saw the Rocky Mountains for the first time, he wrote in his journal that they were "awfully grand—very much similar to dark rain-like clouds rising up above the horizon on a fine summer's evening." A month later, Fidler wrote about a "remarkable high cliff, very much resembling a Pyramid, from which near resemblance I shall call it by that name." Based on his description, the mountain in question was what is now called Mount Glasgow, a 3,000-metre pyramid-shaped peak located in Kananaskis Country between the Little Elbow River Valley and the Elbow River Valley. The Pyramid name never caught on, it seems, because Fidler neglected to list it on any of his maps.

On 31 December 1792 Fidler achieved his mountain-climbing first when he "climbed up a gentle ascent" for two and one-half hours, and "after much fatigue I got to the top." He described the view as "extensive" and said there were few mountains in the vicinity "higher than the place I stood on." He didn't name the mountain, but it is clear from his description that it was today's Thunder Mountain, a 2,335-metre peak located in the Livingstone Range south of the Oldman River Gap.

Fidler, who has often been called Canada's forgotten explorer because his mapping achievements were overshadowed by those of David Thompson, achieved a number of other significant firsts during his 1792–93 trip. He was the first European to note the presence of coal in Drumheller, the first to write about the cactus and the sun-kissed Chinook winds, the first to trade with and describe the customs of the Kootenay tribe, and the first to record their tradition of driving buffalo to their deaths over strategically chosen cliffs known as jumps. He added to his linguistic prowess by learning the language of the Peigan, helped choose the site of HBC's post at Fort Edmonton, and was one of the first Europeans to write about the sticky black oil sands of the Athabasca region: "Found great quantities of bitumen, a kind of liquid tar, oozing out of the banks on both sides of the river in many places, which has a very sulphurous smell and quite black like real tar, and in my opinion would be a good substitute for that useful mineral."

In the summer of 1793, Fidler was part of another unsuccessful attempt by the HBC to find a short, direct, and navigable water route from Hudson Bay to Lake Athabasca. He then spent two years doing routine clerical work at York Factory and married, "according to the custom of the country," a local Swampy Cree named Mary. He sent several maps to the London committee of the HBC illustrating his 1792–93 journey to the foothills of the Rockies, which prompted the committee to ask his immediate superiors why Fidler was wasting his time at York Factory when he could be "proceeding inland on discoveries."

Fidler made a number of trips to Lake Athabasca between 1799 and 1806 in response to the London committee's orders that the HBC explorers compete more aggressively against the rival North West Company instead of spending their time surveying and mapping. However, it was tough to compete against the large and solidly entrenched NWC contingent at Lake Athabasca, especially when the NWC used "every mean and roguish method" (from burning canoes to scaring away game) to intimidate the small HBC group. "I suppose it was their intention to starve our people out," said Fidler. Things finally came to a head in June 1806 when a dispirited Fidler decided that further competition was unfair and senseless. Abandoning Lake Athabasca, he said later, was the low point in his fur trade career.

Between 1806 and 1810, Fidler filled in many of the blank spaces on the maps of the Pacific Northwest through his surveying work, with much of his cartographic material being incorporated by the London committee into new maps of North America. The committee rewarded him for his efforts by raising his salary to £100 per year, and granting him a paid one-year furlough in England. When he returned to Canada, Fidler was assigned to the Red River Settlement in Manitoba and had the distinction of laying out the first river lots in the colony. He served briefly as acting governor of the colony, remained there until 1817, and then returned to the fur trade as chief trader at the HBC posts in Brandon and Lake Dauphin, Manitoba. In 1821, he learned he was soon to be pensioned off, because the merger of the HBC and NWC had created a surplus of employees. Fidler took the opportunity to settle his personal affairs by formally marrying Mary in the Anglican Church and drawing up a will that provided for the surviving eleven of their fourteen children.

Though his retirement was postponed, and he was allowed to continue working as a clerk at his old salary of £100 a year, Fidler did not enjoy his final years at Dauphin Lake House because he was in failing health. In company papers he was described as "a faithful and interested old servant, now superannuated, who has had a recent paralytic condition and his resolution quite gone, unfit for any charge." He died on 17 December 1822, at age fifty-three, and remained largely forgotten until 1966 when Alberta historian James G. MacGregor published a book about his life, *Peter Fidler: Canada's Forgotten Surveyor*. Today, Fidler is remembered as an important surveyor and mapmaker who travelled more than seventy-eight thousand kilometres by canoe, dogsled, horseback, and on foot, and deserves to stand next to David Thompson as one of the great surveyors of the fur trade era.

The Mystery of the North American Himalayas—1827

Compass-card.

BOTANIST DAVID DOUGLAS REACHES FOR THE TOP

The history of mountaineering in North America began with a miscalculation. On 1 May 1827 a sight-impaired twenty-eight-year-old Scottish botanist, named David Douglas, climbed to the top of a peak in what is now Jasper National Park and recorded in his journal that its height "does not appear to be less than sixteen thousand or seventeen thousand feet above the level of the sea." He described the peak as "the highest yet known in the northern continent of America" and named it Mount Brown after his former teacher and fellow botanist Robert Brown. Looking across at an adjoining peak, Douglas estimated it to be about the same height—five thousand metres—and he named it Mount Hooker after Sir William Hooker, a distinguished Scottish botanist who had once adopted the young Douglas as his protégé.

Douglas's first-person account of his climb was published posthumously by his mentor Hooker in an 1836 edition of *Companion to the Botanical Magazine* two years after Douglas was killed at age thirty-five in a bizarre climbing mishap in Hawaii. For fifty-seven years after that, his story left mountaineers, geographers, and mapmakers believing that at least two Himalayan-sized giants—higher than any peak in the Alps—existed in North America. The tallest mountain in Europe, Mont Blanc, was known to be just 15,771 feet high, while the Matterhorn was only 14,692 feet.

European climbers viewed Douglas's North American giants as

their next challenge once they had scaled the principal summits of the Alps. Maps and geography books told them that the two mountains were located near remote Athabasca Pass, about fifty kilometres southwest of today's Jasper townsite on what is now the Alberta–British Columbia boundary. However, when a Quebec-born geology professor named Arthur Coleman explored the Athabasca Pass region in 1893, doubts about Douglas's 1827 climb began to emerge. Coleman calculated that Mount Brown was only 9,184 feet (2,799 metres) high and that Mount Hooker was no more than 1,600 feet (487 metres) higher. "What has gone wrong with these two mighty peaks that they should shrink seven thousand feet in altitude?" Coleman wrote in his journal. "And how could anyone, least of all a scientist like Douglas, make so monumental a blunder?"

One probable explanation was that Douglas made an arithmetical error based on a flawed premise. He seems to have calculated the heights of his giant peaks from a previous measurement that gave Athabasca Pass an altitude of 11,000 feet above sea level, more than 5,000 feet higher than it actually is. Just where this original incorrect measurement came from has never been conclusively determined. Some say it might have come from the explorer David Thompson, who accidentally discovered the Athabasca Pass in 1811 while searching for navigable routes across the Rockies, and did some crude experiments aimed at measuring the height above sea level. Though normally a conservative geographer, Thompson seems to have grossly exaggerated the altitude of the pass at 11,000 feet above sea level, and placed the tops of the peaks at 7,000 feet beyond that. The British Admiralty gave these measurements to Douglas before he set off on his North American trip, and he accepted them at face value.

Douglas had done little or no mountain climbing before he ascended Mount Brown in 1827. The son of a stonemason who did restoration work for the Earl of Mansfield at Scone Palace near Perth, Scotland, Douglas was apprenticed to the palace gardener at age eleven and worked for the Botanical Gardens in Glasgow until he was in his early twenties. At age twenty-three, Douglas became a botanical specimen collector for the Royal Horticultural Society in London and spent two years travelling America, studying and reporting species of plants and trees. He described two hundred new species and discovered the evergreen conifer that now bears his name: the majestic Douglas fir. He described it as "the most important tree in the American lumber trade."

Douglas was travelling by canoe with a group of Hudson's Bay Company (HBC) traders and voyageurs when he reached Athabasca Pass in 1827 and decided on a whim to climb "what seemed to be

David Douglas F.L.S. 1798-1834
nlarged from a pencil drawing   ætat 30   by his niece Miss Atkinson

Botanist David Douglas as depicted in a pencil drawing by his niece, Miss Atkinson: "The sensation I felt is beyond what I can give utterance to." (Whyte Museum of the Canadian Rockies M106-7)

the highest peak in the north." One has to wonder today about that description because, far from being the highest peak in the Rockies, Mount Brown is not even the highest mountain in the ranges surrounding Athabasca Pass. However, one possible explanation for Douglas's apparent exaggeration is that he suffered from a combination of ophthalmia and snow blindness and thus was unable to clearly see the unnamed peaks that dwarfed Mount Brown.

Douglas had a tough time climbing Mount Brown. Physically frail and weakened by rheumatism that had caused him years earlier to believe he "would shortly be consigned to the tomb," he sank to his waist in the deep snow several times while trying to get above the treeline. However, five hours after he started climbing he reached the top. He spent twenty glorious minutes there, with night closing in on him, and was moved by what he saw around him. "The sensation I felt is beyond what I can give utterance to," he wrote. "Nothing as far as the eye can reach but mountains rugged beyond all description. Such gives us a sense of the stupendous and wondrous works of the Almighty."

It was not the first documented ascent of a mountain in the Rockies. Peter Fidler had already achieved that distinction back in 1792 when he climbed Thunder Mountain in the Oldman River Valley, and David Thompson had also added his name to the tiny list of pioneer climbers when he ascended Loder Peak near Exshaw in 1800. However, mountaineering as a sporting activity did not become popular in Europe until the 1850s, and by that time Douglas was the only climber whose North American achievement was still remembered. So for most mountaineers, Douglas was the man to follow when they started climbing in the Rockies at the end of the nineteenth century.

Arthur Coleman's search for Mount Brown and Mount Hooker began in 1885, when it became possible to travel across Canada by train. His search was motivated by curiosity. Why, wondered Coleman, hadn't the great artist-explorer Paul Kane sketched the two mountains during his horseback trip across the Rockies in 1846? Surely two peaks, towering thousands of feet above all the others, would have attracted Kane's attention. And why did none of the Canadian government surveyors ever mention the peaks when they began looking for possible railway routes through the mountains in 1871? Coleman decided he should "visit and, if possible, climb them."

Coleman's 1885 trip took him by train to a point just west of the Rockies near today's Golden, British Columbia. From there he estimated he would have to travel northward about two hundred kilometres by canoe and portage trail to reach Athabasca Pass. However, when he returned to the area in July 1888 to canoe down the Columbia River from Golden he discovered, to his dismay, that the Athabasca Pass could not be reached by this route and he was forced to abandon his quest.

In 1892 Coleman undertook a more extensive search for the two peaks, starting in the foothills west of Calgary and travelling some eight hundred kilometres northward through the mountains before again failing to reach Athabasca Pass. One of his travelling companions, a Toronto professor of surveying named L. G. Stewart, took advantage of the opportunity to map and name dozens of rivers, lakes, and passes, but the mystery of the two giant peaks remained unsolved. It wasn't until the following summer that Coleman finally reached Athabasca Pass, and only then to discover that the two peaks were not as high as previously believed.

Coleman was disappointed when he discovered "after six weeks of toil and anxiety, and three summers of effort, that Mount Brown and Mount Hooker were frauds." But whether it was a fraud or a simple calculation error, the fact remained that two mythical North American peaks had beckoned as a challenge for mountaineers for more than fifty-seven years following the 1836 publication of Douglas's legendary account of climbing Mount Brown. And legends do not die easily.

While Coleman concluded after his 1893 trip that Douglas's five thousand-metre giants did not exist, other mountaineers—including Walter Wilcox and Norman Collie—felt that more investigation still needed to be done. If the giants were not located near Athabasca Pass, perhaps they might be located somewhere else, in an uncharted part of the Rockies. Or perhaps Coleman's journey through the mountains might have taken him to the wrong pass. The jury would remain out until it could be proven which of the two men, Douglas or Coleman, had made a mistake.

Wilcox, a twenty-seven-year-old outdoors enthusiast from

Washington, D.C., went looking for Mount Brown and Mount Hooker in the summer of 1896. A forestry student at Yale University, he had spent two summers camping near Lake Louise and liked exploring uncharted wilderness. Working on the assumption that Douglas had discovered mountains higher than any ever found in Europe, Wilcox and three companions began their search near the headwaters of the Bow River just northwest of Banff, and proceeded northward from there. "They must be somewhere," Wilcox said. However, while he and his party did blaze a trail that was used by horseback travellers until the first Banff-Jasper road was built in the 1930s, he never did find the elusive peaks.

Collie, a thirty-nine-year-old chemistry professor and climbing enthusiast from London, also found it unthinkable that Douglas, a self-trained botanist and scientist, could have miscalculated the height of the mountains at Athabasca Pass. In 1898 he set out to "rehabilitate the outraged majesty of Mount Brown and Mount Hooker, if the facts will allow." During the trip he and companion Herman Woolley completed the first documented ascent of Mount Athabasca, a 3,500-metre peak located halfway between Banff and Jasper, and from the summit they became the first Europeans to see the greatest body of glacial ice in the Rocky Mountains—the 330-square kilometre Columbia Icefield. But they didn't solve the riddle of Douglas's mountains.

It was only when he got back to London, and re-read the faded copy of *Companion to the Botanical Magazine* containing the description of Douglas's 1827 climb, that Collie found the long-awaited answer to the riddle. It was right there in Douglas's statement that the ascent had taken five hours. "Had this document ever been studied thoughtfully, the absurdity must have been at once apparent," Collie wrote. As an experienced alpine mountaineer, Collie knew that it was manifestly impossible for any climber—much less an unskilled one like Douglas—to ascend a 16,000 to 17,000-foot peak in five hours. Coleman had been right when he estimated that the mountain Douglas ascended had to be less than 10,000 feet high, and Douglas had clearly compounded a previous calculation error that then endured for decades. Collie "with regret, chanted the requiem" of the two fabled giants, and turned his attention to other mountaineering challenges.

But was it fraud or an honest mistake that caused the legend of the North American Himalayas to endure for so many years? In August 2002, Parks Canada and the Alpine Club of Canada organized a horseback expedition to Athabasca Pass to try to answer the question for once and for all. The expeditioners found several discrepancies in Douglas's narrative—including his placement of Mount Hooker to the south of Mount Brown rather than to the east. But they gave Douglas the benefit of the doubt, credited him with completing the historic climb, and put his miscalculation down to error rather than deceit.

"It was a great story and, even if it weren't true, it put the Rockies on the map of the world and lured hundreds of notable climbers," mountain historian Bob Sandford told an *Edmonton Journal* reporter. "I think it justifiable that [Douglas] be remembered not only for the good science that he carried out here, but for the fact that he was America's first mountaineer."

Douglas came to a bizarre and violent end just seven years after his fabled adventure in the Rockies. He was killed in 1834 while mountain climbing in Hawaii when he fell into a pit dug to trap wild cattle and was gored by an enraged bull. Gardeners worldwide now remember Douglas as a father of modern horticulture, while mountaineers remember him as one of the first to ascend a peak for the mere sake of the accomplishment. His name graces a peak in the Red Deer River Valley which, at 3,235 metres, stands as high as the two mythical giants he once thought to be higher than any in the Alps.

Of Missionaries and Treaties— 1840-77

ROBERT RUNDLE, THE MCDOUGALLS, AND TREATY SEVEN

The Natives of the Rockies have a saying: "Before the white men came, we had the land and they had the Bible. Now, we have the Bible and they have the land." Spoken with bitterness, it clouds the fact that the Natives actually welcomed the Bible-carrying missionaries with open arms when they first reached the foothills and front ranges of the Rockies in the winter of 1840.

Stoney oral tradition says that game was scarce that winter, and that the people appealed to their chief, Mah-Min, to do something to ease their hunger. The chief prayed to the Great Spirit for a successful hunt, but then abruptly stopped when a strange voice told him to "watch and listen for a white missionary who will come to this country of yours at the time of the next moon." The voice said that the hunt would be successful if the Stoney listened to the missionary telling them about a "Father God in Heaven," and that his word should be taken as the truth. "You believe in that God and then leave me alone, for I cannot help you any more."

The missionary in question was an English-born Wesleyan Methodist, Robert Rundle, and shortly before his arrival the hunt did improve. The Stoney hunters shot two moose followed by several bison, and then travelled to Rocky Mountain House to meet the missionary. "The Stoney were glad they had known a missionary was to come," said one of Mah-Min's descendants, William Twin, "and they received him kindly." Instead of killing him, as some of the warriors had planned to do, they listened quietly while Rundle preached. Chief Mah-Min was the first to accept the invitation to baptism, and others soon followed.

Rundle was not the only missionary to visit the Rocky Mountains during that period. A Belgian-born Jesuit named Pierre-Jean De Smet worked among the Flathead in Montana, and among the Blackfoot and Cree at Canmore and Rocky Mountain House. Another Roman Catholic missionary, Quebec-born Jean-Baptiste Thibault, travelled across the Prairies to the Rocky Mountains on horseback, preaching the gospel to anyone who would listen. However, Rundle seems to have left the most lasting impression. James Hector of the Palliser Expedition recalled camping with a group of Stoney on a Sunday several years after Rundle's departure and being surprised to hear them praying and singing such Methodist hymns as "In the Sweet By and By," which Rundle had translated for them.

Rundle was an itinerant missionary who spent seven years travelling between Hudson's Bay Company (HBC) forts in what is now Saskatchewan and Alberta, pursuing the Natives and baptizing them with such English names as Benjamin and Jacob and Sarah. While the HBC governor, Sir George Simpson, would have liked the roving missionary to establish permanent mission stations in HBC territories to help civilize the Natives, Rundle preferred to seek his nomadic flock as it wandered. He lived by the Methodist dictum, "Christianity first, then civilization." Like his congregation, he was a child of the sky, with a copse for his cathedral and a tree stump for his altar.

Rundle travelled on horseback in summer, usually accompanied by his pet cat. In winter, he travelled by dogsled, always well protected against the cold. In his diary, he noted that his winter wardrobe included "sealskin cap tied under the chin, moccasins, pair of lambs-wool stockings, flannel shirt, woolen shirt, woolen drawers to foot, thick trousers lined, leggings and black silk gaiters, coat, waistcoat, pilot coat and shawl tied around the neck." Additionally he carried a buffalo robe and two blankets.

During the early years of his mission, before he became fluent in Cree and Blackfoot, Rundle travelled with Métis guides and interpreters. They didn't always get along. Part of the problem was that some Natives believed Rundle to be the white man's god, and this irritated the translators. During one service in 1841, for a large gathering of Natives at Rocky Mountain House, an interpreter named Jimmy Jock (James Bird) got so annoyed at hearing about Rundle's divine qualities that he simply stopped translating. Rundle lost face and a few potential converts on that occasion, but on the whole he was well respected by the Natives, and the seeds he sowed bore fruit for future missionaries.

Captain John Palliser heard so many good things about Rundle's work among the Natives that he decided to name a mountain in the Bow River valley after the popular missionary. The mountain is located ten kilometres southeast of Banff, and there has been some suggestion that Rundle on 9 November 1844 may actually have attempted to climb it. He wrote in his journal that he made a trip to the Rockies on that day and climbed a peak for several hours until overcome by fatigue. But he was obviously unprepared for the climb. He had left camp without eating breakfast and was close to fainting when he reached the limit of his climbing ability. "It was presumptuous of me, I know, but I had to see if I could find a way to scale higher. I could not succeed, so I now abandoned my design and commenced descending." When he reached the bottom, after an unexpectedly difficult descent, he couldn't find the road back to the camp. It was only when someone in the camp fired some signal shots that he was able to make his way back to safety. He wrote that he then "took some medicine and had breakfast about sunset."

The Stoney had no problems embracing the gospel of Christianity as espoused by Rundle. There wasn't much difference between what they already believed and what Rundle preached. As Stoney Chief John Snow writes in his book *These Mountains Are Our Sacred Places*, the Christian concept of sharing was nothing new to the Stoney. "In fact, it was the way of life in the Stoney tribal society. Our community was a sharing community—that is one of the reasons why we survived for so many centuries." The Stoney also believed in the concept of God as creator, and in the concept of heaven as a place where people go after they die. "There were questions regarding the new religion, but it sounded good and its basic teachings were not unfamiliar," Snow writes. "And so we listened to the missionaries and many converts were made."

While several missionaries visited the Rockies from the 1840s onward, it wasn't until 1873 that the first permanent mission station was established in Native territory there. John McDougall, a Methodist clergyman who had followed his father, George Millward McDougall, into the missionary service, knew from having lived in Upper Canada (now Ontario) that advancing white settlement could disrupt the traditional Native way of life, which included the freedom to roam and hunt at will. McDougall hoped that by establishing a mission at Morley, in the ancestral winter camping grounds of the Stoney midway between Banff and Calgary, he would provide a measure of isolation from white society for the Natives of the foothills (estimated to be as many as two thousand) while they adjusted to the coming changes. He would teach them to become farmers instead of hunters, and instill in them the European cultural values that would allow them to participate in the future as full citizens.

The Stoney welcomed the McDougalls—father George and sons John and David and their families—and worked with them to build the mission. The chiefs felt they had to obtain the best possible protection for their people in the face of the new political realities. Canada had become a dominion in 1867 and immediately set its sights on expanding westward toward the British colony on the Pacific coast. In 1870, the HBC transferred "ownership" of its lands to the new Canadian government, which then assumed responsibility for administration and settlement of the West. In 1871, British Columbia became part of Canada, and the federal government promised to build a railway to the Pacific coast to seal the bargain. The Morley mission could not stop these political currents from swirling about the peoples of the West, but it could provide the Natives with their own church and school and perhaps allow them to have a say in deciding their future. Once the Canadian government took over control of the territory, it became clear to the Natives that the missionaries were simply the advance men for the new way of life. It made more sense to make friends with these missionaries than become their enemies.

In the summer of 1874, John McDougall told the Stoney to prepare for the coming of the North West Mounted Police, and thus he helped facilitate what his biographer, James Ernest Nix, has called a "next to miraculous" transformation of the region from a lawless territory, occupied by warring Natives and renegade whisky traders, into a "peaceful country newly opened to civilized settlement." This, Chief Snow observes, "was one action of the white man's government which my people really did appreciate." Scores of Natives had died of alcohol poisoning "as though killed by strychnine" and here was an opportunity to "use the white man's law and order to correct one of the worst conditions and situations in our entire history."

The arrival of the Mounties in what is now Alberta paved the way for the signing of a treaty that was to change the Native way of life forever. In the summer of 1877, the moccasin telegraph carried word that all Natives south of the Red Deer River were to gather at Blackfoot Crossing, on the Bow River east of Calgary, to negotiate the surrender of their hunting lands to Queen Victoria's representatives. Three Stoney bands—the Bearspaws, the Chinikis, and the Goodstoneys, or Wesleys as they came to call themselves (because Rundle was a Wesleyan missionary)—agreed, at John McDougall's instigation, to sit down with their enemies in the Blackfoot Confederacy and participate in the negotiations. McDougall assured the Stoney that it was the aim of the Queen and her servants to deal fairly and justly with them, and they accepted his word. "To our minds, the equation was simple," Snow writes. "The McDougalls were men of God and counsellors or advisers to the Great Queen's representatives. Therefore, what they said about the importance and the promises of the treaties must be true."

Stoney Chief Jacob Bearspaw travelled from Chief Mountain, Montana, part of his band's ancestral hunting territory, to take part in the proceedings. He was a rugged warrior, then about forty years old, who had gained a reputation for fierceness and daring in his youth. According to oral tradition, he "never missed a chance to kill a Blackfoot" because his mother was murdered by a Blackfoot. Respected as a leader and later as a peacemaker who "adhered to what he considered just and right," Bearspaw was the chief who first encouraged the McDougalls to establish their mission station in Stoney territory at Morley.

Bearspaw's brother-in-law, Chief John Chiniki, brought his band members to the negotiations from their lodges adjoining the McDougall mission at Morley. The son of a Cree chief named

Maskepetoon, he had lived with a Stoney family after his parents died, and was the acknowledged chief of the middle band by the time he was in his thirties. Like Bearspaw, he was a strong supporter of the McDougall mission and known to be a devout Christian.

The third Stoney chief, Jacob Goodstoney, brought his band from the northern part of the Stoney territory, near the headwaters of the North Saskatchewan River. According to government records, he was a "moral, sober, honest and industrious" leader who "looked well after his band." He invited John McDougall, who spoke Ojibwa and Cree but not Stoney (Nakoda Sioux), to interpret for the Stoney when David Laird, the Lieutenant-Governor of the North-West Territories, spoke to the assembled tribes in August 1877:

> In a very few years, the buffalo will probably all be destroyed, and for this reason the Queen wishes to help you to live in the future in some other way. She wishes you to allow her white children to come and live on your land and raise cattle, and should you agree to this she will assist you to raise cattle and grain, and thus give you the means of living when the buffalo are no more. She will also pay you and your children money every year, which you can spend as you please. By being paid in money you cannot be cheated, as with it you can buy what you think proper.

Laird outlined the specifics of the treaty concessions as follows: twelve dollars initially for every man, woman, and child; five dollars annually for each person every year thereafter; a suit of clothes, a silver medal, a flag, and a twenty-dollar annual bonus for each head chief signing the treaty; a new "treaty suit" for the chiefs every three years; and a guarantee of reserve land (but not title) "upon which none other will be permitted to encroach." The reserve allotment would be one square mile (2.6 square kilometres) for every family of five, "on which they can cut the trees and brush for firewood and other purposes." Hunting outside the reserve would continue to be available to the Natives until white settlers occupied the land.

After six days of negotiations, the Stoney and the other nations, on 22 September 1877, did "cede, release, surrender and yield up to the Government of Canada for Her Majesty the Queen and her successors for ever, all their rights, titles and privileges whatsoever" to their lands. The area surrendered amounted to 91,000 square kilometres, covering most of what is now southern Alberta. In return, the Natives received 3,600 square kilometres of reserve land—less than five percent of the total ceded.

Jacob Bearspaw was the first Stoney chief to accept the treaty—the seventh such contract to be ratified by Canada's Natives and the Canadian government during the 1870s. With McDougall acting as translator, Bearspaw told a correspondent for the Toronto *Globe* newspaper that he was "pleased with the treaty, the police, and the prospect of getting provisions and money." The correspondent commented that Bearspaw "appeared by his speech to be of a mercenary bent," which meant that the chief seemed to be intent on getting the best deal possible for his people.

McDougall, who had been trying with marginal success to train the Stoney to become farmers, suggested that they accept agricultural implements rather than the cattle for ranching given to the Blackfoot Confederacy and Sarcee bands. At the time, this seemed like good advice because there seemed to be an abundance of rich soil, water, and pasture on the Stoney reserve land, vaguely defined in the treaty as being "in the vicinity of Morleyville." It would soon become apparent, however, that the McDougall mission took up the best farmland in the district, just east of today's Morley townsite. The bulk of the reserve was on rocky ground, unsuitable for sustaining an agricultural economy.

There were other disappointments. Each Stoney chief put his signature mark on the Treaty Seven document, believing that reserve land would be set aside for his band in its traditional hunting areas. However, the seeds of future difficulties were sown when it transpired that the only land being set aside for all three Stoney bands was a small, 375-square-kilometre tract in Morley, with no additional consideration given to the specific needs of the northern and southern bands.

Further misunderstandings arose over the extent to which the Stoney would be able to maintain their traditional way of life. The Stoney believed they were still free to go wherever they wanted in their ancestral hunting territory, to hunt and trap in any season, and also to fish at any time of the year. "We had no idea we would be forced to settle on a small piece of land and become agriculturists," Snow writes. "We thought the missionaries were making the best possible deal for us, but in fact they were working to secure land for white settlers."

McDougall, first viewed by the Stoney as an honest man of God who protected their interests, eventually came to be seen as an opportunist who used the treaty negotiations to secure the best farmland for his family and expand his mission to include an orphanage and residential school. But the Stoney did give him credit for trying to improve conditions for them when they were no longer able to rely on hunting and trapping for their subsistence economy. Acknowledging that he had been too optimistic about the potential of the region for cultivation, and that the best bet for future economic progress on the Stoney reserve was ranching, not agriculture, McDougall lobbied the federal government (albeit unsuccessfully) for additional reserve land to accommodate large numbers of horses and cattle. When he became aware of the various restrictions the government was imposing on the Stoney, he spoke out against such injustices as the pass system that prevented them from leaving their reserve without the Indian agent's permission, and the rule that required them to have the agent's permission before they could sell their farm produce. "Give the Indian full liberty in all matters except the disposition of his lands and the trafficking in intoxicants," McDougall said. The government didn't pay him much heed, however, because it was then more interested in listening to settlers and railway builders than advocates for Native causes.

Despite their many disappointments, the Stoney remained true to their treaty promises. During the Northwest Rebellion of 1885, the chiefs signed a letter affirming their loyalty to the Crown and agreed to have their people act as scouts for the Alberta Field Force. While poverty and deprivation continued to plague them for many decades afterwards, the Stoney did eventually see an improvement in their fortunes. During the early part of the twentieth century, many of them played an important role guiding tourists through mountain wilderness areas.

McDougall continued to live on the Morley reserve with his

wife, Elizabeth, and their six children, until he retired in 1906 at age sixty-four. After that he served as a commissioner for the Department of Indian Affairs, visiting reserves in Alberta and British Columbia to hear the views of the residents on aboriginal title and other matters. He ran unsuccessfully as a Liberal for Calgary Centre in the Alberta provincial election of 1913, and to the end of his days he persisted in annoying the Methodist authorities by arranging for Natives to put on their costumes and dance at various exhibitions, including Banff Indian Days and the Calgary Stampede. When he died, in Calgary in 1917 at age seventy-five, he was hailed for the work he had done at Morley for the betterment of the Stoney. "Their present condition and development," said the *Calgary Herald*, "is due largely to the intelligent and never-ending efforts exercised in their behalf by Rev. Mr. McDougall."

The Wanderings of an Artist through the Northwest 1846-48

PAUL KANE RECORDS A PASSING WAY OF NATIVE LIFE

Paul Kane was the first professional artist to travel the fur-trade routes from the Great Lakes to the Pacific, sketching and making notes as he went. In the process, he created an extensive pictorial record of Native life in the Canadian Northwest during the nineteenth century. From seven hundred field sketches, which he once had to abandon temporarily in the Rockies due to transportation difficulties, Kane created one hundred paintings that survive as a permanent record of a people he believed threatened with extinction because of white westward expansion. No other illustrative record of nineteenth-century Native life begins to approach the wealth or magnitude of that made by Kane.

Born in County Cork, Ireland, in 1810 and raised in what is now Toronto, Kane took a few painting lessons when he was in his twenties and then followed a practice common among emerging North American professional artists by working as a sign painter and furniture decorator while earning the occasional commission as a portrait painter. Between 1836 and 1841, he worked as a journeyman portrait painter in Detroit, New Orleans, and Mobile, Alabama, until he had saved enough money to pay for art study in Europe. He couldn't afford to pay for formal study in an academy so he learned by visiting museums in Rome and Florence and copying into his sketchbook the works of such Old Masters as Rubens, Raphael, and Murillo.

In October 1842, Kane travelled to London where he met George Catlin, a Philadelphia-born artist who had spent six years painting Natives from the American Great Plains to the foothills of the Rockies. Catlin believed that European settlement threatened the Native traditions of roaming, camping, and hunting, and so he dedicated himself to capturing their lives on canvas while this was still possible. Kane, obviously inspired by Catlin's work, decided to do in Hudson's Bay Company (HBC) territory what Catlin was doing in the United States. He would paint the Native tribes of the Northwest before a tide of white settlers swept across their lands and destroyed them.

Kane returned to Toronto in the spring of 1845 and left on 17 June to cross the continent "with no companions but my portfolio and box of paints, my gun, and a stock of ammunition." His aim was to "devote whatever talents and proficiency I possessed to the painting of a series of pictures illustrative of the North American Indians and scenery."

He got no further west than Lake Michigan. After a few weeks of sketching Natives who had assembled along the shores of the Great Lakes to receive gifts of guns, tobacco, blankets, and other items from the British government, Kane arrived in Sault Ste. Marie, where a HBC factor named John Ballenden urged him to turn back: "He strongly advised me against attempting to penetrate into the interior, except under the auspices of the Company, representing it as almost impossible and certainly very dangerous." Ballenden suggested that Kane should apply to Bay governor Sir George Simpson for permission to travel with the Bay's fur brigades when they journeyed westward the following spring. Kane agreed that such protection would allow him "to travel further and see more of the wilder tribes."

Kane met with Simpson in Lachine, Quebec, in March 1846, showed him his sketches, and after extensive negotiations received permission to travel west with the spring fur brigades. Simpson promised him free board and lodging at company posts along the way, and commissioned him to paint fourteen canvases for the Bay when the western tour was over. With his major expenses thus covered, Kane's only costs would be for clothing, blankets, tobacco, rum, and gifts for the Natives, most of which he could pay with skins from the moose and buffalo that he shot along the way.

Kane left Toronto on 9 May 1846 and met up with the voyageurs when he reached Fort William (now Thunder Bay) on 24 May. From there he travelled by river and lake to Lake Winnipeg and then south along the Red River to the Dakota plains, where he witnessed, sketched, and participated in one of the last great Métis buffalo hunts of the nineteenth century. Kane counted five hundred dead and dying buffalo after the first hour of the hunt and calculated that, at this rate, the Dakota hunters must slaughter thirty thousand buffalo a year. "I have often witnessed an Indian buffalo hunt since," Kane wrote, "but never one on so large a scale."

The artist found his "wilder tribes"—specifically, the Assiniboine, Plains Cree, and Blackfoot—as he crossed the Prairies from Norway House, near the northern tip of Lake Winnipeg, to Fort Edmonton. During this part of the journey, he travelled on horseback accompanied by John Rowand, a tough, no-nonsense Bay factor who ruled the Saskatchewan district with his brawn and fists. Kane was grateful for Rowand's protection because, even though his mission was to visit Native settlements and depict them in his sketchbooks, he lived in constant fear of being attacked by hostile tribes.

Kane arrived at Fort Edmonton on 26 September and spent ten days there preparing for what he called "the arduous journey which now lay before us." Crossing the Rockies with winter approaching was a journey fraught with potential rigours and unknown perils, but Kane was determined to press on. On 6 October he left Fort Edmonton with brigade leader Richard Lane, a guide named McGillivray, sixteen packers, and sixty-five horses. The brigade's assignment was to bring packs of otter skins to Fort Vancouver (now Vancouver, Washington) for eventual delivery to the Russian government as payment for Bay trapping rights in Alaska.

After a nineteen-day trip along the Athabasca River, which he characterized as "the most monotonous river that ever I have met with on my travels," Kane saw for the first time "the sublime and apparently endless chain of the Rocky Mountains." On 30 October he wrote in his journal that the packers greeted the mountains with a "hearty cheer" while he sketched the river with the mountains in the distance.

On 2 November, the party reached Roche Miette, a 2,316-metre mass of sheer rock that today guards the Highway 16 east entrance to Jasper National Park. There Kane experienced his first major storm in the mountains, which he described as a "perfect hurricane." It blew the brigade's only boat out of the water, which meant transferring everything onto the horses. After camping overnight in a snowstorm, Kane pushed ahead of the party on horseback and arrived at the Bay's three-hut Jasper House trading post "cold, wet and famished" after fording the ice-strewn Athabasca River four times. There he was greeted by factor Colin Fraser, Sir George Simpson's former piper, who built a fire and cooked Kane a dish of mountain sheep that tasted "far more delicious than any domestic animal of the same species."

Kane didn't think he would be able to cross the Rockies on horseback so he asked one of the Natives who lived in a tipi at Jasper House—a Shuswap chief named Capote Blanc—to make him a pair of snowshoes. These proved to be a boon over the next seven days as Kane travelled over "almost inaccessible crags" and through "gloomy and tangled forest," with the snow building and the temperatures dropping, en route to Athabasca Pass. The horses, as he had feared, were unable to negotiate the snowy mountain terrain and were sent back to Jasper House. After that, the men had to carry their own provisions and blankets.

At the top of Athabasca Pass, near a small lake that Simpson had named Committee's Punch Bowl in honour of the governing committee of the Bay in London, Kane and his companions raised a tin cup of rum to toast "their honours, the nabobs of the fur trade." Simpson, who had travelled through the pass in 1824, regarded the lake as a notable landmark in the Rockies because it fed the headwaters of one stream that eventually connected with the Mackenzie River system flowing into the Arctic Ocean and another stream that eventually connected with the Columbia flowing into the Pacific. Simpson thought it extraordinary that this "little basin should send its waters to each side of the continent and give birth to two of the principal rivers in North America."

Kane and his companions didn't waste any time dallying at

Committee's Punch Bowl. They were already three weeks behind schedule because of the wintry conditions, and leader Lane was concerned he might miss the boatmen from Fort Vancouver who were scheduled to meet the horse brigade at a place called Boat Encampment, in the Upper Columbia Valley, near today's Mica Dam. It was an important rendezvous for the brigade because they were running out of food and the boatmen were bringing replacement provisions.

Getting to Boat Encampment was a matter of sliding down icy slopes and wading through rivers choked with ice. After a dispiriting two days of this, Kane and his companions arrived at their destination on 15 November "almost perishing with cold and hunger." They got there just in time. The boatmen had been waiting for thirty-nine days and were about to return home to Fort Vancouver. Kane expressed his relief in his journal:

> Few who read this journal, surrounded by the comforts of civilized life, will be able to imagine the heartfelt satisfaction with which we exchanged the wearisome snowshoe for the comfortable boats, and the painful anxiety of half-satisfied appetites for a well-stocked larder. We no longer had to toil on in clothes frozen stiff from wading across torrents, half-famished, and with the consciousness ever before us, that whatever were our hardships and fatigue, rest was sure destruction in the cold solitudes of those dreary mountains.

The two-thousand-kilometre river trip through countless rapids and waterfalls from Boat Encampment to Fort Vancouver took Kane and his companions twenty-two days. Before they got there they ran out of food and had to shoot and roast a horse that Kane found "very palatable." From there Kane journeyed on to Oregon and then back to Fort Vancouver, which became his home base for the rest of the winter. During that time he sketched canoes and cedar lodges, painted medicine masks and burial sites, made portraits of important chiefs along Juan de Fuca Strait, and traded for blankets, masks, rattles, tools, and other objects. These sketches and artifacts are now regarded as one of the most important ethnological records of the Native cultures of the Pacific Northwest.

In April 1847, Kane moved to Fort Victoria on Vancouver Island and started making plans to return to Toronto. Before he left he travelled to Washington and sketched the constantly eruptive Mount St. Helens volcano. He had considered the idea of remaining on the Pacific coast and setting himself up as a private trader, but eventually changed his mind.

On 1 July 1847, Kane finally left the coast and started up the Columbia River. Three months later, after sketching extensively in the Lower Columbia Valley, he reached Boat Encampment. He waited three weeks to rendezvous with a horse brigade coming from Jasper House, and then began his second crossing of the Rockies with winter coming on. The leader of the Jasper House group, Thomas Lowe, warned him that the horses might not make it back across the mountains because of the weather, but Kane didn't care. "I was completely wearied with my long inaction," he wrote. Plus, he was running out of provisions "so I had no choice but to cross as quickly as possible."

Kane was leading a brigade of four Métis packers and fifty-six horses when he left Boat Encampment on 30 October 1847. The temperature dropped steadily as they ascended the slope toward Athabasca Pass and Committee's Punch Bowl. "Rather cold punch at present," Kane commented wryly in his journal. He estimated the temperature at –56°F (-49°C), the coldest he had ever experienced. "I endeavoured to thaw myself by melting some snow over the fire but the water froze upon my hair and beard and I actually had to scorch my face before I could thaw the ice out."

When Kane reached Jasper House, on 6 November, he expected to be met by nine voyageurs who would transport him by boat down the Athabasca River to a little fur-trading post, Fort Assiniboine, located one hundred kilometres northeast of Fort Edmonton. However, seven of the men had left without him because the river was starting to freeze over. Kane didn't relish the prospect of spending the rest of the winter in the "wretched accommodation" of Jasper House, with its three tiny log huts, so he asked the remaining two men to build him snowshoes and a dogsled. He resumed his journey on 15 November, when the ice on the Athabasca River seemed hard enough to travel on.

Kane encountered several problems during the 560-kilometre

trip from Jasper House to Fort Assiniboine. One of the three dogs ran away and the two remaining animals proved too weak to tow all his baggage, so Kane reluctantly had to abandon the heavy tin trunk containing the field sketches he had made and the Native memorabilia he had collected during the previous eighteen months. He stashed it on the banks of the Athabasca with the hope that the spring fur brigade eastward bound from Fort Vancouver would eventually retrieve it. He would advise Fort Vancouver about the trunk by dispatching a letter from Fort Edmonton with a brigade travelling west.

On 17 November, Kane fell through the ice and barely avoided drowning or freezing to death. Three days later, he was stricken with severe pain in his insteps, a condition (*mal de racquet*) that often plagued those unused to walking long distances on snowshoes. A week after that, on 27 November, he fell through the ice again. By this time, Kane and his two companions were down to the last of their provisions and debating whether or not they should eat the dogs. "But their thinness saved them—the two would not have furnished us with a sufficient meal. If they had been in better condition, they would most assuredly have gone into the pot."

Kane and his companions reached Fort Assiniboine on 29 November, feasted on a meal of whitefish, and then rested up for two days to allow Kane's feet a chance to heal. He was determined to carry on to Fort Edmonton because it was just three days travel away and contained all the amenities he wanted for a comfortable stay over the rest of the winter. Additionally, it afforded him an opportunity to get back to his mission of sketching Natives because "seven of the most important and warlike tribes on the continent are in constant communication with the fort."

Kane remained at Edmonton until 12 April 1848, when he made one last trip west for sketching purposes. He didn't plan to cross the Rockies this time, but he did intend to spend time at Rocky Mountain House, within sight of the mountains, where a "large band of Blackfeet were shortly expected to visit." He spent over a month there, sketching traditional dances and ceremonials, and returned to Edmonton on 22 May just in time to meet the Fort Vancouver spring brigade. Much to his relief, it had received his letter and was carrying the precious trunk of field sketches and Native memorabilia that he had been forced to leave in the mountains the previous November.

On 25 May, Kane left Fort Edmonton for the last time, travelling eastward with a flotilla of twenty-three boats crewed by 130 men. The Blackfoot and their allies, the Sarcee and Gros Ventre, had recently started attacking Bay brigades for guns and horses, and the leader of the Fort Edmonton group, John Harriott, thought there would be safety in numbers. As it turned out, they faced no attacks—the one war party they met along the way was interested only in pursuing Cree and Assiniboine—but Kane did have a moment of apprehension when an armed Blackfoot chief named Big Snake refused initially to smoke a peace pipe with the brigade. After that, as a goodwill gesture, Kane agreed to spend the night in Big Snake's camp, and was acclaimed as a powerful medicine man when he demonstrated his ability to quickly capture the chief's likeness on paper.

Kane's acceptance as a medicine man marked the last milestone in his journey to meet the Natives of the Canadian Northwest and depict their lives in his sketchbook. After an absence of two and one-half years, he owed a net total of £14 6s 9d. to the Bay for expenses covered, and the greatest hardship he now faced "was the difficulty in trying to sleep in a civilized bed." Soon he would return to his Toronto studio, where he would use his sketches to create one hundred oil paintings that would earn him the approval of the Province of Canada's Legislative Assembly, which purchased twelve of his canvases for £500, and bring him lasting fame as an artist.

Kane never made it back to the Rockies, although he did try. In 1849, he accepted an offer of £200 a year plus expenses from a twenty-three-year-old British military officer, Sir Edward Poore, to accompany him on a trip through the Rockies and on to the Sandwich Islands as "conductor, guide and interpreter." However, the short-tempered Poore dismissed Kane when they reached Fort Garry, Manitoba, alleging that the artist was "impertinent, overbearing and incapable of fulfilling his contract as an interpreter." Kane returned to Toronto, married Harriet Clench—the daughter of a cabinetmaker who had once employed him as a decorator—and had several children. He spent his last years writing about his travels and painting—until the onset of blindness in 1858 forced him to put away his pens and brushes. He blamed his deteriorating sight on, among other things, snow blindness suffered in the high passes of the Rockies during his travels of the 1840s. He died in Toronto on 20 February 1871, at age sixty-one. A 3,090-metre peak in Jasper National Park is named in his memory.

Kicked by a Horse—1858

PETER ERASMUS GUIDES THE PALLISER EXPEDITION

It was called the Palliser Expedition because Captain John Palliser was the man in charge, and it used to be that whenever historians wrote about it they gave co-billing to James Hector, the geologist and naturalist who did much of the expedition's scientific work. They didn't give much weight to the achievements of Peter Erasmus, the Métis interpreter and guide responsible for some of the geographical "discoveries" claimed by Hector. Why? Because Erasmus lacked a publicity agent. His role in the story didn't become widely known until after 1976, more than 115 years after the expedition, when his reminiscences finally appeared in print.

Palliser and Hector became famous after exploring what is now Western Canada because they were accomplished self-promoters, who published articles about the expedition that received wide circulation in England from 1863 onwards. Erasmus's role in the expedition remained hidden until 1920, when he sat down at age eighty-seven and dictated his memoirs to an aspiring newspaper reporter named Henry Thompson. The reporter wanted to know why the existing histories "gave the Native no credit in the building of western history—in fact, very little mention at all." But the public never got to read the story because the *Edmonton Bulletin*, the newspaper that assigned Thompson to interview Erasmus, changed owners and refused to print it. It wasn't until after 1963, when Thompson gave a copy of his manuscript to the Glenbow

Archives in Calgary, that the wheels were set in motion to publish the document. The 1976 publication was a book entitled *Buffalo Days and Nights*.

Palliser and Hector needed the assistance of a local guide like Erasmus because when they first ventured into the hinterland in May 1857 they knew almost nothing about the section of the Rockies that lies between today's Jasper National Park and the American border. Although explorers, fur traders, and missionaries had travelled through the region for years, they dispatched across the Atlantic little of what they learned. The traders kept quiet about the agricultural potential of the West because they didn't want to see it settled or developed. That would have been bad for the trade, they said. "Where the axe of the settler rings, there the trapper must certainly disappear," said Sir George Simpson, the governor of the Hudson's Bay Company (HBC). To keep the homesteaders away, the Baymen insisted that the Pacific coast was unsuitable for settlement, while adding that the droughts and frosts on the Prairies made that region unsuitable too.

Palliser, who came from Ireland, and Hector, who was Scottish, did know about the Athabasca Pass region, in the southwest corner of today's Jasper National Park, because a fanciful account of

Scottish botanist David Douglas's supposed discovery of two Himalayan-sized peaks in the Rockies had appeared in England in 1836. Palliser and Hector also knew about the Lake Minnewanka region, near present-day Banff, because Sir George Simpson had described this region in his 1847

Peter Erasmus: "Historians fail to note these factors in crediting their heroes."
(Glenbow Archives NA-3148-1)

book *Narrative of a Journey Around the World in 1841 and 1842.* But they didn't know anything about the early-nineteenth-century Rocky Mountain travels and discoveries of the great geographer and mapmaker David Thompson, because his writings and maps were not published until long after his death in 1857. And while Governor Simpson could have told them about Thompson's trail-blazing cartographical work, he chose instead to dismiss it as "worthless"—essentially because Thompson had done the unthinkable in 1796 when he jumped from the Bay to the rival North West Company.

So when Palliser and Hector set off, in 1857, to see if the southern prairies and mountains of British North America were suitable for overland travel, settlement, and farming, they were—although they didn't know it—following in the footsteps of many others. While the tendency for some historians has been to regard their findings as groundbreaking and important, it might be more realistic for the Palliser report to be seen today as the product of a group of Europeans who journeyed along well-travelled trails and engaged in an exercise in self-education.

Palliser, then forty years old, had been keen to return to North America since 1847–48, when he spent eleven months hunting buffalo ("a noble sport"), elk, antelope, and grizzly bear in the regions of the United States "still inhabited by America's aboriginal people: that ocean of prairies extending to the foot of the great Rocky Mountains." The son of a wealthy Anglo-Irish aristocrat with estates in County Waterford, he never had to get a real job. (His military title was an honorary militia ranking customarily bestowed on members of the landed gentry.) He listed his occupation as "sportsman," and spent much of his life roaming the world on big-game hunting expeditions. He spent the winter of 1847–48 hunting in the prairies and mountains of the Upper Missouri region, not far from the boundary between the United States and British territory, and when he returned home he promoted the idea that the British should know more about their North American possessions. Were these lands suitable for agriculture? Where did the Plains meet the mountains to the northwest? Was there any way of getting through those mountains to the Pacific? Just what exactly was out there?

In 1856 Palliser pitched his exploration idea to the Royal

Geographical Society, asking for money to finance a solo trip to the southern prairies of British North America, and the adjacent passes through the Rocky Mountains, to collect scientific and geographic information. He initially planned to pay his own way, but his family's finances took a beating after the Irish potato famines of the 1840s and his father had to sell some estates to pay down debt.

Captain John Palliser: "Just what exactly was out there?" (Glenbow Archives NB-29-1)

The Royal Geographical Society members, who were aware of American attempts to discover railway routes to the Pacific, took immediate action. The members liked Palliser's plan, but thought that trained scientists should accompany him because his own knowledge of science was limited to a couple of engineering courses he had taken at Dublin's Trinity College. That's how Hector, at age twenty-three, became involved with the expedition; he was recognized as an expert in geology and natural history as well as being a qualified physician. Other members of the expedition included French-born botanist Eugène Bourgeau, astronomer John Sullivan, and naturalist Thomas Blakiston. The British Treasury approved a grant of £5,000 to fund the expeditioners, who were to spend up to two years (later extended to three) exploring the area between Lake Superior and the Pacific coast.

During the first part of their survey, the explorers received expert advice and assistance from a Métis guide and interpreter named James (Big Jimmy) McKay, a heavy-set, 136-kilogram adventurer who joined them in August 1857 when they reached Fort Ellice, just east of the present-day Manitoba–Saskatchewan border. McKay prevented the explorers from venturing into dangerous Blackfoot country, near the international boundary, and guided them safely to Fort Carlton, near today's Duck Lake, Saskatchewan, where they spent their first winter.

In December 1857, Hector travelled by dogsled from Fort Carlton to Fort Edmonton to recruit Métis drivers and guides for the expedition's spring and summer work on the southern prairies and in the Rocky Mountains. A couple of months later he met Peter Erasmus, and the two men—who were both in their early twenties—took an immediate liking to one another. Hector could see that Erasmus had strong leadership, interpreting, and guiding skills, and Erasmus liked the fact that Hector—far from being a pampered and condescending Brit—could hold his own in any outdoors situation: "He could talk, ride or tramp snowshoes with the best of our men, and never fell back on his position to soften his share of the hardships."

Erasmus was both cultured and well educated. Of Danish-Cree parentage, he was born in the Red River Settlement, a colony in what is now Manitoba, and studied to become an Anglican clergy-man. However, he was drawn to the free life farther west and in 1855 agreed to serve as an interpreter for a Methodist missionary, Thomas Woolsey, in the Fort Edmonton region. Erasmus was well suited to the job; he spoke six Native languages, English, Latin, and Greek.

Erasmus began his two-season stint with the Palliser Expedition in the summer of 1858 and, while he was destined to become a tower of strength for Hector, he was under no illusions as to who would get the credit when it was all over. Many of the earlier visi-tors would have been "hopelessly lost, starved or frozen to death without the guidance and advice of the Indians and half-breeds," Erasmus wrote in *Buffalo Days and Nights*. "Historians fail to note these factors in crediting their heroes and glorifying their charac-ters in their stories. The Indians and half-breeds were paid servants and thus not entitled to any praise for their deeds, which were quite frequently at the risk of their own lives."

The expedition divided into three parties for the 1858 journey from Fort Carlton to the Rocky Mountains. Hector, Erasmus, three Métis voyageurs, and a Native hunter nicknamed Nimrod (because Hector couldn't pronounce his actual name, which trans-lated roughly as "the one with a thumb like a blunt arrow") searched the Bow River system for passes through the Rockies, using a crude birchbark map that Erasmus had acquired from a Stoney friend—whom he didn't name in his memoirs. Bourgeau travelled with Hector for a while and then dallied in the foothills to collect and study plants. Blakiston did some exploring around what is now the Waterton Lakes area. Palliser explored the western and southern limits of what would later become known as Palliser's Triangle, a drought-prone stretch of southern Alberta and Saskatchewan that Palliser considered ill-suited for agriculture, though later explorers and botanists, most notably the Irish-born naturalist John Macoun, would disagree with him. Palliser also crossed the Rockies somewhere near the United States boundary, by a pass he named Kananaskis. Geographers have had difficulty pinpointing this location—some think it was today's North Kananaskis Pass, others think it could be Elk Pass—because Palliser travelled quickly and left notes so sketchy that they were later considered to have almost no geographic value.

Hector named several landmarks as he wandered through the mountains. They included Vermilion Pass, Mount Ball, the Sawback Range, Mount Murchison, Castle Mountain (which carried the name Mount Eisenhower from 1946–79), and Kicking Horse Pass, which received its unusual name after a saddle horse kicked Hector in the chest, and which later became the route through the mountains for the Canadian Pacific Railway line.

There are a few recorded versions of the horse-kicking incident, which took place on 29 August 1858. Erasmus reported that the incident happened when Hector went to retrieve his saddle horse after helping pull a pack horse out of what is now the Kicking Horse River. The saddle horse reared on its hind legs and kicked Hector so hard with its front hooves that he lay unconscious for two hours before recovering. Hector added a note in his journal to the effect that after he regained consciousness the men "covered me up under a tree, and I sent them all off to try and raise something to eat." Later on, he embellished the account to say that his companions "proceeded to dig my grave, but lucky for me I revived before being buried alive." Another version of the story, which has become part of the folklore of the Rockies, says that Hector was actually placed in the shallow grave by his companions, and that they had started to shovel dirt on his body when he winked at them!

Hector spent two days recuperating before he felt strong enough to continue travelling. During that time the rest of the party went hungry because Erasmus and Nimrod came back empty-handed from hunting trips. Hector dipped into his emergency supply of pemmican to tide them over but it wasn't until 3 September 1858, five days after the horse-kicking incident, that the starving men were able to sit down to their next full meal—a moose shot by Nimrod. They continued to journey through the mountains for another month, returning to Fort Edmonton on 7 October 1858.

Hector and Erasmus spent the first part of 1859 exploring in the Athabasca Pass region, following in the footsteps of botanist David Douglas. By this time Erasmus had added geological surveying to his repertoire of wilderness skills because Hector had instructed him "in the use of those instruments which rendered me useful as a surveyor's assistant." After they returned to Edmonton, Hector and Erasmus headed south toward today's Red Deer and then eastward to the Cypress Hills, where the partnership abruptly dissolved in August 1859.

The partnership ended because Erasmus didn't want to accompany Hector back to the Rockies. Palliser had ordered Hector to return to the mountains, cross them "by the pass you explored last year, and endeavour to explore a route practicable for horses to the westward." However, Erasmus remembered how the group had nearly starved during their previous trip to the Rockies, and he didn't want to repeat the experience. "If you consider the condition of the stock, the lateness of the season, and the scarcity of pemmican and dried meat supplies to take along, you

Dr. James Hector: "Lucky for me I revived before being buried alive." (Glenbow Archives NA-1618-2)

might understand my refusal," he told Hector. "We would have to depend on game in the region. To take from the supplies on hand for your needs will make the other members of the expedition dependent on day-to-day hunting for food. I'm sorry but I just cannot do it."

Hector forged ahead regardless. With Erasmus gone, his travelling companions now included two Métis guides, a couple of gold seekers from California who hoped to strike it rich on the western side of the Continental Divide, and Hector's old hunter, Nimrod, who brought along his wife and child. When they reached the Banff area, Hector seems to have made a discovery that would have a profound impact on the history of the Bow Valley region. "To the right of the trail," wrote Hector, "I observed some warm mineral springs which deposited iron and sulphur, and seemed to escape from beds of limestone." (In 1886, two Canadian mineral prospectors, Billy McCardell and Frank McCabe, would tell a federal mining inquiry that they were actually the ones who "discovered" the hot springs, ensuring future mention in the history books when the springs would precipitate the establishment of Banff National Park and the beginnings of an international tourism industry.)

As it turned out, Hector did make it across the Rockies without running out of food, but he ran into difficulties when he tried to find a pass through the Purcell and Selkirk ranges on the other side. He didn't reach the Pacific coast until he took a more southerly route, through United States territory, and he returned to England with Palliser in June 1860. The three-year expedition cost £13,000—more than two and one-half times the original estimate—and opposition politicians accused the government of squandering money. Palliser came to be seen as an adventurer who prolonged the expedition just to get in a little hunting on the side, and his reports were viewed as useful only insofar as they documented what Natives, fur traders, and missionaries had previously communicated orally. However, the reports did provide some geographical information for such later travellers as the North West Mounted Police, railway surveyors, and planners.

Palliser never returned to North America. He died in poverty in Ireland in 1862 after one adventure in the West Indies and another in Russia. Hector went to New Zealand, became director of the

Geological Survey there, and received a knighthood. He returned to Canada for a brief visit in 1903, after being invited by the CPR to point out the place where the kicking-horse incident had occurred and "see my grave." A memorial cairn honouring Hector's discovery now stands near the Kicking Horse Pass location. Hector died in New Zealand on 5 November 1907.

Erasmus never forgave himself for abandoning Hector in the Cypress Hills in August 1859. Forty-one years later, on 27 June 1900, he wrote Hector a letter saying "if I had not been induced by some fair promise, which I did not realize, I would not this day regret having done the like." It turned out that the real reason Erasmus left the expedition was not so much due to worry about declining food supplies (although that was indeed a concern) as to the fact that he had an opportunity to do some gold mining in British Columbia, from which he made "a snug little sum of money." Hector, for his part, doesn't seem to have borne a grudge. He named a 3,265-metre peak in Banff National Park after Erasmus.

Erasmus returned to service with the Methodists, helped build a mission northeast of Edmonton at Smoky Lake, and spent three years working as an interpreter for the pioneering missionaries George McDougall and his son John. In 1865 Erasmus settled with his wife, the former Charlotte Jackson, at Whitefish Lake, northeast of Smoky Lake, and worked as a trader, trapper, and hunter. He also worked as an interpreter for the federal Indian Affairs department, after having served as an interpreter at the negotiations for Treaty Six, the most comprehensive of the agreements calling for the Canadian government to assume responsibility for the "protection" and "wellbeing" of Canada's Native peoples.

Erasmus died in 1931 at his home in Whitefish Lake, at age ninety-seven, having lived long enough to become the last surviving member of the Palliser Expedition. The *Edmonton Journal* called him "one of the province's most notable citizens" and said he deserved wider recognition for his achievements: "He played a much larger role in shaping the history of the country than has been credited to him." The old log cabin that became Erasmus's Whitefish Lake home in 1861 is now preserved as a heritage building in Fort Edmonton Park.

A Railway Runs through It— 1881-85

WALTER MOBERLY AND MAJOR ALBERT ROGERS FIND THEIR MOUNTAIN PASSES

In the summer of 1865, a thirty-two-year-old British Columbia engineer and government surveyor named Walter Moberly was looking for potential railway routes through the mountains near present-day Revelstoke, in southeastern BC, when he saw a flock of eagles winging its way eastward. He knew that eagles tended to follow a river valley or search for a gap in the alpine wall to fly through, and so he tracked the route of the birds through the Gold Range of what are now called the Monashee Mountains, between Shuswap Lake and the giant Columbia River. When he found what he and the birds were seeking—a corridor through the mountains—he named it Eagle Pass. Excited by his discovery, he hacked some bark from a tree and wrote on it what turned out to be prescient words: "This is the Pass for the Overland Railway."

However, there was no actual transcontinental railway on the books when Moberly made his prophetic announcement in 1865. It was only in 1871, when Prime Minister John A. Macdonald lured British Columbia into Confederation with the promise of a railway across the Northwest to the Pacific, that a transcontinental line became a possibility. And even then, the likelihood of Eagle Pass becoming a railway route through the mountains seemed remote. The Canadian government had decided that the western part of the line connecting Canada's commercial heartland in southern

Ontario and Quebec to the Pacific Ocean should follow the traditional route taken by the explorers and fur traders on their journeys
from Lake Winnipeg to Fort Vancouver. This route led north and
west to Fort Edmonton, through the Yellowhead Pass in the north-
central Canadian Rockies near present-day Jasper, and then down
the valleys of the Thompson and the Fraser rivers to Burrard Inlet
on the Pacific. It was only when this northern route was eliminated
from contention that Eagle Pass did indeed become a railway route
through the Monashee Mountains as Moberly had forecast.

Prime Minister Macdonald fell from power in 1873 because of
the Pacific Scandal, which had to do with the ruling Conservatives
accepting large sums of money in campaign funds from the railway
promoters. When he was returned as prime minister in 1878, he re-
surrected the transcontinental railway project, which went forward
as a private enterprise with some government involvement. The
Canadian Pacific Railway was incorporated as a privately owned
syndicate in February 1881 and for the first few months its major
stockholders seemed happy to go along with the recommendation of
the company's chief engineer, Sandford Fleming, that the new railway be built across the parklands of the northern prairies—referred
to in some exploration reports as the "fertile belt"—through the
Yellowhead Pass to British Columbia. A compelling argument for
this route had already been made, albeit indirectly, some twenty
years earlier when Captain John Palliser led his scientific expedition
through what is now southern Alberta and reported to the Royal
Geographic Society in London that the weather in the southern
prairie region was too dry for farming. The CPR officials said this
meant the land would be unappealing to potential settlers, and so
they initially supported the northern railway route.

But then suddenly, in May 1881, they changed their minds. Instead
of following Fleming's carefully surveyed northern route they settled
on a route through the southern Canadian Rockies, where at least two
potential passes—the Howse and the Kicking Horse—were already
known to exist, and then across the mysterious Selkirk Mountains,
where no pass of any description had yet been found.

Why the change of route? Historians can only speculate. Pierre
Berton, in his classic CPR history *The National Dream*, notes that
the official reason given by Railways Minister Charles Tupper in

1882 was that it would shorten the line by 127 kilometres and give the CPR a greater advantage over its American rivals to the south. However, Berton doubts that this was the chief reason because, if no pass through the Selkirks had been found, then the Canadian railway would have had to circumvent those mountains, and almost all the advantages over the northern route would have been lost.

Nor does Berton think much of the theory advanced by some historians that the change of route was pushed by the Canadian government in an effort to stop American railways from sending feeder lines north of the border and cutting into CPR profits. "This is scarcely tenable," Berton says, "since it was the government that had authorized and surveyed the northern route at great expense."

A more likely reason, says Berton, was the CPR's desire to run the line through largely unsettled prairie territory rather than through country where communities such as Battleford and Prince Albert already existed and where real estate speculators stood poised to make a profit from land sales. By going through virgin territory the railway company was in a position to dictate where key passenger and maintenance depots would be located and, Berton says, "Woe to any speculator who tried to push the company around." As for Palliser's claim that the southern prairie was unsuitable for agriculture, the CPR now had a contradictory and more credible (albeit exaggerated) claim from an Irish-born naturalist named John Macoun to the effect that the region was "one of unsurpassed fertility . . . literally the garden of the whole country." Macoun, who worked for the natural history branch of the Geological Survey of Canada, conducted five surveys of natural vegetation in the region between 1872 and 1881, and each survey reinforced his belief that the entire Northwest—including the arid southern plains—was an agricultural Eden.

With the northern route thus removed from the drawing board, the challenge now for the CPR was to settle on a pass through the Rockies and find a pass through the apparently impassable Selkirks. Walter Moberly had concluded that there was no pass through the Selkirks after tracking the Illecillewaet River along the western slopes of the range in 1865–66 and exploring the route again in the winter of 1871–72. However, an American-born CPR surveyor named Albert Bowman Rogers proved him wrong.

Rogers, who acquired the military title of major when he served with the United States army in the 1860s, was an engineer from Minnesota who earned the nickname "The Railway Pathfinder" for his location work with the Chicago, Milwaukee and St. Paul Railroad. This brought him to the attention of the executive committee of the Canadian Pacific Railway, which hired him in late February 1881 to take charge of all mountain location work for the company.

In May 1881, Rogers took up where Moberly had left off and after a few weeks of hiking and climbing east of the Eagle Pass he reached a point high in the Selkirks where his surveyor's intuition told him that a pass might exist. "Such a view, never to be forgotten," wrote his nephew, also named Albert Rogers, who accompanied the major on the trip. "Our eyesight caromed from one bold peak to another for miles in all directions." From this vantage point, in late June 1881, Rogers thought he saw a way through the barrier, but could not verify this because he had run out of supplies and thus was not able to explore the remaining thirty kilometres.

Major Albert Rogers: "His driving ambition was to have his name handed down in history." (Glenbow Archives NA-1949-1)

The major returned the following summer to approach the ridge from the eastern side and, at a height of 1,370 metres, confirmed the existence of the pass that would forever afterwards bear his name. "His driving ambition was to have his name handed down in history," said his packer, Tom Wilson. "For that he faced unknown dangers and suffered privations. To have the key pass in the Selkirks bear his name was the ambition he fought to realize."

With a route through the Selkirks thus identified, the next question to be resolved was how the railway would cross the southern Rockies east of the Selkirks. The Yellowhead Pass was now out of contention because it was too far north. (It would later become a route through the mountains for both the Grand Trunk Pacific and Canadian Northern railways.) That left the railway builders with a choice between the Howse Pass, which Moberly had favoured, and the still unsurveyed Kicking Horse Pass, which Rogers had boldly pinpointed in 1881 as a possible route, although he secretly harboured doubts about its feasibility.

The Howse Pass, discovered by the explorer David Thompson in 1807, became Moberly's choice for a route through the Rockies when he theorized that the railway would have to circumvent the Selkirks by following the hairpin-shaped Columbia River valley northward and then southward through the Gold Range by way of the Eagle Pass, which led to Fort Kamloops and the canyons of the Fraser River. However, Sandford Fleming first eliminated the Howse Pass from contention when he recommended the northern route through the Yellowhead Pass, and then Major Rogers rejected the Howse in favour of the Kicking Horse Pass located west of present-day Lake Louise. Rogers didn't give much thought to the matter before rejecting the Howse as a southern route through the Rockies. He simply decided on a whim that the Kicking Horse Pass, although located at an elevation of more than fifteen hundred metres, would be a more practical route. But it was a hunch that would give him a great deal of anguish during the months that followed.

Rogers spent the late summer and fall of 1882 satisfying himself that the Kicking Horse Pass was indeed the best choice. Explored in 1858, by James Hector of the Palliser Expedition (it derived its name from an incident in which Hector was kicked in the chest by his saddle horse), the Kicking Horse was known to have severe inclines that might prove difficult for a railway engine to traverse. However, when Rogers's packer, Tom Wilson, returned from an arduous solo trip to the Howse Pass and reported on the extreme difficulties he encountered while getting to the summit and back, Rogers decided that the Kicking Horse Pass should be the preferred route. That would not be the final say on the matter—other

CPR surveyors would have to do some further checking before construction of the line could actually proceed—but for all intents and purposes Rogers had given his bosses both the pass through the Rockies and the pass through the Selkirks that they needed to take the railway from the Prairies to the Pacific. (The severe inclines of the Kicking Horse Pass did, as feared, prove to be a problem. In 1909, after twenty-four years of using three and four locomotives to get trains over the pass, the CPR cut two spiral tunnels into the valley sides to extend the track and reduce the gradient by half.)

Although Moberly had never found a pass through the Selkirks, he tried to pretend that he did and insisted for years that he, not Rogers, discovered the pass that now bears the latter's name. However, there was one achievement that could never be taken away from Moberly. On 7 November 1885, twenty years after he discovered and named Eagle Pass, both he and Rogers were in attendance when the last spike of the CPR was driven at Craigellachie in Eagle Pass. A cairn at Craigellachie commemorates Moberly's discovery of the pass, and a 2,340-metre peak in the Columbia River valley bears his name.

Early Guides and Outfitters—
1881-1972

TOM WILSON, WILLIAM TWIN, BILL PEYTO, AND JIMMY SIMPSON SHOW THE WAY

The railway brought the hotels to the Rockies and the hotels brought the visitors. "If we can't export the scenery, we will import the tourists," said William Van Horne, managerial mastermind behind the Canadian Pacific Railway's construction. The first of them arrived bearing well-oiled hunting rifles and ammunition in September 1887, when Van Horne's "castle in the Rockies," the Banff Springs Hotel, was still a work in progress. They needed a local guide to lead them to the best hunting grounds, and twenty-eight-year-old Tom Wilson was the man recruited for the task.

Wilson had been living and working in the region for six years when assigned to lead the first known guided sport-hunting trip in the Rockies. Raised on a farm north of Toronto, he joined the North West Mounted Police in 1880 at age twenty and was posted as a constable to Fort Walsh in the Cypress Hills, which straddle the borderline between today's Alberta and Saskatchewan. He lasted only a year there. In 1881, he secured a discharge from the police force to join a CPR survey crew working its way westward into the Rockies. Wilson signed on as a packer, to help transport supplies by horse and wagon from a trading post at Fort Benton, Montana.

Wilson spent three summers in the mountains with the railway survey and building crews, working closely with Major Albert Rogers, the American-born surveyor after whom the Rogers Pass is named. The railway workers detested Rogers, a quick-tempered, tobacco-spitting, hard-swearing eccentric who made many enemies. "The labourers hated him for the way he drove them and the packers for the way he abused the horses," Wilson said. However, after volunteering to accompany Rogers on his first exploration trip to the Kicking Horse Pass in 1881, Wilson grew to like the gruff surveyor. "Very few men ever learned to understand him, yet he had a generous heart and a real affection for many. He wore a thick mask, and it was in being able to see beneath it that my dislike for him changed to affection."

Wilson achieved a number of firsts during his early years in the mountains. In the summer of 1882, accompanied by a Stoney guide he named "Gold Seeker," Wilson became one of the first white men to visit and take note of Lake Louise. He described his "discovery" as "the gem of beauty beneath the glacier" and named it Emerald Lake. It appeared under that name on the first geological map of the region, published in 1886. However, by that time, the Geographical Society of Canada had named it Lake Louise to honour the wife of the Marquis of Lorne, Governor General of Canada. The Emerald Lake name did survive, though, when Wilson subsequently gave it to another scenic gem he "found" in the Rockies, near today's Field, British Columbia.

In 1884, Wilson became the first white man to push through a pass into the Yoho Valley, east of Field, and gaze upon the magnificent Takakkaw Falls. (Takakkaw is actually the Cree word for magnificent.) The following year he took time out from his mountain adventures to serve with Sam Steele's Scouts, helping put down the Northwest Rebellion. He was back in the mountains, however, in time to witness the driving of the last spike of the transcontinental railway at Craigellachie, and to be included in the famous photograph of the event. After that, Wilson made the mountains his permanent home. He married Minnie McDougall, a cousin of the pioneering Methodist missionary John McDougall, and established the region's first guiding and outfitting business, supplying horses and equipment for wilderness trips.

By 1890, two years after the Banff Springs Hotel opened, Wilson had been granted the right to call himself "guide to the CPR." His clients included such prominent mountaineers and explorers as

Walter Wilcox, R. L. Barrett, and, most famous of all, Sir Edward Whymper, the English-born conqueror of the Matterhorn. Although Whymper's fondness for alcohol prevented him from accomplishing anything significant during his trips to the Rockies between 1900 and 1905 or in 1909, two years before his death at age seventy-one, he did draw a lot of international newspaper publicity that helped consolidate Wilson's reputation as the top white outfitter and guide in the Rockies.

While Wilson was earning Whymper's approval as the best white guide in the mountains, a Stoney named William Twin was quietly establishing himself as the exemplar of the Native as mountain guide. Born in 1847 as Ne-sho-dao (a Stoney name meaning "embers") into the Chiniki Band, Twin received his English name from the Methodist missionary Robert Rundle and was one of the only members of his tribe to enter the new trade of guiding when the tourists arrived on the first scheduled passenger trains. While others in the tribe attempted to become farmers or ranchers—not easy for a society that had been nomadic for centuries—Twin quickly adapted to new possibilities and lived a full life in the mountains.

In 1893, a group of Philadelphia tourists hired Twin to bring saddle ponies from the Morley reserve to Laggan (the Lake Louse train

station) so they could ride in comfort the three kilometres from the station to the lake. One of the group, Mary Schäffer, recalled that she gave Twin a half dollar to provide her with a dependable horse, and he offered her what seemed like "one of the most forlorn horses in the group." However, the horse,

Tom Wilson in the doorway of his cabin at Kootenay Plains: "The gem of beauty beneath the glacier." (Whyte Museum of the Canadian Rockies V701/LC-36)

named Joshua, proved to be the best of the bunch. "While all the other horses were wandering all over the trail, taking every advantage of a bunch of easterners who had no idea on earth how to make them go, my woolly, skinny Joshua marched steadily ahead." The Philadelphians dismounted so they could wander around Lake Louise for a while and when they returned to the horses to continue their journey, Schäffer was disturbed to find another member of the party trying to mount Joshua. Twin quickly took care of that situation. He shook his fist at the interloper and ordered her back on the horse she had used for the trip to the lake from the train station. "Dear old William Twin had not forgotten the piece of silver which had changed hands," said Schäffer.

The following summer Twin helped a friend of Schäffer, a young Philadelphia linguist and explorer named Samuel Allen, give appropriate Stoney names to the mountain features he was exploring and mapping. Some of the features were later renamed, but many have survived. They include such peaks as Hungabee (chief) and Wiwaxy (windy), a pass and a valley named Wastach (beautiful), and a small mountain lake named Minnestimma (sleeping water).

When the first New York Sportsman's Show was held in Madison Square Garden in 1895, the Canadian Pacific Railway decided to exhibit in the show and asked missionary John McDougall to recommend a "real grizzly bear hunter." McDougall chose Twin because the guide had already shown himself capable of getting along with tourists, and he could speak English. Twin travelled to New York by train—something he had never done before—and when the train stopped at Winnipeg, Twin accompanied McDougall to an evening service at Grace Church that featured organ music and a choir singing in four-part harmony. "What I have seen and heard tonight is greater than all my dreams," he told McDougall. The missionary reported afterwards that it was a delight to see how this man, who had spent all his life in the mountains, reacted to such new experiences as eating and sleeping in a moving train. "Now I am in an unknown land," said Twin, "but you know where we are going, and I have faith in you."

While the sights and sounds of Winnipeg impressed Twin, he did not find much good to say about New York. "Many canyons of buildings," he said. "Walk many miles, find no stream, find no lake, find no poles for lodge. Not very good place for camp."

Twin worked as a guide and outfitter in the Rockies until he was well into his seventies, and frequently supplied horses from the Morley reserve to Wilson's expanding guiding and outfitting business in Banff. As Wilson's business grew, so did his need to hire good assistants and some of these went on to establish reputations for themselves as both accomplished guides and colourful characters. They included William (Wild Bill) Peyto, a crazy Englishman from London who, it is said, once let a lynx loose in a Banff saloon just to see how quickly the drunken patrons could get to their feet, and Jimmy Simpson, a rogue from Lincolnshire, England, who helped break the monopoly of the CPR by building one of the first independently owned hotels in the Rockies.

Peyto (1848–1943) was a farm boy, from what is now Greater London, who left England at age eighteen because he thought his part of the world was becoming too industrialized and he wanted to live in the Canadian wilderness. After travelling west, on the recently completed Canadian Pacific Railway line, Peyto worked as a railway labourer at Golden, British Columbia, did some copper prospecting in what is now Yoho National Park, and then settled on a plot of land near Cochrane, Alberta, where he thought he might take up ranching.

Peyto soon realized that he preferred being in the mountains, prospecting, hunting, and trapping. He moved to Banff in the early 1890s, built a log cabin home, and established himself as a horse outfitter and packer, guiding tourists drawn by the romance of the Rockies. Climbers and hunters sought his services because he knew the terrain so well, and were invariably surprised to discover that this quintessential North American mountain man spoke with a broad English accent. "Peyto assumes a wild and picturesque though somewhat tattered attire," wrote American mountaineer Walter Wilcox. "But he is one of the most conscientious and experienced men with horses that I have ever known."

As Peyto's reputation as an outfitter and guide grew (he billed himself as "the most reliable and experienced guide in the Canadian Rockies—I make a specialty of ladies' camping outfits"), so did his reputation as a colourful eccentric with a peculiar sense of humour. One of his habits was to snowshoe into Banff from his copper claim near today's Sunshine Village ski resort, buy a steak at the butcher shop, and make a big show of eating it raw while snowshoeing back to Sunshine. He never used a razor, always shaving himself—badly—with his hunting knife. It is also claimed that he once killed a grizzly bear with his pistol and blew away an alarm clock with his gun because he didn't like the sound of the ringing bell.

Although Peyto cultivated a reputation both as a heavy drinker and as an eccentric, he performed efficiently and responsibly when working as a guide and outfitter. Climbers and hunters sought his services because he knew the terrain so well, and such young guiding assistants as Jimmy Simpson, who was thirty years Peyto's junior, looked up to him as a mentor.

Simpson (1877–1972) was a remittance man sent to Canada by his uncle in hopes that he would earn a respectable living as a farmer, after failing at the various trades he tried in England. However, he wasn't cut out to be a farmer. He arrived in Winnipeg in 1896 as a red-haired nineteen-year-old, took one look at the homestead his uncle had arranged for him to buy, and spent the money on booze instead. After the money ran out, he pawned his gold watch and bought a ticket to Calgary on a cattle train. From there he stowed away on a passenger train bound for Golden, British Columbia, where he hoped to work for the CPR. However, a conductor found him hiding aboard and kicked him off the train near Lake Louise.

Simpson worked as a CPR labourer around Lake Louise and fell in love with the mountains. However, he still had some more of North America to see before settling in the area. After a few months in Lake Louise, he headed for San Francisco "to see the sights on fifty dollars." When he returned to the Rockies, in the summer of 1898, after working as a logger in Oregon and then as a seaman aboard a schooner hunting seal off the West Coast, Simpson "decided then and there that Banff was the place for me." He joined Tom Wilson's outfit as a trail cook and began to learn the basics of horse packing and guiding from Wilson and his assistant Peyto. Simpson would later describe Peyto as his "teenage hero," whom he was "determined to emulate or die in the attempt."

One of Simpson's first jobs for Wilson was to help cut a trail north of Lake Louise through the Bow River Valley along today's Highway 93, which links Lake Louise to Jasper. When he "discovered" Bow Lake, picturesquely located beneath the blue ice of Bow Glacier (which has since disappeared from view due to climate change), Simpson described it as "the most beautiful thing I've seen in Canada" and said, "I'll build a shack here sometime." Over the next twenty years, it would become his favourite camping spot.

A bequest from an English relative allowed Simpson to start building his own guiding and outfitting business in the early years of the twentieth century. Like his hero, Peyto, he cultivated a reputation as a hard-drinking eccentric. He wore the Stetson and fringed buckskin shirts that the "dudes" (as he called his clients) expected of a genuine mountain cowboy, and he claimed in later years that water never passed his lips. "This whole country was built on rum," he said. "Nobody drank any water when I came here. They all said the Good Lord made it for running under bridges."

By 1916, Simpson was well established as a guide, trapper, horseman, self-taught naturalist, and wilderness traveller in the Rockies. The Stoney called him Nashan-esen ("wolverine go quick") because of his speed on snowshoes. Resolutely independent, he seemed content to live the single life forever. However, at age thirty-nine he surprised his friends by getting married. His bride was Williamina (Billie) Ross Reid, a twenty-five-year-old Scottish immigrant who worked in Calgary at a dry goods store. They raised two daughters, who grew up to become accomplished figure skaters, and a son they named Jimmy Jr.

In 1919, Simpson made preparations to build a lodge at his favourite camping spot near Bow Lake. It was to be much more elaborate than the "shack" he had talked about twenty years earlier. In a letter to the Commissioner of Dominion Parks, Simpson asked to lease ten acres for construction of "suitable buildings for development of the tourist business." He received four acres and put two small log cabins and a boathouse on the site. A bequest, from his uncle in England, helped pay for the $5,000 in improvements. Simpson named the camp Ram Pasture and used it in the summertime as a base for his guiding and outfitting operations.

During the early 1930s, the federal government put unemployed men to work building a long-awaited road between Banff and Jasper.

Simpson's Bow Lake camp now assumed strategic importance as a tourist destination because it was located along the new route. Simpson, however, couldn't capitalize on the situation by developing an expanded tourist facility because he lacked the cash. It wasn't until his talented daughters gave him the money that he was able to proceed.

Margaret and Mary Simpson had been doing well as figure skaters ever since they made their pre-adolescent debuts as the Simpson Sisters at the 1928 Banff Winter Carnival. After appearing across Canada as amateurs during their teens, they turned professional in 1937 when their mother, Billie, negotiated a contract with an American touring ice revue, Gay Blades. Dressed in Mountie-style uniforms, they performed as the "Sweethearts of the Canadian Rockies" and jointly earned between US$350 and $450 per week. (Taking inflation into account, that works out to around $5,000 a week in 2004 American dollars.) With a share of that money Simpson was able to carry on with his expansion project. In 1940, he completed work on a $15,000 stone and log lodge with six guest rooms that he named Num-Ti-Jah (the Stoney word for pine marten) and acquired a permit to operate it as a summer hotel.

Simpson was sixty-three when the first phase of Num-Ti-Jah was completed, and the lodge became his primary focus during the years following. He turned his guiding and outfitting business over to his son, made one of the original Ram Pasture cabins a summer residence for himself and Billie, and began expanding the main lodge to accommodate the increased tourist traffic. By 1950 a second storey had been added to the building and the number of guest rooms had grown from six to twenty-five. Jimmy Jr. lived year-round with his wife in a four-room suite on the second floor. Jimmy Sr. and Billie continued to live at Ram Pasture during the summer and moved back to Banff when the tourist business began to drop off in winter. Daughter Mary, meanwhile, spent her summers helping out at the lodge until she retired from skating, married, and settled in Fort St. James, British Columbia. Her sister, Margaret, also helped at the lodge for a few summers until she died, unexpectedly, of complications relating to a tubal pregnancy.

The work of running a lodge proved too burdensome for Jimmy Sr. and Billie as they got older. They passed the torch to Jimmy Jr.

while Jimmy Sr. settled into a new role as the lodge's resident "grand old man of the mountains," telling stories to the tourists about his years in the Rockies.

When Jimmy Simpson died, in October 1972 at age ninety-five, he was hailed as the last of the early guides and outfitters. His old boss Wilson had died in 1933, his hero Peyto had died in 1943, and William Twin died in 1944. Wilson had left guiding in 1904 because he couldn't make enough money from it to support his wife and five children, and had operated a horse ranch and trading post in the Kootenay Plains for several years before returning to Banff in 1927 to spend his last years giving talks about his guiding experiences to the guests at the Banff Springs Hotel. Peyto had left guiding in 1913 to become one of the first park wardens to work in what is now Banff National Park, and had worked for the warden service until 1936 when he retired due to ill health. Twin had worked as a guide until he was in his late seventies and spent the last twenty years of his life telling stories to tourists, as the *Crag & Canyon* described it, "about the real Indian days, which have gone, never to return."

Wilson, Peyto, and Simpson (but not Twin) have mountains named after them in the Rockies. Mount Wilson stands just north of Saskatchewan River Crossing, midway between Banff and Jasper. Peyto Peak is located near the Wapta Icefield, halfway between Saskatchewan River Crossing and Lake Louise. Mount Jimmy Simpson overlooks the lakeside area where Simpson's Num-Ti-Jah Lodge is situated, still looking much as it did when completed in 1950.

Jimmy Simpson painting at his kitchen table: *"I'll build a shack here sometime."* (Whyte Museum of the Canadian Rockies V577/IID/PA/27)

A National Park is Born— 1885

FORTUNE HUNTERS FRANK MCCABE AND BILLY MCCARDELL FORCE THE CANADIAN GOVERNMENT'S HAND

C anada's national park system began as a romantic idea in the mind of CPR chief engineer Sandford Fleming, who said after a trip to the Rockies in 1883 that the federal government should create, for future tourists, "retreats of quiet repose amid some of the grandest scenes of wild nature." However, when the idea became a reality in 1885, it wasn't because the government wanted to protect the environment or set aside tracts of unspoiled wilderness for the enjoyment of tourists. It was to stop a group of speculators from exploiting the commercial potential of the hot mineral springs in the Banff area.

Word of the hot springs first reached Ottawa in early 1885 when a Nova Scotia-born railway construction worker and part-time mineral prospector named Frank McCabe applied to the federal Interior ministry for ownership rights to what his prospecting partner, Billy McCardell, would later call a "mysterious grotto where warm clear water bubbled from its depths." The grotto, which is now part of the Cave and Basin national historic site, was located on the lower slopes of Sulphur Mountain, just south of the present town of Banff. McCabe and McCardell, accompanied by McCardell's younger brother Tom, claimed to have "discovered" the springs in 1883 while looking for the fabled Lost Lemon Mine, an elusive gold find that had drawn prospectors to the region for a dozen years.

McCabe and the McCardell brothers were not the first white visitors to come upon the bubbling hot springs known to local Natives for centuries. In 1875, two American fur hunters, Willard Younge and Benjamin Pease, spent a season trapping near the hot springs after members of the local Stoney tribe told them where to find the thermal waters. Before that, in 1859, James Hector of the Palliser Expedition wrote in his journal that he observed the hot springs while looking for a way to cross the Rockies on horseback. However, McCabe and the McCardells were the first to try turning the hot springs into a commercial enterprise. They knew that hot-water bathing would appeal to the workers building the transcontinental railway, and also to the wealthy tourists who would visit the area in the future. They asserted squatter rights by building near the Cave and Basin, a crude shack that they called a "hotel," and then built a fence around the cave with the intention of eventually charging admission.

By the time McCabe's letter arrived in Ottawa, various other claimants were seeking a piece of the hot springs action. Archie McNeil, a squatter who rewrote and mailed the letter on McCabe's behalf, added his signature to the claim without McCabe's knowledge. A squatter named Theodore Siebring also filed a claim, as did a squatter named David Keefe, who built a makeshift raft to provide "access" across the Bow River for potential visitors to the springs. A further claim was filed by a visiting Nova Scotia Member of Parliament named Douglas Woodworth, who duped McCabe into signing over his interest and that of the McCardell brothers, and financed construction of some trails around the hot springs.

Ottawa, however, was not about to recognize any exclusive rights to the springs. The lead shown by the Americans in setting aside the Arkansas Hot Springs and Yellowstone National Park for public use had set a precedent for Canada to follow. A New Brunswick MP, Peter Mitchell, was assigned to investigate the matter, and he immediately recognized the value of the Banff springs as a potential spa. He reported to Prime Minister John A. Macdonald that the site, when developed, could be worth "at least half a million dollars." CPR general manager William Van Horne subsequently visited the site and declared, "These springs are worth a million dollars." Van Horne envisaged Banff becoming the new Switzerland. Faced with such profit potential, Prime Minister Macdonald decided that the springs should belong to the people of Canada. "No squatting should be allowed," he wrote in a letter to Deputy Interior Minister Alexander Burgess, who had recommended that the springs be reserved for public use. "And any attempt to squat should be resisted."

Interior Minister Thomas White visited the site in October 1885 and told the squatters that no ownership rights would be granted for the springs, although he added that some compensation might be given for "improvements" made to the site. He wrote to the prime minister saying, "It would be a great misfortune to permit the springs to get into the hands of any of these claimants." He directed William Pearce, of the Dominion Lands Branch, to prepare a plan of the proposed reserve area, amounting to about twenty-six square kilometres on the north face of Sulphur Mountain. He submitted the plan to the Privy Council for approval and, on 28 November 1885, the world's third national park (after Yellowstone and Australia's Royal National Park) came into being. The enabling clause of the Order-in-Council was worded as follows:

> His Excellency by and with the advice of the Queen's Privy Council for Canada has been pleased to order, and it is hereby ordered, that whereas near the station of Banff on the Canadian Pacific Railway, in the Provisional District of Alberta, North-West Territories, there have been discovered several hot mineral springs which promise to be of great sanitary advantage to the public, and in order that proper control of the lands surrounding these springs may be vested in the Crown, the said lands in the territory, including said springs and in their immediate neighbourhood, be and they are hereby reserved from sale or settlement or squatting.

Pearce posted signs around the hot springs forbidding further construction on the site, and convened a hearing, called the Hot Springs Inquiry, to settle the various claims. Although Pearce didn't think the claims had any legal standing, he recommended that token payments be given to buy the silence of the claimants and thus allow government development of the park reserve to proceed without hindrance. He awarded a total of $1,350 to McCabe and the McCardells for "improving" the site, and gave $100 to Keefe for his makeshift ferry. (McNeil, who had signed the McCabe letter, didn't make an appearance at the hearing.) MP Woodworth, who demanded $4,397 for building the trails and buying the shack "hotel" from McCabe and the McCardell brothers, received $1,000. Other claimants received nothing. Squatter Siebring was advised that his cabin was more of an eyesore than an improvement. Willard Younge, who attended the inquiry to claim credit for "discovering" the springs in 1875, was denied compensation because he had done nothing to develop the site.

With the claimants thus dispatched, the government was left free to choose its own business partners and, as Interior Minister White said, "make of the reserve a creditable national park." The CPR, which was already planning to build a luxury tourist hotel in Banff, arranged for a chemical analysis of the thermal waters and reported that the "million dollar" springs were filled with sulphur and other curative minerals. The CPR called for immediate development of the springs, and the government responded by building a carriage road from the Banff train station (then known as Siding 29) to the Cave and Basin site. A second road was built to the Upper Hot Springs, located at the fifteen-hundred-metre level on Sulphur Mountain. For a Bow River crossing, the government put in a temporary pontoon bridge at a cost of six hundred dollars. It was later replaced by a sturdier steel structure.

George Stewart, a federal land surveyor and soon-to-be first superintendent of what was now called Banff Springs Park, oversaw the construction work. Operating from a tent pitched near the train station, he surveyed and laid out a grid-patterned townsite on the north side of the Bow River, as well as pushing through roads to the hot springs and to the site of the new Banff Springs Hotel. He arranged for a government-owned bathhouse to be built at the Cave and Basin site, and leased the Upper Hot Springs to a couple of private operators. They paid fifteen dollars a year for the water rights and built bathhouses with adjoining hotel accommodation.

Stewart reported to Ottawa that a large tract of land beyond the original park reserve, encompassing Lake Minnewanka (then Devil's Lake) and Spray Lakes, presented "features of the greatest beauty" and should be added to the reserve. As a result, when the Rocky Mountains Park Act was enacted in 1887 to formally change the status from reserve to actual park and retroactively approve the government expenditures on its development, the legislation covered an area that had grown from 26 to 673 square kilometres. (In 1930, following years of back-and-forth boundary movements, the renamed Banff National Park would grow to ten times that size.) Prime Minister Macdonald visited the region with his wife, Lady Agnes, in the summer of 1886, and immediately became one of the park's biggest supporters. He predicted that it would bring prestige and money to Canada. The water from the hot springs would "recuperate the patients" and the rental of the waters would "recoup the Treasury."

Opposition MPs suggested that the government should stay out of the park development business, and that the CPR should build the needed infrastructure to support a future tourist industry. However, Macdonald insisted that the government had a responsibility to make the park "useful" for the country, not just for the CPR. "The Canadian Pacific Railway would be only too glad to take the land and make 1,000 percent profit out of it." If the park was to be a showplace for Canada and a "place of great resort," Macdonald said, it was clear that the government must regulate and administer it.

The Rocky Mountains Park Act received royal assent on 23 June 1887. The baby born in 1885 now became a toddler. The dedication clause said the parkland should be "reserved and set apart as a public pleasure ground for the benefit, advantage and enjoyment of the people of Canada." In the years following, the region would become a subject of debate between those who would try to stop further tourism and recreation facilities from being developed, and those who would try to continue exploiting the parkland for commercial gain. In 1902, for example, it would expand enormously to include Kananaskis Country and a large part of the eastern slopes, only to be cut back again in 1911—following a backlash from ranchers and resource developers. However, for the moment, it was a place where hot springs and townsite development could occur without, in Macdonald's words, "interfering with the beauty of the park as a whole."

Banff Indian Days—
_1889-1978_

WALKING BUFFALO AND THE STONEY ESTABLISH A
MOUNTAIN TRADITION

A rockslide on the CPR line in the summer of 1889 brought rail
transportation to a standstill, stranded tourists at the new sixty-
room Banff Springs Hotel, and paved the way for an impromptu
celebration of Native culture that continued annually for the next
eighty-nine years. When the hotel management discovered that the
track crews would take more than ten days to repair the damaged
line, they asked CPR guide Tom Wilson if he could arrange for
some entertainment to keep the stranded guests amused. He rode
his pony sixty-five kilometres to the Morley reserve and asked his
friends in the Stoney community if they could help. They instantly
offered to ride up to the Banff Springs Hotel and put on a show for
the visitors.

Two hundred and fifty Stoney arrived in Banff over the next
couple of days, bringing cayuses, tipis, travois, ceremonial feath-
ered headdresses, and other Native regalia. They camped along the
Bow River below Bow Falls and remained there for about a week,
offering horse races, foot races, tugs-of-war, dance demonstrations,
and a rare opportunity for the "white savages"—as a witty eighteen-
year-old Stoney named Walking Buffalo called them—to visit the
tipi homes of the once-nomadic tribe and inhale the pleasing scents
of sweetgrass and poplar smoke.

Walking Buffalo had already witnessed a number of important

firsts, and experienced something of the white way of life, when he took part in that first informal display of Native culture that later came to be called Banff Indian Days. The grandson of two Stoney tribal chiefs and the son of a warrior named Wolf Ear, he was born in a tipi at Morley before the reserve was established and attended the historic signing of Treaty Seven in September 1877. Though only six years old at the time, Walking Buffalo retained vivid memories of the signing, recalling that until that time he had no idea there were so many people in the world. One of the signatories to the treaty was his uncle, Chief Jacob Bearspaw.

A restless and troublesome student at the McDougall mission school in Morley, Walking Buffalo, at age nine, was adopted and given the name George McLean by a visiting Methodist missionary named John McLean. His maternal grandmother, Jane, who had raised Walking Buffalo from infancy after his mother, Leah, died of a childbirth-related illness, readily agreed to give the boy up for adoption when the Rev. McLean said he could give him the opportunities to become a church minister or doctor.

With the Rev. McLean's support, Walking Buffalo attended a government residential school in Red Deer, after completing his elementary schooling in Morley. When the CPR line pushed through Stoney territory in 1885 the fourteen-year-old Walking Buffalo rode on the first eastbound passenger train from Morley to Calgary. He told his friends afterwards that while he enjoyed the experience, he still preferred travelling on horseback.

From Red Deer, Walking Buffalo moved to Winnipeg to study at St. John's Methodist School and, during a trip home in the summer of 1886, he had an opportunity to visit a newly organized Calgary agricultural fair that later evolved into the annual Stampede. Shortly after that, his formal schooling ended. Rev. McLean wanted him to carry on with his studies in Winnipeg, but Chief Bearspaw insisted that Walking Buffalo return home for good. "White men's schools may be all right, but you can get too much of anything," Bearspaw told McLean. "If he stays longer at school, he will never come back to us. We want him here; we need him now as an interpreter."

A powerfully built individual, Walking Buffalo worked briefly as a blacksmith in Calgary before returning to the reserve. By the time the first Banff Indian Days was held in 1889, he was re-established at Morley, about to marry Flora, the daughter of a Stoney medicine man named Hector Crawler, teaching at the reserve school, building a log house, and starting to acquire cattle and horses for a ranch.

The first Banff event in 1889 was so successful that the Stoney were invited to return the following year to participate in the sports days held annually in conjunction with Queen Victoria's birthday on 24 May, and Dominion Day on 1 July. After that, more and more Natives from Morley came each year to pit their equestrian and running talents against those of local Banff residents. By 1902, it was clear that a larger site was needed, both for the Stoney camp and for the activities. The new location was the flats near Minnehappa, a waterfall at the base of Cascade Mountain, which had once been the site of a racetrack.

In 1908, Walking Buffalo was one of five accomplished Stoney equestrians from Morley chosen by Rev. John McDougall to appear in Calgary as guest performers with the Miller Brothers' 101 Ranch Wild West Show, one of the more successful of the travelling Buffalo Bill show imitators. Guy Weadick, an enterprising young cowboy showman who would later become the architect of the Stampede, asked Rev. McDougall to let the Stoney perform, along with half a dozen Sioux from the United States, in a "wild Indian" act that included the dramatization of an attack on white "settlers" travelling across the arena in an ox-drawn covered wagon. Walking Buffalo and his friends were happy to do the "warpath" scenes for a couple of dollars each and, when Weadick returned in 1912 to stage the first Stampede, he asked Rev. McDougall to bring together a much larger gathering of Natives for the event. Weadick understood the importance of staging sideshows that would contribute to the overall excitement of the main rodeo program, and he thought that thousands of Natives in full ceremonial dress would make for a great spectacle.

It was uncertain at first whether or not the federal government would allow the Natives to participate in the Stampede. The government was trying to turn Natives into farmers and ranchers and didn't think they should be taking time away from their duties to participate in public exhibitions and rodeos. However, Weadick managed to convince several important people, including Senator James Lougheed and future prime minister R. B. Bennett, that a

Native presence was key to the Stampede's success. In August 1912, a month before the Stampede was due to start, the government backed down and more than five thousand Natives—the biggest such gathering since the signing of Treaty Seven—came to the Stampede to present their dances and compete in the rodeo events. Walking Buffalo competed in the steer roping events and, though he did not win any prizes, he did take home a souvenir—a medal presented to him by the Duke of Connaught, Canada's Governor General—that he wore with pride for the rest of his life.

Banff Indian Days was a well-established institution by the time the Stampede became an annual event—starting in 1923. Directed by Norman Luxton, a Banff entrepreneur and adventurer who once tried, unsuccessfully, to sail across the Pacific in a dugout canoe, Banff Indian Days expanded over the years to include such events as dance competitions, rodeos, concerts, and pageants. The Banff Springs Hotel built a grandstand for the spectators and, while the Stoney in later years would come to regard the event as exploitative, featuring Natives in a spectacle put on just for white visitors, they saw it in the early years as a welcome opportunity to showcase their heritage. As author Jon Whyte wrote in his book *Indians in the Rockies*, "Indian Days at Banff allowed them to be proudly Stoney, to revel in a noble past, apologizing to no one for the grandeur of their costumes, the sublimity of their music, the richness of their culture."

Walking Buffalo was a popular figure at both Banff Indian Days and the Stampede, where the Indian Village, with its tipis, pow-wows, and displays of historical artifacts, was a major attraction. Whyte recalled visiting Walking Buffalo's tipi as a child, on a trip to the Calgary Stampede during the 1940s, and being awed by his "medicine-man costume of hides, his headdress of bison horns, and his necklace of claws." Author Hugh Dempsey, in his book *Indians of the Rocky Mountain Parks*, reported that Walking Buffalo became so familiar with cameras, as a result of being one of the most photographed figures at Indian Days, that he was always ready to assist a flustered photographer: "On one occasion, when an amateur photographer was having trouble, he took the camera, made the necessary adjustments, and handed it back. He then resumed his pose as a stoic Indian."

While the Banff and Calgary events gave Walking Buffalo a chance to relax every July, he remained busy with serious matters in Morley for the rest of the year. Chosen chief of the band in 1920, following the death of his cousin Moses Bearspaw, Walking Buffalo spent his fifteen years in office working to bring a high school to the reserve "so that our boys and girls will not have to live in an unsympathetic community where people consider them inferior." He also brought modern agriculture techniques, electrical power, and gas heating to his people, and took a strong stand against allowing liquor on reserves. He retired as chief in 1935, at age sixty-four, to devote the rest of his life to reflection and spiritual renewal. The same year, he was introduced at Indian Days to a visiting American evangelist, Frank Buchman, who was to have a profound influence on him. Buchman was the founder of Moral Re-Armament, an international non-denominational revivalistic movement based on moral absolutes and the "life-changing" of individuals through personal growth. Norman Luxton told Walking Buffalo that Buchman was a "man of good will who holds high ideals," and suggested that he make him a blood brother. Walking Buffalo agreed, and spent the next several years studying Buchman's teachings and promoting his philosophy.

In June 1958, when he was eighty-seven, Walking Buffalo accepted an invitation to attend Buchman's eightieth birthday celebration at the American Moral Re-Armament headquarters on Mackinac Island in Lake Michigan. He went on from there to see a play about Moral Re-Armament at the National Theatre in Washington, D.C., where he was accorded a seat in the presidential box. When he returned home to Morley, Walking Buffalo told the tribal councillors that he was prepared to travel the world to promote the cause of peace and understanding and goodwill. "All the nations are lost in darkness, bumping their heads together," he said. "We have got to change the minds and hearts of men so that all nations will be united."

Walking Buffalo began the first of three international tours in October 1959, and spent the next three years travelling back and forth to twenty-seven countries on four continents, talking to more than one million people about peace, aboriginal culture, and spirituality. He met with Prime Minister John Diefenbaker in Ottawa, met the vice-president of the West German government, Victor-Emanuel Preusker, in Bonn, spoke at a civic reception hosted by the mayor of Johannesburg, dined with the king and queen of Bunyoro-Kitara in Uganda, and signed the visitors' book at Buckingham Palace. When he returned to Morley, he suggested that it might be a good idea for someone to build a "university of nature" in the region, where people could learn about aboriginal cultures and the Natives' view of humans as an integral part of the natural world.

In 1962, Walking Buffalo became part of an informal group called the Buffalo Nations Cultural Society, formed to pursue his "university of nature" idea. It was drawn from members of the various Native groups who had signed Treaty Six and Treaty Seven, including the Stoney, Sarcee (Tsuu T'ina), and the Nations of the Blackfoot Confederacy. They encouraged intertribal cooperation, and discussed the possibility of having a Native cultural park or heritage facility located between Calgary and Banff.

Walking Buffalo died before his dream of a "university of nature" could become a reality. He suffered a stroke on 26 December 1967 and died the following day at age ninety-six. "Something of greatness has been removed from us," said historian Grant MacEwan, who published a book about Walking Buffalo two years later.

Banff Indian Days was in trouble at the time of Walking Buffalo's death. The Stoney were exploring their own cultural traditions at home in Morley rather than bringing horses to Banff for the parades, so the spectacular sight of many chiefs on horseback was no longer part of Indian Days. The few Stoney still travelling to Banff were doing so to participate in the rodeo events, which led Indian Days' committee member Claude Brewster to observe, "Most Indians today prefer to be cowboys." In 1970, the rodeo aspect of Indian Days disappeared due to the difficulty of getting stock to Banff for the events, and in 1978 Banff Indian Days finally went out of business due to organizational problems and changing attitudes toward having Natives put on public display for tourists. "We all, I believe, are poorer for the festival's demise," wrote Jon Whyte. "The landscape has lost a human element it harboured for many centuries."

The tradition of celebrating Native culture in the Rockies did not die, however, at that time. In 1989, the Buffalo Nations Cultural Society was registered as a non-profit organization. Invoking the spirit of Walking Buffalo, the society members, who included Stoney Chief George Labelle and Red Thunder dance group organizer Lee Crowchild, revived Indian Days as Buffalo Nations Tribal Days, staging rodeo events and dances at the Rafter Six Ranch Resort adjoining the Morley reserve. The society assumed ownership of the Luxton Museum of the Plains Indian in Banff to keep it from closing because of financial difficulties, and announced that it hoped some day to build a Native cultural park between Calgary and Banff, just as Walking Buffalo had envisaged. "Through these and other projects, the Buffalo Nations Cultural Society continues the tradition promoted by Walking Buffalo," said Luxton Museum executive director Pete Brewster, "encouraging understanding and harmony between human beings and nature through the presentation of aboriginal oral histories, artifacts, songs, dances and crafts."

What's in a Name?—1896

HA LING FINALLY GETS HIS DUE RECOGNITION

It was a wager that precipitated a lengthy controversy over the naming of a mountain in the Rockies. In October 1896, a twenty-eight-year-old Chinese immigrant named Ha Ling accepted a fifty-dollar bet to climb an unnamed 2,680-metre peak about three kilometres south of what is now Canmore, with the understanding that he would complete the ascent and descent within ten hours. He started his climb at 7:00 AM on a Saturday, planted a small flag on the summit, and returned shortly after noon to collect his bet. However, his friends refused to believe he had actually made it to the top, because he came back after little more than five hours and they were unable to see the flag through their field glasses.

Ha Ling's friends insisted on accompanying him back up the mountain the following day. When they found his little flag they acknowledged Ha Ling's achievement, agreed that he had reached the summit, and gave him his fifty dollars—a sizeable sum for that time. They then removed the flag and replaced it with a larger, scarlet model, two metres square with a three-metre pole. "The flag and flagstaff can now be seen by the naked eye," reported the *Medicine Hat News* on 22 October 1896. "As the peak has no name, let it henceforth be called 'Ha Ling Peak' in honour of his daring intrepidity."

The newspaper's call fell upon deaf ears. Within a few years of his mountain-climbing feat, the name of Ha Ling was forgotten. Locally, the mountain became known as Chinamans Peak. But it wasn't an official name; there was no mention of it in either the federal government's gazetteer of Canadian geographical names or in the provincial gazetteer. For more than eighty years, the peak stood nameless as far as Ottawa and Edmonton were concerned.

In 1965, the Historical Society of Alberta reprinted the 1896 *Medicine Hat News* article in the spring issue of its quarterly journal. This prompted Jon Whyte, a Banff poet and historian, to write a column in the *Banff Crag & Canyon* newspaper deploring the fact that the mountain had become informally known by the archaic and derogatory name of Chinamans Peak. "Reader, you are as aware as I that 'Chinaman' is considered a term of disparagement," Whyte wrote. "Since the story has the ring of authenticity to it, I think it quite in accord with its facts that the name of the mountain ought to be Ha Ling Peak. And so, fuelled by the story and by some sense of propriety, I am going to submit the name to the proper authorities to register it in honour of Ha Ling."

The authorities did not go along with Whyte's suggestion. In fact, they moved in the other direction, bowed to local custom and gave the Chinaman name legal recognition. In 1980, both the Canadian Permanent Committee on Geographic Names and the Alberta Historic Sites Board formally ratified Chinamans Peak as the official name. Whyte warned them that the name was deeply offensive to members of the Chinese community and urged them to choose something less pejorative. "If it is not the worst of racist terms, it is still racist," he wrote. The Chinaman name, he said, served only as a reminder of Western Canada's long history of racial discrimination—"a heritage we infrequently refer to proudly."

However, the Historic Sites Board said there was no evidence that the name offended anyone aside from Whyte. To Whyte's surprise, the board rejected his argument that the name fell into the board's own prohibited category of "derogatory, obscene or blasphemous," and noted that the name was already "in current local usage"—the first criterion used by the board when making a name official. "No formal submission has been received to rescind the name," he was told. The board had no comment when Whyte responded that the word "Chinaman" was classified as offensive by virtually every known English-language dictionary because people of Chinese ancestry considered the word a racial slur against them.

Although Whyte kept up the pressure by reminding the Historic Sites Board that it had changed the name of Nigger John Ridge (a geographic landmark honouring the memory of a famous black Alberta cowboy) to the more palatable John Ware Ridge when the name began to offend local sensibilities, he couldn't persuade the board to do the same with Chinamans Peak. Whyte was additionally disappointed to see 1,522 Canmore residents sign a petition urging that the Chinaman name be retained. "The mountain has been known by this name for a very long time," resident Patricia Parker said. "It's part of our history."

When Whyte died in 1992 the mountain still bore the name Chinamans Peak. Five years later, a group of British Columbians of Chinese ancestry successfully petitioned the BC government to have four geographic names with "Chinaman" in the titles removed from the province's gazetteer. That set the scene for a similar initiative in Alberta. In April 1997 members of the Canmore and Calgary Chinese communities formed an ad hoc group with a mission to formally ask the province to rename Chinamans Peak. "We have not been given a fair opportunity to present our case that the term 'Chinaman' is an insult to Chinese people," said Alex Leong, a Calgary medical doctor. "It is degrading. It is disgraceful."

Leong and his colleagues encountered some opposition as they prepared to bring their case to the Alberta Historical Resources Foundation (successor to the Historic Sites Board). Brian Evans, the Member of the Legislative Assembly for Canmore, described Chinamans Peak as a "well-known piece of geographical history in a very well-travelled part of Alberta. It has historical significance. It is a reminder of the Chinese who worked on the railway there in the late 1800s. It has not been seen by the vast majority of people to be offensive." Canmore mayor Bert Dyck said he would only support a name change if a majority of residents demanded it. "If there's a consensus—and I don't mean one person—but if the community comes to see that name as racist, then I won't stand in the way of a change. But I haven't seen the term as racist up to this point."

The Historical Resources Foundation moved quickly to remove Chinamans Peak from the map after Leong and sixty other petitioners of Chinese ancestry presented their case saying the name had to go. The decision came at an appropriate time—on the fiftieth anniversary of the 1947 repeal of the Chinese Immigration Act, a federal law (informally known as the Chinese Exclusion Act) enacted in 1923 to impose severe limits on Chinese immigration to Canada. The Historical Resources Foundation knew it couldn't turn back the clock and wipe out the errors of the past by striking the name of Chinamans Peak from the map, but it could make things better for the future by taking into account the feelings of a previously unheeded community of Chinese-Canadians.

Jettisoning the name turned out to be the easy part. Finding a new name for the mountain proved to be somewhat more difficult. Some Canmore residents said that the man who first climbed it was actually named Li Poon and that he should be honoured accordingly. Others said it should be called Towers' Peak in tribute to the ancestors of former provincial lieutenant-governor Gordon Towers, whose family had a long-time association with the town and mountain. Meanwhile, Stoney residents from the nearby Morley reserve suggested that the peak should be given the traditional Native name for Canmore, which is loosely translated as "shooting at an animal in the willows."

After deliberating for more than a year, the province announced in July 1998 that it would follow the century-old suggestion of the *Medicine Hat News* (and the 1965 recommendation of the late Jon Whyte) and name the mountain Ha Ling Peak. The entire range, which included as many as five other unnamed peaks, would be called Ehagay Nakoda, meaning "the last human." Another peak would be called Miner's Peak in recognition of Canmore's coal mining heritage.

Little is known about Ha Ling aside from the fact that the *Medicine Hat News* credited him with climbing the mountain. It has been speculated that he reached the Rockies either during the construction period of the Canadian Pacific Railway or shortly thereafter, and that he is the Chinese-born man identified as "Hong Ling" in the 1891 census for Canmore. (Census takers didn't always get the names right when dealing with immigrants.) Ling was one of three individuals listed in the census as being born in China. His age was given as twenty-three and his occupation listed as "cook." It is thought that he worked either in a mining camp or at the Oskaloosa Hotel in Canmore.

The First Climbing Casualty— 1896

Three centuries ago, people didn't care much for mountains. They called them "warts," "excrescences," and "boils on the earth's complexion." Superstitious souls considered them forbidding and forbidden, the domains of dragons and other scary beasts. Travellers crossing the Swiss Alps wore blindfolds so they wouldn't have to see the monsters. But then public attitudes changed. By the nineteenth century, mountains had become sublime. Poets such as Wordsworth and Shelley sang their praises. Scientists climbed them in search of knowledge, and mountaineers climbed them in search of thrills.

In the Rockies, the first big wave of recreational mountaineering occurred during the late 1880s, when the recently built Canadian Pacific Railway gave tourists easy access to new unclimbed peaks. The early arrivals included the British, the Swiss, and members of the Boston-based Appalachian Mountain Club, one of the oldest alpine recreation and conservation organization in North America. The Americans made their first climbs west of the Rockies in what is now Glacier National Park, close to where the CPR built a small hotel, Glacier House, to eliminate the need for hauling heavy dining cars through the mountain passes. After scaling such challenging Glacier peaks as Mount Sir Donald and Uto Peak, the Americans turned their attention toward the higher mountains to the east.

In the summer of 1895, three Appalachian Mountain Club members—Philip Abbot, Charles Fay, and Charles Thompson—became the first climbers to reach the top of Mount Hector, a 3,394-metre Rocky Mountain peak located twenty kilometres northwest of Lake Louise. The view from the summit, said Abbot, "cannot be matched in any other mountain system in the world except in Asia." It stimulated his appetite for further first ascents. The following August, the trio returned to the Rockies, accompanied by an Appalachian Mountain Club member named George Little. They planned an assault on unconquered Mount Lefroy, a 3,423-metre peak located ten kilometres southwest of Lake Louise.

All were experienced mountaineers. Fay, a fifty-year-old professor of Romance languages at Tufts University in Boston, had been climbing at Glacier for six years. Abbot, a twenty-eight-year-old Boston lawyer, had done a lot of climbing in the Swiss Alps, accompanied by guides. Thompson and Little had also climbed extensively in the Alps.

But, as mountaineering writer and climber Chic Scott has observed in his definitive book *Pushing the Limits: The Story of Canadian Mountaineering*, the Americans were rank amateurs when it came to alpine climbing in the Rockies. "Lacking the crampons, curved ice axes and ice screws that modern-day climbers now employ, they had little real security."

This lack of security turned into tragedy when the party drew near the summit of Lefroy. Abbot asked the others to untie themselves from the ropes so that he could advance upward without restriction. He lost his footing and fell into a basin (now called Abbot Pass) hundreds of metres below. The others found him lying there unconscious after they had spent several hours gingerly descending without ropes, and he died before they could get medical help. A recovery party retrieved the body several days later.

It was North America's first mountaineering death, and it sent shock waves not only through the Appalachian Mountain Club but also through the mountaineering fraternity around the world. It sparked a fierce debate about the safety of the sport and prompted public calls for its abolition. (The calls echoed those heard thirty-one years earlier when the deaths of four climbers on the Matterhorn prompted Charles Dickens and others to denounce mountaineering as a "depraved taste.")

Fay, however, was not about to let the sport be banned "at the very dawn of a new era of genuine alpine climbing." While saddened by Abbot's death, he felt that the act of dying had conferred a majesty upon him, and that this one casualty "should not call a halt in American alpinism." Climbing knowledge and safety were the answers, not the elimination of an outdoor recreation particularly needed "in an age of growing carefulness for ease and luxury."

At the request of Abbot's father, who had always supported his son's climbing activities, Fay arranged for a memorial ascent of Mount Lefroy in August 1897, on the anniversary of Abbot's death. The party included six Americans and three British members of the Alpine Club of London. Also in the party was Peter Sarbach, a professional mountain guide from Switzerland. He was the first guide recruited from Europe to work in the Canadian Rockies.

There were no mishaps during the second climb. Two days after scaling Mount Lefroy, the British and American party made the first ascent of nearby Mount Victoria. A couple of weeks later, they ascended Mount Gordon, a 3,203-metre peak in the Yoho River Valley at the western edge of Wapta Icefield. The Americans then left for home while the British climbers, Norman Collie and George Baker, carried on to make the first ascent of a 3,155-metre peak located near the confluence of the Mistaya and North Saskatchewan rivers. Collie named the peak Mount Sarbach in honour of their guide.

Sarbach returned to Switzerland at the end of the 1897 climbing season, after showing the climbers how a trained guide could help make climbing safer for inexperienced mountaineers. When CPR officials recognized the value of having such alpine expertise in the Rockies, they hired two Swiss guides, Christian Häsler and Edouard Feuz, to work full-time for the railway company, starting in the spring of 1899. The guides were stationed, initially, at Glacier House in the Rogers Pass and their job was to show inexperienced climbing enthusiasts how to get up and down mountains without killing themselves. In the process, the CPR helped foster the development of mountaineering as a sport for the untrained masses. As alpine historian Bob Sandford wrote in his book *At the Top: One Hundred Years of Guiding in Canada*, a person now needed only a sense of determination and adventure to try mountaineering in one of the most stunning alpine settings in the world. "If a domestic interest in climbing in Canada has a birthplace and date, it is Rogers Pass, 1899."

Swiss guides remained a part of Rocky Mountain life for the next fifty years, leading tourists up unscaled peaks and teaching safe travel techniques to thousands of Canadians. In the meantime, the Alpine Club of Canada came into being as an organization similarly dedicated to keeping novices safe in the mountains.

The Alpine Club of Canada was the brainchild of A. O. (Arthur Oliver) Wheeler, an Irish-born land surveyor who learned climbing techniques from the Swiss guides at Glacier House during the summer of 1901 when the CPR assigned him, at age forty-one, to do a topographical survey of the railway right-of-way through the Selkirk Mountains. Wheeler met Charles Fay at Rogers Pass that summer and became interested when Fay told him about his involvement with the Appalachian Mountain Club, an organization devoted to promoting climbing knowledge. At the time, Fay was also helping establish the American Alpine Club, and Wheeler thought Canada should have a club too. However, he couldn't find much support for the idea. The only Canadians interested in climbing, it seemed, were fellow mountain surveyors, and there were only about a dozen of those in the entire country.

In 1905, Wheeler published a report of his survey work in a book entitled *The Selkirk Range*. In it he proposed that Canadians form a chapter of the American Alpine Club because a Canadian club didn't seem feasible. A Winnipeg newspaper columnist named Elizabeth Parker roundly rebuked him for this. Reviewing Wheeler's book for the *Manitoba Free Press*, Parker wrote that Canadians should not be playing second fiddle to the Americans: "We owe it to our own young nationhood, in simple self-respect, to begin an organized system of mountaineering on an independent basis. It is simply amazing that for so long we have cared so little."

Parker's interest in the subject stemmed from the fact that she had left Winnipeg temporarily in 1904 to spend eighteen months in Banff for health reasons, and during that period she had become what she called a "mountain pilgrim." When she returned to Winnipeg, she wrote a series of articles calling on Canadians to become aware of their mountain heritage, which she characterized as a "national asset."

Wheeler accepted Parker's criticism, acknowledging that she had "declaimed my action as unpatriotic, chided my lack of imperialism, and generally gave me a pen-lashing in words sharper than a sword." He wrote to the *Manitoba Free Press*, saying he would work toward the creation of a Canadian alpine club—if the newspaper would support the plan. The editor, John Wesley Dafoe, had no interest in mountaineering but the prospect of supporting a Canadian initiative appealed to him. (At a time when it promoted Winnipeg as the "gateway to the West," the *Free Press* considered that its circulation reach covered the entire region between Manitoba and the Rockies.) Dafoe gave his blessing to Parker when she proposed writing to the federal government for help (though he didn't expect a favourable response) and was surprised when Prime Minister Wilfrid Laurier "gave the proposed movement his benediction, if nothing else."

Other prominent Canadians soon followed suit and pledged their support for a Canadian alpine club. By March 1906 the proposed club had seventy-seven charter members. "Nothing since the formation of the Lord Strathcona Horse has so appealed to the Canadian feeling for Empire," Wheeler said. Twenty-six delegates, representing six

Arthur O. Wheeler: "Nothing since the formation of the Lord Strathcona Horse has so appealed to the Canadian feeling for Empire."
(Whyte Museum of the Canadian Rockies NA66-299)

provinces, attended the founding meeting of the Alpine Club of Canada on 28 March 1906. The CPR did its bit for the cause by providing twenty free rail passes to bring the out-of-town delegates to Winnipeg.

Wheeler became the first president of the new club and Parker, at age fifty, became the secretary. Though not a mountaineer herself ("I scale the rock and cut the ice stairway in imagination only"), she became a passionate advocate for Canadian climbing, describing it as "an ennobling, ethical and aesthetic pastime."

Parker remained active with the Alpine Club of Canada until her death in 1944 at age eighty-eight. Her name graces a backcountry hut in the Rockies at Lake O'Hara, fifteen kilometres southwest of the Lake Louise townsite. Wheeler died the following year at age eighty-five. A peak in the Selkirks carries his name.

The arrival of the Swiss guides and the founding of the Alpine Club of Canada marked two significant milestones in Rocky Mountain history, coming after an accidental death that might have precipitated a ban on climbing and a consequent limit on travel in the mountains. Today, Canada is recognized as one of the world's great countries for alpine recreation, with its own distinctive mountain culture and heritage.

Elizabeth Parker: "We owe it to our own young nationhood to begin an organized system of mountaineering." (Whyte Museum of the Canadian Rockies CAJ 1938, p. 92)

The Weatherman of Sulphur Mountain—1896-1932

NORMAN SANSON ASCENDS THE SAME PEAK
ONE THOUSAND TIMES

N orman Sanson always said he wanted to have the words "gone higher" inscribed on his grave marker in the Banff cemetery but, for whatever reason, the words never made it onto his tombstone. They would have made a fitting epitaph. During his thirty-six years as Banff's resident meteorologist, Sanson hiked up 2,270-metre Sulphur Mountain more than one thousand times to service a weather station at the top.

Sanson became Banff's official weather observer in 1896, four years after arriving there from what is now Saskatchewan, and twenty five years after Canada first established a national meteorological service to record climatological data and issue weather warnings. A veteran of the Riel Rebellion, Sanson was a self-taught naturalist and taxidermist who left an office job in Toronto at age twenty-three because he wanted to learn about the flora and fauna of Western Canada.

Sanson was thirty when he arrived in Banff. He parlayed his nature-studying hobby into a job as assistant to curator George MacLeod when Western Canada's first natural history museum opened in Banff in July 1895. The Geological Survey of Canada (GSC) established the museum to showcase the flora, fauna, and mineral specimens collected in the region during the 1870s by John Macoun, a GSC naturalist assigned to survey the agricultural potential of the Canadian northwest. The specimens included 259 mounted birds and 814 plants, which Macoun described as "an almost complete representation of the birds and flowering plants found within the limits of the park."

When asked by park superintendent George Stewart who should be the curator for the new Banff museum, Macoun wrote, "You should have a man of wide intelligence who could give information on many subjects when showing the specimens of the museum. He should be energetic (not a hotel lounger), should know the species of fish in the park, and ought to be able to skin a bird or mammal. In short, you should want an intelligent, educated, good, energetic young man, who would talk natural history, mineralogy, geology or anything else to the visitors. A political bloke should be the last man for that place."

Park employee MacLeod, an amateur naturalist, was the first choice for curator, but he was ill with cancer when he accepted the job. He died in March 1896 and Sanson, who was similarly qualified, replaced him as curator. Sanson also took over MacLeod's duties as Banff's meteorological observer. In that capacity, he maintained a journal of temperature, barometric pressure, humidity, wind direction, and precipitation readings in the Bow Valley, and relayed the data by telegraph to Ottawa. He did this manually for seven years until an automatic weather station was built on Sulphur Mountain in 1903. After that, Sanson's job was to climb the mountain every two weeks to check the instruments and replace the recording paper. He was given a thirty-year supply of paper to record the meteorological data. The paper ran out before he completed his service!

In summer, it took Sanson an average of two hours to hike up Sulphur Mountain. In the winter, travelling on snowshoes, the journey could take up to nine hours. Avalanches and other weather-related conditions never stopped him, though lightning storms sometimes marooned him at the top. During one such storm in the 1920s, lightning struck a weather vane and set off a chain reaction, burning out three recording machines at the station, coursing through the wires supplying electricity to the station, and causing a small fire in the Banff Upper Hot Springs bathhouse located at the 1,500-metre level on the mountain. Sanson later characterized the incident as a "narrow squeak."

Additionally, Sanson walked and rode thousands of kilometres along mountain trails, collecting flowers, butterflies, minerals, wood samples, and other specimens for the museum. He spent his evenings drying, pressing, arranging, labelling, and cataloguing the plant specimens for inclusion in the museum's herbarium. Operating without a clear mandate, Sanson collected materials illustrating the human history as well as the natural history of the park. These included such items as Native artifacts, logging material from the Eau Claire Lumber Company in Calgary, and a picture of the pioneering Methodist missionary Robert Rundle. By 1903, Sanson had gathered so much material that a new museum building had to be constructed to accommodate his collections. The distinctive, pagoda-style log structure, later preserved as a national heritage site, was described by the *Crag & Canyon* newspaper as "that magnificent structure located on the north bank of the Bow River, close to the bridge."

Sanson lived alone, and over time he developed a reputation as a colourful eccentric who kept skunks and porcupines as pets, always wore English tweeds, drank ginger ale because he couldn't be bothered making coffee or tea, and rarely did the dishes. If a visitor dropped in unexpectedly, he would take unwashed plates from the sink, turn them upside down, and serve sandwiches and cake on the underside! Banff historian Eleanor Luxton characterized him as a droll individual who could quote poetry freely and liked to tell a good story.

On 1 July 1931, when he was sixty-nine, Sanson celebrated Dominion Day by completing his one-thousandth official ascent of Sulphur Mountain. He was accompanied by sixty members of the Banff Rotary Club who travelled with him by pony (Sanson insisted on walking) and timed the journey so they could watch the sun rise when they reached the top. They ate a commemorative breakfast catered by the Banff Springs Hotel, presented Sanson with a medal, and granted him the "freedom" of Sulphur Mountain, with tongue-in-cheek permission to catch all wildlife on the mountain—"provided he use only his bare hands." Sanson quipped that this meant he would only be able to catch "mountain rats."

Sanson talked of retirement at the breakfast, and said there would

Norman Sanson leading a snowshoe group: "A man of wide intelligence." (Whyte Museum of the Canadian Rockies V484-NA 29-38)

be no more winter ascents for him because they were proving to be too difficult. However, he did complete one more season of winter climbing to March 1932, when he reached his seventieth birthday and finally retired from his positions as government meteorologist and museum curator. After that, he continued to climb Sulphur, in both winter and summer, just to enjoy the panoramic view of Banff and the surrounding Bow Valley. He made his last trip in 1945, at age eighty-three, to observe a solar eclipse. Three years later, he received word from the Canadian Board on Geographical Names that the highest peak on Sulphur Mountain would be named in his honour.

Sanson wasn't replaced after he retired. The weather station was closed and the museum ended the magpie work of indiscriminately collecting and documenting specimens of all kinds, because such an eclectic endeavour was now considered to have little scientific or educational merit. While other natural history institutions focussed on scientific analysis and particular fields or genera such as mammals, birds, or botany, the Banff museum covered all forms of natural life, including human life, and thus exemplified an early catch-all approach to the interpretation of natural history that was no longer considered valid in Canadian museum circles.

While Sanson's collecting work was discontinued, his trips up Sulphur Mountain set a pattern for others to follow. In 1940, a

Swiss-born mountain guide named John Jaeggi opened a teahouse on the summit of Sulphur Mountain, to serve the growing numbers of hikers who wanted to visit the old weather station and enjoy the view. Five years later, Jaeggi built a halfway station on the mountain and began offering his guests a choice of lunch or bed and breakfast.

In 1947, Jaeggi began ferrying tourists up Sulphur Mountain on a modified tractor with a platform that could hold eight passengers. This increased his business to such an extent that he started thinking of more elaborate ways to take people up the mountain. During the early 1950s, Jaeggi enlisted the support of Calgary investors to build a European-style aerial lift on the mountain, and saw the idea finally come to fruition in 1959—two years before his death at age seventy-two—when the Banff Sulphur Mountain Gondola opened as one of the first cable-driven lifts in Canada.

Sanson died in 1949 at age eighty-seven. The notes from his various field trips were destroyed, because nobody seemed to know what else to do with them, and his collection of about six thousand pressed plants was donated to the University of Calgary, which sorted and catalogued them and incorporated them into its own herbarium collection. Sanson's other natural history specimens were retained by the Banff Park Museum, which was declared a national historic site in 1985 to coincide with the one hundredth anniversary of the establishment of the national park. As part of the year-long centennial celebrations, the first of a series of annual Sanson memorial hikes up Sulphur Mountain was held to commemorate the contributions of the pioneering weatherman and naturalist. In 1992, the old stone weather station was refurbished in period style by the federal government at a cost of $90,000, and opened to the public as a heritage building with easy access by boardwalk from the upper terminal of the Banff Gondola. Visitors can see some of the weather station's original contents, such as Sanson's pot-bellied stove and some Campbell's Soup cans from the 1920s.

How She Spent Her Summer Holidays—1904-47

GERTRUDE BENHAM, PHYLLIS MUNDAY, GEORGIA ENGELHARD, AND KATIE GARDINER MAKE THEIR MARKS

July 1904 was to have been a significant month for American mountaineering pioneer Charles Fay, the founder of the American Alpine Club. Two years previously, at the invitation of the Geographic Board of Canada, he had chosen an unclimbed mountain in the Valley of the Ten Peaks, ten kilometres south of Lake Louise, to be named after himself. Now, he was set to become the first climber to ascend Mount Fay. However, a British climber named Gertrude Benham beat him to it.

Benham was a thirty-seven-year-old adventurer from London, a single woman of independent means who climbed 130 peaks in the Swiss Alps before setting her sights on the Rockies. Arriving in June 1904, she planned to spend the summer climbing in Canada before moving on to New Zealand in October.

The story goes that Benham walked into the CPR-built log cabin named Chalet Lake Louise, hired two Swiss guides, brothers Hans and Christian Kaufmann, and ordered them to "be ready at midnight." The ensuing twenty-seven-hour trek across the Continental Divide, which included an ascent of the 3,199-metre Mount Stephen near Field, British Columbia, typified what this energetic woman would be doing for the rest of that summer. The two guides were so hard pressed to keep up with her that they fell down exhausted when they staggered into Field at 3:00 AM.

Fay arrived in July 1904 to claim the mountain that bore his name. Already renowned in the Rockies for having made the first ascents of Mounts Hector, Lefroy, and Victoria, the fifty-eight-year-old Fay intended to make this climb his crowning achievement. He scheduled his ascent of Mount Fay, formerly known by the Native name of Heejee (Peak Number One), for 20 July. Benham, however, stole the spotlight by launching her own assault, accompanied by Christian Kaufmann, on 19 July.

While Benham did climb one of the valley's ten peaks on 19 July, it turned out not to be Mount Fay. Undeterred, she rescheduled her attempt for the following day. She and Christian would launch their attack from the northwest via a steep narrow gully known as the Hourglass Couloir, while Fay and Christian's brother, Hans, would approach the 3,235-metre peak from Consolation Valley, northeast of the mountain.

The going was tough for both parties. Soft snow and falling rock bogged them down. Fay and Hans finally turned back. Benham and Christian pushed on and made it to the top. Fay was enraged. Someone else had claimed victory for what he thought should be rightfully his. He talked about writing to the Geographic Board and asking that another of the valley's ten peaks, Shappee, be named after him instead. However, when he discovered that Benham and Christian had already climbed Shappee (now Mount Allen) a few days previously, Fay decided to leave well enough alone. Because there was no other unclimbed peak in the valley that he could ascend and name for himself that summer, he settled for making a second attempt on Mount Fay on 5 August, which he achieved successfully.

There has been some suggestion, often repeated but never verified, that the Kaufmann brothers—as a practical joke—conspired to let Benham make the first ascent, and that when Fay found out about it he asked the CPR to fire them. It is known, nonetheless, that the Kaufmann brothers were no longer in the picture when Fay made his ascent on 5 August. Accompanying him on that occasion were guides Christian Häsler Sr. and Frederick Michel. Hans Kaufmann returned to Switzerland at the end of the 1904 climbing season and never worked in Canada again. His brother, Christian, carried on for a few more years in Canada and then moved back to Switzerland.

Benham never had a mountain named after her in the Rockies. She spent only that one summer in Canada before moving on to other adventures. But what a summer it was. As well as climbing Mounts Fay and Allen, she also became the first woman to climb 3,618-metre Mount Assiniboine, the so-called Matterhorn of the Rockies. Additionally, she ascended such major Rocky Mountain peaks as Victoria, Lefroy, and Balfour. Then she moved west to the Selkirk and Purcell ranges, where she climbed such peaks as Sifton, Dawson, and Mount Sir Donald.

Benham spent more than thirty years travelling the world after she left Canada, "enjoying to the utmost the spirit of wanderlust that has entered my soul," and climbing the highest mountains she could find. In 1908, she walked across South America from Valparaíso to Buenos Aires. The following year, at age forty-two, she became the first woman to conquer 5,895-metre Kilimanjaro, the highest mountain in Africa. "My first feeling up there was that of being absolutely on top of the world," she said. During seven solo trips around the world, her constant companions were a Bible, R. D. Blackmore's *Lorna Doone*, Kipling's *Kim*, a pocket Shakespeare, and her knitting. Though she travelled alone, she was never lonely. "How can I be when there is so much to see and admire in the world?" She died at sea in 1938 at age seventy-one while returning from one of her many walks across Africa. The Plymouth City Museum, which holds a collection of artifacts she gathered while travelling, referred to her as a "doughty traveller."

While Benham spent only one summer in Canada, and was not even the first woman to climb a major peak in the Rockies (Mary Vaux of Philadelphia quietly achieved that distinction in 1900 when she ascended Mount Stephen), her widely heralded 1904 achievements, in the largely male world of North American mountaineering, inspired generations of women to follow her. By the 1920s, dozens of women had crashed the alpine gender barrier in the Rockies. Among the most notable were Phyllis Munday, Georgia Engelhard, and Katie Gardiner.

Munday made her mountaineering mark in 1924, at age thirty, when she became the first woman to climb 3,954-metre Mount Robson, the highest peak in the Rockies. Just a few years previously, the all-male B.C. Mountaineering Club had reluctantly granted her a conditional membership, saying they would only accept her as a full member if she completed two climbs and had them properly witnessed. Munday had no difficulty satisfying the membership requirements. She had been climbing mountains since she first hiked up Vancouver's Grouse Mountain with her parents, at age twelve, fifty years before the hill acquired chairlifts and became an internationally famous ski resort.

Munday's ascent of Mount Robson came at a time when women were still expected to wear skirts in public. For a while she got

Phyllis Munday and her daughter, Edith: "Domed with snow and bristling with gleaming icicles." (British Columbia Archives 1-61701)

around the dress code (which even applied to hiking women) by wearing bloomers under her long skirt until she was away from public view, then removing the skirt and stashing it under a rock. However, by the time she tackled Robson, she had traded in the skirts and bloomers for the pants, cleated boots, and leggings worn by the men.

She climbed with a group of others, including her husband, Don Munday, an experienced mountaineer, freelance journalist, and First World War veteran. They had met when she was working as a stenographer at the Vancouver Veterans Hospital and he was recuperating from wounds suffered overseas. They married in 1920 and introduced their daughter Edith to climbing when she was just three months old. The baby rode in a canvas carrier on her father's back.

Edith accompanied her parents on several ascents but not on the Robson climb. That would have been much too dangerous for the child. The "big climb" was even considered to be more than a woman could handle; however Phyllis managed without any problems. The Robson summit, said Phyllis, was "domed with snow and bristling with gleaming icicles; they were a never-to-be-forgotten sight. Fairylike, perhaps, but sinister, hostile and menacing."

The Mundays climbed a few more mountains in the Rockies after that, but mostly confined their subsequent mountaineering activities to the rugged Coast Range of northwestern British Columbia. They spent a dozen years trying to reach the top of an unmapped 4,016-metre peak, located 280 kilometres northwest of Vancouver, which they dubbed "Mystery Mountain." They never did reach the summit, which Don described as a "nightmare moulded in rock," but they did complete ten other first ascents in the Coast Range. The Geographic Board eventually gave the name Mount Waddington to the Mundays' mystery mountain, and gave the name Mount Munday to a neighbouring 3,367-metre peak that Don and Phyllis first conquered on skis.

While the Mundays were writing their names into the mountaineering records of British Columbia during the 1920s and 1930s, Georgia Engelhard and Katie Gardiner were matching one another peak for peak as the females with the greatest number of first ascents in the Rockies. Both did better than most of their male counterparts. Only three males, not counting professional guides, exceeded their records of thirty-two first ascents for Engelhard and thirty-three for Gardiner.

Engelhard, a New York City socialite, first started climbing in the Rockies at age twenty in the summer of 1926, and caused a sensation in the Lake Louise area by climbing the 3,067-metre Pinnacle Mountain in less than three hours. Her guide, Edward

Feuz Jr., was astonished by her speed. "She just stuck her head in my rucksack and so I ran," he said. His brother, Ernest Feuz, noted that when Engelhard started uphill "she goes like a rocket. What she needs is a mountain goat, not a guide." Engelhard explained that she had "enormously strong legs and great endurance." The idea was not to dally on the mountain, she said, but to hasten to the top, where she would be "seized by an indescribable ecstasy, filled with the joy of conquest."

Engelhard was still scampering up mountains like a mountain

Georgia Engelhard and guide Ernest Feuz on Mount Victoria: "What she needs is a mountain goat, not a guide." (Glenbow Archives NA-4868-195)

goat in 1929, when she climbed nine Rocky Mountain peaks in nine days, and again in 1931, when she climbed a total of thirty-eight mountains in the Rockies and the Selkirks. She stood on the summit of 3,464-metre Mount Victoria eight times that summer. Seven of the ascents were for the filming of the promotional movie *She Climbs to Conquer*, shot by CPR cameraman Bill Oliver. CPR officials thought Engelhard's name would add lustre to the movie because she came from a distinguished American family. Her uncle was the influential photographer Alfred Stieglitz, and her aunt was the famed artist Georgia O'Keeffe. Engelhard spent so much time with her aunt as a child that she was given the nickname Georgia Minor.

Engelhard continued to climb in the Rockies until 1947 when, at age forty-one, she married one of her regular climbing companions, a Philadelphia banker named Eaton "Tony" Cromwell. They moved to Switzerland and spent the next forty years enjoying the Alps together. Engelhard never came back to the Rockies after her marriage, but she did have a mountain named after her. The 3,270-metre Mount Engelhard, rising from the headwaters of the Athabasca River in the southern end of Jasper National Park, stands as a lasting memorial to the silver medallist in female first ascents.

The gold medallist, Katie Gardiner, was born to climb. Her father, Frederick Gardiner, was a distinguished British climber, the first to reach the summit of 5,642-metre Mount Elbrus in Russia. She climbed with him in the Alps as soon as she was able to walk. At age ten, she climbed 3,782-metre Mount Breithorn in Switzerland.

Gardiner did her first serious climbing in New Zealand. In 1928, she became one of the first women to reach the summit of 3,754-metre Mount Cook. A year later, at age forty-four, she visited Canada for the first time. Accompanied by Swiss guide Walter Feuz and two packers, she explored the country between the Bow Valley and Crowsnest Pass, made five first ascents, and also reached the summit of Mount Assiniboine. This set a pattern that continued for the next ten years. Gardiner spent the Canadian winter climbing in New Zealand, and spent the summer climbing in Canada. Invariably accompanied by Feuz, and sometimes by Ken Jones—the first Canadian to become a certified guide in the

Rockies—she achieved fourteen first ascents in the Kananaskis area and nineteen in other parts of the Rockies and Selkirks.

Compared to Engelhard, Gardiner was a tortoise in the mountains. Jones described her as a slow but steady climber with great stamina. "She walked sort of funny, like she was going to fall over her own feet." There was no doubting her sure-footedness, however, once she left the trail behind and started to climb. In one notable season, 1930–31, she made nine first ascents in New Zealand and half a dozen more in Canada.

The Second World War ended Gardiner's climbing career in Canada. She worked for the Red Cross at an auxiliary convalescent unit in northwest England. After the war, she did some climbing in Switzerland and New Zealand and completed her last ascent, in the

Alps, in 1951 at age sixty-six. A companion said she "went as well as anyone half her age." There is no mountain or other feature in the Rockies commemorating her gold-medal achievement, but she does have an alpine hut named in her memory near Mount Cook in New Zealand.

Katie Gardiner in 1932: "A tortoise in the mountains." (Whyte Museum of the Canadian Rockies V225/PD9 (317))

Shoot Every Mountain— 1906-24

BYRON HARMON PHOTOGRAPHS THE PEAKS

In August 1924, a forty-eight-year-old American-born mountain photographer, Byron Harmon, set off on a seventy-day, 800-kilometre trek along the Columbia Icefield to complete the last part of an assignment he had set for himself twenty years earlier: to photograph every major peak, glacier, and valley in the Rocky Mountains. He was accompanied by Lewis Freeman, a *National Geographic* writer, who subsequently published an exaggerated account of the trip in a book titled *On the Roof of the Rockies: The Great Columbia Icefield of the Canadian Rockies*. ("The greatest opportunity ever presented to film one of the most stupendous of Nature's manifestations.") There was nothing exaggerated, however, about the sentiment expressed in the book's dedication: "To Byron Harmon, who, through his photographs, has given the Canadian Rockies to the world."

Harmon was the first professional photographer to make his home in the Rockies, the first to make shooting in the mountains his life's work, and the first to send his images around the world. He did so at a time when roadways into the mountain parks were almost non-existent, and only Western Canadians and a few wealthy world travellers knew of the wondrous beauty of the mountains. Travel was by pack train in summer and by dogsled or snowshoes in winter.

Born near Tacoma, Washington, in 1876, Harmon became interested in photography when the Eastman Kodak Company of Rochester, New York, was marketing its Brownie box camera at a

retail cost of one dollar. He couldn't afford to buy one of the advertised Brownies—his single mother had barely enough money from
her housekeeper's job to clothe and feed her three children—but
he was handy with tools and was able to fashion a crude pinhole
camera out of a wooden box. When he was older and chronic
asthma forced him to quit his job as a mill worker, he turned to
photography as an alternative way to make a living.

Without any photographic training, Harmon set himself up in
business as a portrait photographer. He rented space in a Tacoma
office building, used all his available cash and credit to equip his
studio, and hung out his shingle. He didn't have enough money to
buy film, but he solved that problem by pretending there was film
in the camera when his first client walked in the door. He accepted
the client's down payment, shot several frames with the empty
camera, and told the client the prints would be ready the next day.
When the client came back, Harmon said the session would have
to be repeated because the pictures hadn't turned out. He took
some more pictures, this time using film he had purchased with the
client's down payment, and the following day his first customer
walked away satisfied.

After three years of studio photography, Harmon closed his
Tacoma shop, packed his camera gear into a couple of suitcases,
and hit the road as a travelling photographer. He went across the
United States by train to New York, and then westward across
Canada, paying his way by taking people's pictures. When he
reached Banff, in 1903, he decided the mountain air would be
good for his asthma and the town itself good for his career
because it didn't have a photo studio. This mountain frontier
could be commercially viable, he thought, because it had five
first-class hotels and was rapidly becoming a haven for alpinists
and scientist-explorers. He made plans to return the following
year to establish himself in what he called "that part of Canada
which stands on end."

Harmon stopped in High River on his return journey to Banff.
There he snapped an impromptu picture of a wanted American
gunman that brought him widespread publicity across North
America. He climbed onto a hotel roof, hid behind a chimney, and
surreptitiously photographed the outlaw as he walked along the

main street with six-shooters drawn. The resulting Wild West image ran on the front pages of several newspapers as if it were a wanted poster. It brought Harmon his first brush with fame and eventually led to the capture of the fugitive.

Harmon rented a storage shed in Banff, converted it into a studio, and advertised his services as a portrait photographer. But he wasn't able to attract much business from the well-heeled people who could afford to have their pictures taken, because his appearance turned them off—he dressed like a hobo, in overalls and without socks. It was only when he turned his lens away from people and directed it toward the Rockies that he began to earn a decent living. He produced a line of Rocky Mountain postcards to sell to the tourists who came to Banff on the train, offering a selection of "over 100 assorted views" for the visitors to choose from. Harmon continued to take pictures of people while developing his postcard business, but only when they agreed to be photographed in a mountain setting. "I'd rather shoot mountains than people," he said, "because mountains, at least, stand still." (He was obviously being mischievous when he said this. His catalogue of mountain characters reveals a love of faces, particularly Native faces, and a childlike delight in having alpinists model for him in goofy poses.)

The 1906 founding of the Alpine Club of Canada gave Harmon an opportunity to broaden his photographic range. He had become an enthusiastic hiker and climber during his two years in Banff, always toting his large-format 5 x 7-inch view camera, heavy glass plates, and cellulose-nitrate negatives, and now he had a chance to further his goal of capturing every Rocky Mountain peak, glacier, and valley on film. He became a charter member of the Club and its first official photographer. That meant he was able to participate in all the climbing, exploring, scientific, and hunting expeditions sponsored by the Club. It also meant he was able to publish his pictures in the Club's *Canadian Alpine Journal*, circulated internationally. During a hunting trip through the forests of the Purcell Range in 1910, Harmon photographed Himalayan climbing veteran Tom Longstaff bagging three grizzlies in one afternoon—a feat that Longstaff later chronicled in the *Journal* and Harmon turned into a best-selling postcard.

Harmon was the Alpine Club's official photographer for seven years. His most extended Rocky Mountain tour during this period was a three-month trip to the Rainbow Range, in what is now Mount Robson Provincial Park, during the summer and fall of 1911. He climbed more than thirty peaks, photographed an avalanche in progress, became part of the first party to travel the mountains "from steel to steel" (from the Grand Trunk Pacific Railway line at Jasper to the CPR line at Lake Louise), and achieved the first ascent of 3,425-metre Resplendent Mountain, accompanied by guide Conrad Kain.

While the Alpine Club expeditions took Harmon up peaks he might not otherwise have scaled, they didn't always suit his purposes as a photographer. To do his best work he needed the freedom to wander and linger, and this was not always possible when he was roped to a group of climbers. There were times when he needed to stop at one location for several days until he had just the right light and weather conditions for his picture. Because of this, Harmon soon took to organizing his own expeditions into the mountains. Always the perfectionist, he told a friend that when he had completed shooting every notable geographic feature in the Rockies he planned to start over and try to do them better.

As well as making trips into the mountains, Harmon established himself in Banff as an industrious businessman who converted an old livery stable into a photo studio, darkroom, and curio shop, and then expanded his holdings to include a movie theatre, drug store, tea room, bookstore, beauty parlour, and lending library. As a druggist—without any pharmaceutical training!—Harmon dispensed patented medicine to customers and their pets. He also functioned as the town veterinarian, again without any training. When Prohibition came into force in Alberta in 1916, Harmon dispensed liquor on prescription to his customers for "medicinal" reasons, and noted with amusement that "a large proportion of ailing people, especially Shriners, have bad health in Banff."

In January 1917, Harmon's photo studio and adjoining movie theatre burned to the ground. The fire, caused by a faulty oil heater, cost him thirteen thousand dollars in damage and the loss of several photo stills. He also lost much of the movie collection that had allowed him to advertise "fresh films daily" in his theatre. The night of the blaze, Harmon's wife (the former Maud Moore, whom he had married in 1910) gave birth to their third child, son Don. "Worst time of my life," Harmon said afterwards to tease his son. "Two disasters in one night."

Harmon soon rebuilt the burned-out block, using local cobblestones, and named it "Harmony Lane" as a gentle play on his last name. His shops boasted the first neon signs in Banff, the first gas lights, the first ice cream machine, and the only automatic postcard machine in Western Canada—calibrated to turn out as many as four thousand cards a day. Harmon designed and built his own darkroom equipment, as well as the screen for his movie theatre, and kept the theatre aired with a mechanical ventilation system of his own invention.

In addition to showing movies, Harmon also made movies. He insisted on action in his films and when he couldn't find it he created it. During a 1920 trip to the Selkirks with a group of hunters, he planned to film a mountain goat being killed, but he didn't have enough light for the camera when an animal was shot at dusk on a cliff high above a glacier. The following day, Harmon staged an elaborate re-enactment. He propped the frozen carcass of the goat against a ledge, and filmed the hunters from several angles as they fired at the lifeless animal. A concealed string to the animal's hind legs caused it to topple at the moment the hunters "hit" their target. Then came a spectacular "leap of death" as the ninety-kilogram goat dropped three hundred metres to the glacier below. Harmon was so mesmerized by the sight of the falling animal that he almost forgot to jump out of the way. The hurtling body missed the cameraman by centimetres and a stray hoof knocked his camera off its tripod, damaging it slightly!

Harmon received his greatest recognition as a photographer in 1920, when the federal government invited him to represent Canada at the World Congress of Alpinism in Monaco. He stopped in Ottawa on his way to Europe and, according to Banff's *Crag & Canyon* newspaper, "did a good stroke of business which should materially benefit Banff." He exhibited 150 of his mountain prints on the floor of the House of Commons, and "sold copies to practically every member of Parliament." In Monaco, his prints and films proved to be so popular that he was invited to return to Europe a couple of years later to show them in France, Germany, and Great

Britain. He picked up so many orders for reprints during his second European trip that he was able to live comfortably for the next several years.

Harmon's 1924 pack train odyssey along the length of the Columbia Icefield was his last extended trip into the mountains. Aside from his photographic goals, he also wanted to see if homing pigeons could find their way through the mountains back to Banff (they couldn't) and if he could pick up radio reception in the mountains (he could). His companion, Lewis Freeman, brought along a Radiola, one of the early "talking machine" radio receivers manufactured by RCA, and it proved to be most useful for planning photo shoots because it picked up the Pacific Coast weather bulletins broadcast by the powerful KGO station in Oakland, California. After one bulletin, Harmon waited eight days for the skies to clear so he could get a good shot of 3,747-metre Mount Columbia, the second highest peak in the Rockies. When he finally got the light he needed, Harmon shot picture after picture for forty minutes until the discarded paper covers from his film packs were, in Freeman's words, "piled up behind his tripods like the brass shells around a hard-pumped machine gun at the end of a battle."

Harmon brought back more than four hundred stills and two thousand metres of movie footage from his trip to the Columbia Icefield. Most of the movie footage was later lost or destroyed but the stills, combined with more than six thousand other images Harmon shot in the mountains over the previous twenty years, now form an important historical document of a fascinating transitional period in the mountain West, between the time of the earliest explorers and the age of commercial tourism. The fur traders, missionaries, and railway builders had long gone by the time Harmon first arrived in Banff, but as mountain historian Bart Robinson has written, "the multitudes of highly mobile, middle-class sightseers racing through the mountains at ever-increasing speed and in ever-increasing numbers had yet to arrive." During the early 1900s, Banff was still a haven for people who were in no great hurry to leave the nineteenth century behind.

Harmon continued to make trips into the Rockies after 1924, but his photographic work there was largely done, and now he had other parts of the world—Mexico, Guatemala, Hong Kong, the

American southwest—that he wanted to see and photograph. When he came home, he invariably told friends that nothing could beat the Rockies for photographic opportunities.

During Harmon's last years, he was troubled by high blood pressure and failing sight and hearing, but his sense of humour never failed him. Shortly before his death at age sixty-seven in 1942, his son Don noticed that he was swatting at flies on the outside of a screen door, and asked him why he was bothering to kill them. "I'm not really killing them," replied Harmon. "I just stun their legs,

Byron Harmon at Fortress Lake, in what is now Hamber Provincial Park, in 1924: "I'd rather shoot mountains than people." (Whyte Museum of the Canadian Rockies V263/2400)

then they fall to the sidewalk and break their necks."

For a time, it seemed that Harmon would have no photographic successor. He had always intended that Don should become a pharmacist, and had taught him how to make ice cream when he might have been teaching him how to use a darkroom. However, when Don returned to Canada after serving as a flight lieutenant with the RCAF during the Second World War, he decided to follow in his father's footsteps. He studied colour photography in California and established a successful business in Banff, publishing his father's black-and-white images in calendars, postcards, and souvenir booklets, as well as publishing his own images.

Like his father, Don Harmon had a special interest in the Columbia Icefield, with its many glaciers, crevasses, ridges, and shifting blue ice. He photographed the area from helicopters as well as on foot and eventually compiled enough photographs to fill a book, *Columbia Icefield: A Solitude of Ice*, published in 1981 by Altitude Publishing, a press co-founded by his daughter, Carole Harmon.

Don Harmon died in 1997, by which time his daughter, Carole, had become part of the third generation of Harmons to become involved in the mountain photography business. Starting in the mid-1970s, she took on the task of restoring and printing her grandfather's collection of 6,500 glass plates and negatives, which she had arranged to be donated to the Whyte Museum of the Canadian Rockies. She copied the highly flammable and unstable cellulose nitrate negatives onto safer modern film, and presented them in an exhibition that toured Canada and the United States. She also was involved in the editing and production of a book, *Great Days in the Rockies: The Photographs of Byron Harmon, 1906–34*. In an accompanying essay, the poet Jon Whyte wrote that Byron Harmon's photos revealed, among his other special interests, a passion for the mountain country above the tree line: "a black-and-white world so perfectly suited in its contrasts to his medium." Because Harmon was constantly drawn to the sensuousness of snow and glacial ice, said Whyte, "we might suspect a Snow Queen fable had some personal significance . . . His achievement was to array the elements of the picturesque and then place people in the scene to humanize the setting, which made his people larger than life and allowed them to enter the perpetual present of mythic time."

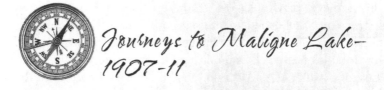

Journeys to Maligne Lake— 1907–11

MARY SCHÄFFER FINDS HER "STRING OF PEARLS"

As she sat in her Philadelphia drawing room, poring over books and journal articles about explorations in the Rocky Mountains, Mary Schäffer wondered why men were doing all the reporting. Why weren't women venturing into uncharted territory and writing about it? Surely females could brave wilderness hardships as well as males? Why did it always have to be the Pallisers, the Hectors, the Collies, and the Outrams who claimed the glory for going where no whites had ever gone before? Schäffer talked it over with her friend and fellow outdoors enthusiast Mollie Adams, and they started planning their own expedition to the Rockies—"a four-months' trip during the summer of 1907 with a vow made 'not to return till driven back by the snows.'"

Schäffer had previously done some travelling in the Rockies during the ten years when she accompanied her husband, a wealthy physician and botany enthusiast named Charles Schäffer, on short summer trips to collect and study alpine wildflowers. But these trips could hardly be classified as adventures in exploration because her husband's weak heart always necessitated that they stay "within sound of the shrieking engines and passing trains of the mountain division."

Dr. Schäffer, who was twenty-three years Mary's senior, died in 1903 of heart failure at age sixty-five. Mary wasn't particularly robust either—she suffered from acute neuralgia—but she was adventurous. After her husband's death, she had continued to make summer trips to the Rockies, venturing deeper into the wilderness as she completed his botanical fieldwork and had it documented for publication in a book with her watercolour paintings and hand-tinted photographs. But still she felt that she had not fully experienced the peace and joy of being in a wilderness place where "silence is deafening, time expansive, and physical effort its own reward." So now, at age forty-six, she was about to "delve into the heart of an untouched land, to tread where no human foot had trod before, to turn the unthumbed pages of an unread book, and to learn daily those secrets which dear Mother Nature is so willing to tell to those who seek."

Her friends and relatives thought she was mad. Ten years before, Mary and her husband had spent a frigid night in a tent near Lake Louise, emerged with "chattering teeth and shivering bodies, and vowed never again to camp in the Canadian Rockies." Plus, she had a pathological fear of horses and bears. Why would she want to risk life and limb for the sake of some foolhardy camping adventure in the wilds of northern Canada? Schäffer, while "scared stiff at rocks or precipices," was not to be deterred. She had done her share of "sitting with folded hands and listening calmly" while men told her about exciting journeys through unexplored country. Now she was going to do some exploring for herself.

The party included, along with the two Philadelphia women, an English-born guide named Billy Warren who had accompanied Schäffer on some of her botany trips to the mountains, and Warren's assistant, Sid Unwin, a Boer War veteran who had left his job as a clerk in London to seek adventure in Canada. The women planned to explore the headwaters of the North Saskatchewan and Athabasca rivers in Banff and Jasper national parks. They wanted to search for an uncharted lake that the local Cree and Stoney called Chaba Imne (Beaver Lake) and which no white person had ever explored. Schäffer had learned about this hidden lake during one of her previous trips to the Rockies in the early 1900s, when guide Jimmy Simpson mentioned it. He couldn't tell her much about the lake, because the Natives were "too afraid about the white man trespassing upon their hunting grounds," but his brief description was enough to make her want to find it.

The 1907 trip took the party northward by pack train from the railway station at Laggan (today's Lake Louise) through mountain passes and valleys where no non-Native woman had ventured before. The major stops along the way—Fortress Lake, Mount Columbia, Wilcox Pass, Brazeau Lake, Howse Pass—had all been previously explored and named by men. There was no sign of the elusive lake mentioned by Simpson.

Schäffer asked about the lake at a dinner party thrown for the group by an outfitter named Elliott Barnes as they neared the end of their trip in September 1907. One of the guests, a Stoney hunter named Samson Beaver, told her he had visited the lake with his father when he was fourteen, and he remembered it as a great place for game. He said the Natives didn't want the white man hunting in there, but he did agree—at Schäffer's urging—to draw a map of the area. She said she would be back the following summer to resume the search.

Schäffer spent the winter of 1907 giving talks at lecture halls in Philadelphia, showing hand-tinted lantern slides of her summer explorations in the Rockies, making travel plans, and stocking up on clothing and supplies for the return trip. This time, she and Mollie—a wealthy widow like herself—would travel with Stewardson Brown, a Philadelphia botanist who had helped Mary develop and publish the alpine flora guide based on her late husband's fieldwork. Also taking part in the expedition would be Brown's assistant, Reggie Holmes, guides Warren and Unwin, twenty-two horses, and a dog.

The party began their trail ride from Laggan on 8 June 1908. Beaver's hand-drawn map wasn't easy to follow—Schäffer had to remember that "a very scribbly spot was a pass, and that something which looked like a squashed spider he called a mountain"—but it did give them a general idea of where they had to go. After a month on the trail they reached Brazeau Lake, northeast of the Columbia Icefield, which they believed was in the general vicinity of the unmapped lake. After searching for another four days, Schäffer became dispirited and wondered about the accuracy of Beaver's map. However, guide Unwin wasn't ready yet to give up. He said he would climb "something high enough to see if that lake is within twenty miles of here, and I'm not coming back till I know." The

Mary Schäffer: "To tread where no human foot had trod before."
(Whyte Museum of the Canadian Rockies V439/PS-5)

strategy worked. Eight hours after ascending what is now named Mount Unwin, the guide returned to camp and announced that he had spotted the elusive lake.

The lake, as it turned out, had been visited at least once before by a white man, a Canadian Pacific Railway surveyor named Henry MacLeod, who reached it after a long and difficult hike in 1875, named it Sorefoot Lake, and said the area around it would not make a suitable route for a transcontinental railway. For Schäffer and her companions, however, it was a jewel in the wilderness, even more precious than Lake Louise, and never seen by any of the camping tourists who littered the forest with their tin cans and "desecrated as they go." Lake Louise, said Schäffer, was a pearl. Chaba Imne, or Maligne Lake as it is now called, was a "whole string of pearls." (The name Maligne, French for "wicked," comes from the river that flows out of the lake, and is so named because its slippery boulders presented fording difficulties for horses.)

Because the shoreline seemed too soft for horse travel, guides Warren and Unwin built a log raft so the party could explore the length and breadth of what we now know to be the longest natural lake in the Canadian Rockies, located forty-eight kilometres south-east of the town of Jasper. They christened the craft HMS *Chaba*, loaded it with tents, blankets, and food for three days, and set off to enjoy what Schäffer said was "the finest view any of us had ever beheld in the Rockies."

Mary Schäffer and guide, Billy Warren: "The finest view any of us had ever beheld in the Rockies." (Whyte Museum of the Canadian Rockies V439/PS-6)

The lake journey took them past one peak that Schäffer named Mount Warren after the guide "through whose grit and determination we were able to behold this splendour" and another that she named Samson Peak—in honour of the Stoney hunter whose map had brought them there. She also named the lake's Samson Narrows after Beaver. At the end of the voyage, she carved her initials on a tree—an impulsive gesture she came to regret later. She shouldn't have done it, she said, because it made her the same as the camping tourists she detested for disfiguring nature with their "personal names and personal remarks."

After abandoning the raft on "those lonely shores where other travellers some day may find and use her," Schäffer and her companions did some exploring north of Maligne Lake and then headed westward to see Mount Robson, the highest peak in the Rockies. Botanist Brown and his assistant, Holmes, left the party during this part of the trip, having seen enough of the wilderness for one summer. But Mary and Mollie were determined to press on until the snows drove them back. By the time they returned to Philadelphia, in early September, the women had travelled much of the historic Yellowhead Trail (today's Highway 16), the route taken by the Overlanders who trekked in 1862 from Manitoba to the Cariboo gold fields in British Columbia, and Schäffer had filled her diaries with enough information for a book.

She started writing the book during a trip she and Mollie made to Japan during the fall and early winter of 1908. It was a sad trip for Mary because Mollie contracted pneumonia while the pair were travelling by boat from Japan to Taiwan and died during the return journey. Mary used some of Mollie's diary entries and several of her photographs for the 380-page book, and dedicated it to her friend "who with me followed the old Indian trails but who has now gone on the long trail alone."

Schäffer had already published articles about her mountain travels in Canadian and American newspapers and magazines, so she had no trouble persuading a New York publisher, G. P. Putnam's Sons, to take on the book. It appeared in 1911 as *Old Indian Trails of the Canadian Rockies* and was an instant success. (The Peter and Catharine Whyte Foundation reprinted it in 1980 under the title *A Hunter of Peace*.) A review in the *New York Times* said it was "difficult to decide just what impresses us most: the excellence of the writing, the picturesqueness of the country described or the personality of the author herself."

No sooner was the book published than Schäffer was on her way back to Maligne Lake, this time at the invitation of the Geological Survey of Canada, to conduct a topographical survey of the lake for tourism purposes. The recent establishment of the Jasper Park Reserve and the coming of the Grand Trunk Pacific and Great Northern railways were expected to bring many visitors to the area. Schäffer, with her profile as the most experienced female explorer in the Rockies, was seen as the ideal person to help promote the region as a tourist destination. Although she had no experience as a surveyor, Schäffer agreed to give it a try when a Geological Survey official, Dr. Donaldson Dowling, offered to teach her the necessary technical skills.

To accompany her on the 1911 trip, Schäffer invited her nine-year-old nephew, Paul Sharples. The boy had been stricken with whooping cough and Mary thought a summer in the mountains would restore him to full health. His mother, Caroline Sharples, wasn't keen on the idea of having her son go to a place where he might get killed by wild animals. But she yielded to Mary's persuasion and said she would travel with the boy rather than have news of any mishap telegraphed back to her in Philadelphia.

The trio travelled aboard the new Grand Trunk Pacific train to Edmonton, where they rested at a hotel for a few days, and then on to Edson and Hinton, where they met their guides, Sid Unwin and Jack Otto. They followed the old Yellowhead Trail on horseback to the Jasper townsite, from where government workers had facilitated their journey by blazing a trail up to the lake. The guides assembled a boat from long cedar planks carried on the horses, and young Paul smashed an empty vinegar bottle on the prow, christening the punt HMS *Chaba II*.

Schäffer spent a month at the lake, measuring, charting, and identifying various natural features whose names would be registered with the Geographic Board of Canada. She also spent the time showing young Paul some of what she had discovered during previous trips to the mountains, and telling him that he should respect the wildlife by not shooting indiscriminately with his .22-

calibre rifle at every mountain goat, beaver, and gopher that came near the camp. She said she would name a mountain after him if he remained on his best behaviour for the trip and, true to her promise, did name Mount Paul to honour him as the first white child to navigate the lake.

The Edmonton newspapers gave extensive coverage to Schäffer's expedition. The Canadian government had recently reduced the size of Jasper Park to exclude Maligne Lake and other significant features, and Schäffer warned that such action would "throw open what have hitherto been the best game preserves in America." She urged the government to protect the lake before it "fell under the fatal breath of improvement," and suggested that it put a "steam launch" for tourists on the lake rather than allow any commercial developments that the advancing railways might bring.

Paul and his mother returned to Philadelphia after Schäffer finished her survey work at Maligne Lake, while she journeyed on to Banff, where she remained until November 1911. The summer trip marked the end of her active exploration work in the Rockies but now she had other work to do in the mountains—helping preserve a disappearing wilderness within protective national park boundaries. She returned to Banff for a longer visit in the fall and winter of 1912 and, after discovering she had no reason to fear Canadian winters, decided at age fifty to make it her permanent home. She asked her long-time guide Billy Warren to find her a property in Banff and in 1913 she moved into a house on Grizzly Street that she named "Tarry-a-while." (Today, the Peter and Catharine Whyte Foundation runs it as a bed and breakfast.) Two years later, she and Billy married. Her friends found it amusing that her first husband had been more than twenty years her senior while her second husband was twenty years her junior.

The federal government answered Schäffer's call for the return of Maligne Lake to the jurisdiction of Jasper Park in 1914 when it expanded the size of the park from the reduced 2,600 square kilometres to 11,400 square kilometres—close to what it had been originally. After that, Schäffer turned her attention to helping her husband get established in Banff as the proprietor of such business concerns as the Alberta Hotel, Cascade Garage, Banff Motor Company, and Rocky Mountain Tours and Transport. She also became involved in the First World War relief effort, creating slide shows of her mountain travels for the entertainment of wounded Canadian soldiers in English hospitals.

During the 1920s, Schäffer was active with such organizations as the Alpine Club of Canada and the Trail Riders of the Canadian Rockies. Her worsening neuralgia and other health problems prevented her from making further long trips into the mountains, but her reputation as a wilderness expert brought many people to her door, asking for advice while they planned their own trips.

When she died of pneumonia at age seventy-seven on 23 January 1939, the *Banff Crag & Canyon* hailed Schäffer as the town's "greatest friend." After that, she was temporarily forgotten in a town and province preoccupied by the events of the Second World War. However, during the late 1940s Schäffer's reputation began to grow again when author Dan McCowan mentioned her in his book *Hill-top Tales*. Then came magazine articles and a play, Elsie Park Gowan's *Jasper Story*, which acknowledged Schäffer's contributions as an early conservationist and explorer in the Rockies. (A second play inspired by the Schäffer story, Sharon Stearns's *Hunter of Peace*, was produced in Vancouver and Calgary in the 1990s.) In 1970, Parks Canada installed an interpretive walk at Maligne Lake to recognize her as the pioneer who put the lake on the map. Today, tourists can cruise the lake in glass-enclosed and heated pleasure boats, considerably more sophisticated than the "steam launch" Schäffer envisaged in 1911.

Scaling the Highest Peak— 1908-13

REVEREND GEORGE KINNEY ATTEMPTS TO CLIMB MOUNT ROBSON

Mount Robson was the prize, the highest peak in the Rockies, still unclaimed at the dawn of the twentieth century. American and British climbers had slipped into town earlier and grabbed other alpine trophies at a time when mountaineering still held little appeal for Canadians. But now things were different. The founding of the Alpine Club of Canada in 1906 had helped foster a new domestic interest in the sport. Now Canadians were eager to take their place in the winners' circle alongside the Americans and the British, and Robson gave them the opportunity to reach for the crown.

The first Canadian to launch a serious assault on Robson was George Kinney, a thirty-five-year-old Methodist minister from New Brunswick and a founding member of the Alpine Club. In September 1907 he was part of a four-man exploration party that reached the foot of the mountain, eighty kilometres northwest of Jasper on the British Columbia side of the Continental Divide. He didn't try climbing the mountain then because snow fell and food supplies ran out before he and his companions could find the best approach. But they did learn enough about Robson to decide that a route up the north face was probably their best bet for success.

Kinney returned to Robson with the same group in August 1908, and this time he made it to the top of the north shoulder, about a thousand metres short of the 3,954-metre summit. The rest of the journey to the top would have involved more rock climbing and ice cutting than Kinney and his companions were prepared to do at that time, so they turned around and headed back to Edmonton.

Kinney made his third trip to Robson in June 1909, now travelling alone because the outfitter from the previous expedition, John Yates, thought it too early in the season for mountain travel. Kinney, however, didn't want to wait, because he had heard "foreign parties were about to attempt Mount Robson." With just $2.85 in his pocket, three packhorses, and provisions for three months, he set off through the bush country west of Edmonton. Along the way he met Donald "Curly" Phillips, a twenty-five-year-old trail guide from Dorset, Ontario, who had never climbed a mountain before. Dressed in wrangler's clothing and cowboy work boots, and carrying a walking stick instead of an ice axe, the oddly equipped bushwhacker volunteered to accompany Kinney on his quest to reach the summit.

They made it to what Kinney believed was the summit, via the west slope, on 13 August 1909 after five failed attempts over the previous seven weeks. Kinney reported that he doffed his hat and said, "In the name of Almighty God, by whose strength I have climbed here, I capture this peak, Mount Robson, for my own country, and for the Alpine Club of Canada." He couldn't find any rocks at the summit to build a cairn for his trip log, and a snowstorm made it impossible for him to take photographs of the peak. But during his descent he found a "splendid natural cairn, a few hundred feet below the peak" where he stowed a borrowed Canadian flag and a tin canister containing his trip log.

While many in the climbing community hailed Kinney's ascent as an epic achievement, Arthur Wheeler, president of the Alpine Club, refused to believe that the clergyman could have scaled the mountain without an experienced guide. He wrote him a letter demanding that he "produce evidence that the world cannot challenge." Kinney replied that a snowstorm had prevented him from taking pictures on the summit, and offered to get signed affidavits from the Robson-bound "foreign parties" (a group of British climbers) he had met while returning to Edmonton. But this was not enough to satisfy Wheeler.

Why was Wheeler being difficult? One reason, it seems, is that Kinney had violated the gentlemanly code of the Alpine Club by racing ahead in an unauthorized bid for solo glory. As author Chic Scott has written in his book *Pushing the Limits: The Story of Canadian Mountaineering*, "that confounded parson had got in the way and stolen the first ascent before the cameras and the Alpine Club were ready."

Wheeler became even more skeptical in 1911 when he led a scientific expedition to the foot of Robson and got a closer look at the west slope that Kinney and Phillips had used as their route to the top in 1909. Although Kinney and Phillips accompanied Wheeler on the 1911 expedition, they still were unable to convince him they had been successful in 1909. Wheeler wrote in the *Canadian Alpine Journal* that the west route looked impossible to traverse and that Kinney and Phillips were lucky not to have been killed in the attempt. He criticized Kinney for taking the risk, saying he should never have tried such a dangerous climb with an untrained companion. Wheeler concluded that the 1909 climb should be discounted, and said the Alpine Club would organize its own ascent of Robson with an international team of experienced mountaineers and guides in the summer of 1913.

Aside from the Canadian contingent, which included the popular Phillips—but not Kinney—the 1913 team included several

George Kinney, Conrad Kain, and Donald "Curly" Phillips together during 1911 scientific expedition to Mount Robson: "I capture this peak for my own country and for the Alpine Club of Canada." (Whyte Museum of the Canadian Rockies V263 NA71-1148)

distinguished American climbers including Charles Fay, founder of the American Alpine Club, and Charles Thompson, who, with Fay, had completed the first ascents of Mount Hector and Mount Lefroy. The team leader was Conrad Kain, a thirty-year-old professional mountain guide from Austria.

To accompany Kain to the summit, Wheeler chose a Canadian, Billy Foster, and an American, Albert "Mack" MacCarthy. Foster was British Columbia's deputy public works minister and a future military hero of the First World War. MacCarthy was a banker from Summit, New Jersey. When they reached the top, via the eastern flank on 31 July 1913, Kain said to Foster and MacCarthy, "Gentlemen, that's so far as I can take you." They spent fifteen minutes on the summit, "ten of pure pleasure and five of teeth chattering."

Byron Harmon, official photographer for the Alpine Club, took pictures of the victorious trio when they returned to base camp. Phillips offered his congratulations and then surprised the party by blurting out that he and Kinney had never made it to the top during their 1909 ascent. Elizabeth Parker, founding secretary of the Alpine Club and another member of the 1913 expedition, wrote in *Scribner's Magazine* that Phillips's admission was spontaneous and unequivocal. Kain corroborated Parker's account in an article he wrote for the *Canadian Alpine Journal*. He quoted Phillips as saying, "We reached on our ascent, in mist and storm, an ice-dome fifty or sixty feet high, which we took for the peak. The danger was too great to ascend the dome."

The Phillips admission gave Wheeler the ammunition he needed. The Alpine Club promptly stripped Kinney of his prize and awarded it to Kain, Foster, and MacCarthy.

But what about Kinney's insistence that he had captured the peak "for my own country" and for the Alpine Club of Canada? Was he lying or deluded? This was shaping up to be a repeat of the 1827 controversy when botanist David Douglas claimed to have ascended a Himalayan-sized giant in the Rockies, higher than anything "yet known in the northern continent of America."

While Phillips did manage to survive the controversy—he had, after all, been just a twenty-five-year-old novice when he first climbed Mount Robson—his admission had the effect of turning

Kinney into a pariah. Kinney resigned from the Alpine Club in disgrace, gave up mountaineering, became a stretcher-bearer in the First World War, and spent the rest of his life ministering to the poor and the oppressed in the interior of British Columbia. He died in Victoria in 1961 at age eighty-nine.

Many historians, including Esther Fraser, dismissed Kinney's first-ascent claim as the fictional concoction of an obsessed loner who couldn't let the facts stand in the way of a good story. "Perhaps the great clergyman-climber was a much happier man when he finally conceded, nearly fifty years later, that he had probably been mistaken and that he had been a few feet short of the summit," Fraser wrote in her book *The Canadian Rockies: Early Travels and Explorations*. But there were some, including author Chic Scott, who felt Kinney had been given a bad rap. He noted that Fraser cited no documentary sources to support her contention that Kinney eventually admitted probable error, and nor did any of the other writers who sought to discredit Kinney. Kinney's son, Don, on the other hand, went to his grave asserting that his father had reached the top of Mount Robson. "There was no doubt in his mind at all."

The argument was finally settled in 2000, just as Scott was about to go to press with his book *Pushing the Limits*. Scott was fully prepared to contradict the naysayers, restore Kinney's reputation, and credit him with making the first ascent of Mount Robson, when he learned that the Harvard Mountaineering Club had recovered Kinney's long-lost climbing log during an ascent of Robson in 1959. A member of the Harvard club, Leo Slaggie, told Scott he had found the missing canister in a rocky bowl "far below the summit and on the wrong side of severe difficulties that lay ahead." After reading the log, Slaggie concluded that Kinney and Phillips could never have reached the top, given the poor weather conditions and the climbing difficulties involved. At best, they could have reached a ridge along the west slope "that in zero-visibility conditions Kinney might have mistaken for the summit." Nevertheless, added Slaggie, Kinney had come very close to capturing the prize, and should be recognized for that achievement. "If he had gone up the right side instead of the left, he might well have made the summit." Scott revised his manuscript accordingly.

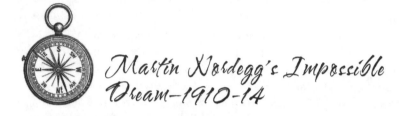

Martin Nordegg's Impossible Dream—1910-14

BUILDING A MODEL TOWN IN THE ROCKIES

M artin Cohn (later Martin Nordegg) was well established as the manager at a Berlin printing house in 1906 when a visiting Canadian politician asked him some pointed questions about his education, his job, and the salary he was making. "In Canada a man like you would have great chances," commented Onésiphore-Ernest Talbot, a Liberal MP from Quebec. "And, if you had some capital, you would have tremendous opportunities."

Cohn, then thirty-eight and married with a baby daughter, didn't have capital, and he didn't know anything about Canada. But his interest was piqued when Talbot offered to introduce him to Canada's prime minister, Sir Wilfrid Laurier, and to "many other people who will be of great use to you." Cohn discussed the matter with the only capitalist he knew, his employer Georg Büxenstein, and asked if he would provide financial backing. A day later, Büxenstein called Cohn into his office, gave him a big cigar, and said, "That country, Canada, is just now in great fashion; a great favourite here." He advanced Cohn $60,000 that he had collected from a hastily formed syndicate of Berlin businessmen, Deutsches Kanada Syndikat. "Go with God and come back with many good Canadian dollars," Büxenstein said.

Cohn, who had lived in Britain and was fluent in English and French, left Germany for Canada in May 1906. Talbot, true to his word, introduced him to Prime Minister Laurier when he arrived in Ottawa. "Have you got large capital?" Laurier asked. "I am being financed by substantial interests," Cohn replied. Laurier suggested that Cohn might consider mining in Canada as a potentially lucrative investment opportunity.

After spending the summer and winter of 1906 looking at nickel and silver prospects in northern Ontario, Cohn decided not to invest. He also passed up an opportunity to go into partnership with the Italian inventor Guglielmo Marconi, who was then conducting experiments with wireless radio transmissions across the Atlantic from Nova Scotia to Ireland. Instead, Cohn set his sights on exploiting the coal deposits identified by a Canadian geologist, George Dawson, along the eastern slopes and foothills of the Rockies, south of the Athabasca River. Cohn had listened to a debate in the House of Commons about two railway companies, the Canadian Northern and Grand Trunk Pacific, that were proposing to run transcontinental lines west of Edmonton through the Yellowhead Pass, and he felt that coal from that region would be "very useful and necessary" for their locomotives.

In the summer of 1907 Cohn began his search for coal along the eastern slopes of the Rockies. He didn't know much about coal beyond the fact that it was important to the economy of Silesia, the Prussian coal-mining province where he was born in 1868. But he did have an expert, Donaldson Dowling of the Geological Survey of Canada, travelling with him. Dowling had done some surveying in the Rockies east of Jasper and concluded that the coal deposits he found there would be "good for railway fuel," if available in commercial quantities.

Cohn and Dowling travelled by train from Ottawa to Canmore and Banff, where they looked at coal mines operating in the vicinity, and then on horseback, accompanied by guides and pack train, northward toward Jasper. They were still several hundred kilometres short of Jasper (which they never actually reached) when they made their first major coal discovery, in the Bighorn Range of the Rockies, 115 kilometres west of Rocky Mountain House. "My dream has come true," Cohn wrote in his journal. "I cannot sleep any more. I can see nothing but mountains of coal." After staking one claim there and another claim twenty-five kilometres to the northwest, in the cliffs above a tributary of the South Brazeau River, Cohn made plans to return to Germany to secure additional financing. Dowling estimated it would cost at least two million dollars to develop the coal deposits they had discovered.

It took a while before the dream came true. In order to convince his German backers that he was on to a good thing, Cohn brought with him a fourteen-kilogram lump of coal from the South Brazeau claim. He placed it on the desk of Syndikat president Georg Büxenstein and said, "This is our coal which will be needed badly by the expanding railways in Western Canada." Büxenstein said he would need to obtain an opinion from a coal expert, Henri Potonié at the Prussian Geological Survey in Berlin, before he could ask the other shareholders for the needed two million dollars.

Potonié, author of a book about the origin of coal, refused to believe that Cohn's sample could be from the Rockies. "The Rocky Mountains are from the Cretaceous geological era," he declared. "There is *no* coal in the Cretaceous. This is one of the greatest swindles that ever came to my observation, and you are one of the most impudent swindlers and impostors I ever heard of." He picked up a bamboo pole, chased Cohn out of his office, and threw the coal sample out onto a landing where it broke into smithereens.

Cohn was in tears when he reported back to Büxenstein. He pointed out that working coal mines were already operating in the Rockies, in the Banff region and in the Crowsnest Pass, and he suggested that Büxenstein should send a cable to the Geological Survey of Canada asking for confirmation of the location of Cohn's coal claims.

The reply from Ottawa was unequivocal: Not only was there a "very large deposit" of semi-bituminous coal along the Bighorn and South Brazeau rivers, but coal also existed in plentiful quantities all along the foothills of the Rockies down to the forty-ninth parallel.

The good news from Ottawa was not enough to convince the other syndicate members that they should give Cohn the two million dollars. One of them, Fritz Friedländer-Fuld, already had extensive coal investments in Silesia and in the Ruhr valley, and he couldn't see any point in putting money into a coal venture in the Canadian wilderness. However, Büxenstein was able to persuade a firm of London bankers, Lazard Brothers, to invest in the project, and Cohn was given the green light to return to

Canada to secure the necessary leases.

Cohn spent the summer of 1908 restaking the first coal claims, and staking new claims, to conform with newly enacted Canadian government mining laws. Then he took a two-month holiday in France and Spain and started making arrangements to bring his wife, the former Berthe-Marie Brand, to Canada. She had been living in New York, where their daughter, Marcelle, attended a private girls' school, while Cohn was exploring in Western Canada. Cohn decided that their new Canadian home should be in Toronto, where he planned to have his office. He had registered a company, the German Development Company, as a Canadian arm of the Berlin syndicate because he felt it would be easier for him to do business in Canada with Canadian investors and a Canadian corporate address.

In April 1909, Cohn changed his last name, and that of his wife and daughter, to Nordegg. The reason for the change has never been conclusively established. Cohn's biographer, W. John Koch, has theorized that the name could have been derived from the German words for "north" (*nord*) and "corner" (*ecke*), and that Cohn chose it because he saw a life of prosperity for himself in the "northern corner" of the Rocky Mountains.

Martin Nordegg, as we'll now call him, approached three railway companies with proposals for them to purchase coal from mines he had yet to develop. First he contacted the Canadian Pacific Railway, because its transcontinental line ran close to the Kananaskis region, southeast of Banff, where Nordegg had staked one of his claims. However, the CPR was already well served by an existing mine located near Banff at the now defunct town of Bankhead. Former CPR president Sir William Van Horne suggested that Nordegg would be better off spending German Development's money in Cuba, where Van Horne was promoting a railway construction scheme.

The Grand Trunk Pacific Railway did express interest in Nordegg's proposal but said that German Development would have to build its own branch line from the coalfields to the railway company's main transcontinental line. Nordegg was receptive to this idea but didn't want German Development to be stuck with the full cost of building what could be a six-million-dollar railway.

His last option, therefore, was to seek a partnership agreement with Canadian Northern, the other major railway operating in Western Canada.

Canadian Northern, which already owned two coalfield leases in Alberta, offered to combine its leases with those of German Development and build the branch line in exchange for a joint ownership arrangement using the name Brazeau Collieries Ltd. The branch line would either run south to the coalfields from Canadian Northern's proposed Edmonton-Vancouver line, or west from the company's Calgary-Edmonton line, depending on which proved to be the cheaper option. The railway company also extracted an undertaking from Nordegg that he would develop the mines and supply coal only to Canadian Northern, not to its railway competitors. The Syndikat in Berlin approved the deal after the London bankers and other financiers guaranteed backing with a total of $9.5 million in bond issues.

In the summer of 1910, Nordegg hired workers to start developing a mine and townsite at the South Brazeau River location. However, he soon abandoned that project when he accidentally discovered what would become the Nordegg Coal Basin, thirty-five kilometres to the east. He was riding on horseback toward Rocky Mountain House, through what for him was unknown territory, when he found what turned out to be a very promising coal deposit. He quickly registered the new claim and told his railway partners that there was a change in plan. They had no problems with this because it meant building a shorter branch line than originally envisaged, and saving as much as two million dollars in construction and coal transportation costs.

Nordegg then launched into "the most important work of my life"—the design and construction of a "modern and pretty town" to accommodate the Brazeau Collieries's mineworkers and officials. Every resident's cottage would have a bath, and the town's facilities would include the "best-equipped" hospital west of Calgary and Edmonton. Nordegg set up a temporary office in Red Deer, just south of a junction from where his railway partners were building a line westward toward the Rockies. That line would be used for the transportation of construction materials and mining equipment too heavy to be hauled to the new townsite by pack train or sleigh.

The Khaki Suit.

Martin Nordegg: "My dream has come true." (National Archives of Canada C-035065)

A trained draughtsman, Nordegg filled an album with sketches of the buildings he planned to have in the new town. There would be a company store, butcher and baker shops, poolroom, dance hall, Methodist church, movie theatre, doctor's office, and a residence for the two members of the Royal North West Mounted Police who were to be permanently stationed there.

Nordegg spent the winter of 1911–12 working on his vision of the new town. He lived in the Banff Springs Hotel and made frequent trips to the townsite by train and horse to see how the town and mine were progressing. Berthe-Marie, meanwhile, had moved back to Europe, having decided that if she and her husband were to be separated for long periods, she would prefer to be somewhere other than Toronto, where she had no friends or family. Daughter Marcelle continued to attend boarding school in New York.

No detail was too small for Nordegg to consider as he brought his dream of a model town to fulfillment. For the paint on the cottages, he chose "soft pastels which proved very pleasing to the eye." For the water tower, unsightly and protruding from a grove of spruce trees, he experimented with shades of green until he found one that "hid it so completely that one could not see the tower at all."

Nordegg was so proud of having "created something for the benefit of mankind" that he invited daughter Marcelle, then fourteen, to spend seven weeks visiting with him in the summer and fall of 1912. He showed her the mine, the growing town, and the mountain scenery "that is unsurpassed even in Switzerland. The greatness and the beauty of what you have seen will remain in your memory forever."

Construction work on the branch line between Rocky Mountain House and the townsite was completed in February 1914, and Nordegg advised his railway partners that he had 91,000 tonnes of coal ready for shipment from the new Brazeau Collieries's mine. The chief executive of Canadian Northern, Sir William Mackenzie, marked the occasion by naming the new town after Nordegg. "He had decided to erect a monument to me which would be living and more lasting than one made out of stone or bronze," Nordegg said. "There was no doubt that I was considered an important man west of the Calgary-Edmonton railway line." The official photograph of the proceedings showed Nordegg standing on the rear platform of Mackenzie's private rail car, dressed in a military-style khaki gabardine suit, with left hand on hip, surveying the scene like a conquering general.

Nordegg revelled in the role of town father. He rode around town on his horse, glad-handing, chatting with the folks, instantly recognizable with his waxed moustache and Boy Scout-style hat. He wanted his town to be unlike any other company town—an equitable place where every cottage had electricity and running water, and all classes and creeds lived together in peace and harmony. However, because the railway line bisected the town and the best cottages were built on a slope above the tracks, there was a gulf created between the workers who lived in the "lower town" and the company officials—including Nordegg himself—who lived up on the hill. There was also a clash of lifestyles. Nordegg was shocked to discover that some miners' families were storing coal in the bathtubs and bathing their babies in the toilets. Others wanted the plumbing installations pulled out to give themselves more bedroom space. "I had to give in," Nordegg said.

Alcoholism, dance hall fights, backyard garbage dumps, and other social problems abounded as the population increased with the arrival of every passenger train from the east. There was one problem, however, that Nordegg could laugh about afterwards. The respectable women in town were horrified when they discovered that an itinerant madam had established a tent brothel on the edge of town, and they demanded that Nordegg rid the area of this unwanted menace. Nordegg checked with police and forestry officials only to be told there was "no law preventing ladies from camping in the woods and gentlemen from visiting them." The women of the town were not pleased with this response but the company store operator was happy to see an immediate increase in perfume sales to the madam and her girls!

Nordegg had less than a year to enjoy the satisfaction of being the most important man in town. In August 1914, the British Empire, including Canada, went to war against Germany. Throughout Canada, German nationals were interned in large numbers. Nordegg wrote to Ottawa requesting that he be "protected from arrest or molestation on account of being a German citizen" and was relieved when he received that assurance in writing. However, there were no assurances in terms of continued financial backing for Brazeau Collieries. The London bankers closed off the money supply to the Berlin syndicate and Nordegg found himself scrambling to pay the bills. Canadian Northern provided temporary relief by offering to cover the mine payroll and other expenses.

In May 1915, with anti-German sentiment escalating in Canada, police raided Nordegg's cottage and confiscated his hunting weapons and a number of documents, including his protection letter from Ottawa. A telegram from Ottawa assured him that the protection was still in place, but the experience rattled Nordegg. A month later, he was summoned to Ottawa for questioning by a national security committee about his German business connections. His lawyer, Andrew Haydon, managed to convince the committee that Nordegg should not be interned because of his dealings with the enemy nation, but the committee ruled that he had to leave immediately for exile in the United States. "What a difference between my first arrival in Ottawa and this departure," Nordegg said. "My heart was heavy."

Nordegg headed for New York, where he reunited with his wife and daughter. His wife was suffering from heart problems and depression so Nordegg decided, after consulting with a Manhattan physician, that she should live by the sea in Atlantic City. Marcelle, who was out of school for the summer, stayed with her mother at an Atlantic City hotel. Nordegg came down and visited with them every second weekend.

His railway partners were now prepared to let Nordegg run the affairs of Brazeau Collieries from New York by correspondence, but he felt he was losing control of the company and soon he started looking for other opportunities. Between 1915 and 1917 he helped sort out the financial problems of a German-owned coal company in Pennsylvania, Lehigh Coke, and he facilitated the sale of that company to the giant Bethlehem Steel Corporation.

Nordegg's railway partners and the financiers eventually took advantage of his absence from Canada to remove him from the board of directors of Brazeau Collieries. Because he was unable to regain control of Brazeau, he sold to the London bankers the shares held by his Toronto-based German Development Company, and that resulted in "many hundreds of thousands of dollars" for the Berlin syndicate. The sale made Nordegg a wealthy man. After that, he felt free to "roam the world to my liking and to help and assist mankind."

Nordegg spent the 1920s dabbling in various business ventures and travelling the world with Sonia Meisel, a Polish-born actress he met and wooed after a theatrical performance in Atlantic City. He married her in 1924, a few months after Berthe-Marie died of pneumonia while seeking medical treatment in Switzerland for respiratory problems. One of the places Martin and Sonia visited was China, where Martin's daughter, Marcelle, settled after her marriage to an American oilman named Arthur May. Martin and Sonia also visited the town of Nordegg, to which Martin would always have a strong sentimental attachment. He was deeply disappointed when railway officials decided in 1919 to change the name of the train station from Nordegg to Brazeau, to correspond with the name of the local colliery.

In 1928, Martin and Sonia bought a large home in Ottawa that later became the residence of the Sri Lankan High Commissioner.

(Nordegg's status as a deportee had been lifted by Canada after the war.) Martin did some contract work with the federal government dealing with the problems of political refugees, and he published a book, *The Fuel Problem of Canada*, about the difficulties facing the Canadian coal industry. He also wrote a sentimental chronicle, *To the Town that Bears Your Name*, of his daughter's 1912 visit to Nordegg.

Martin and Sonia lived in Ottawa for nine years. In 1937, they relocated to New York, and Martin started writing his memoirs, in German. He was never able to find a publisher for the memoirs during his lifetime—he died in 1948 at age eighty—but they did appear in translation in 1971 under the title *The Possibilities of Canada Are Truly Great*. In the last paragraph of the book, edited and translated by Saskatchewan historian Ted Regehr, Martin recalled how later in life he often "longed for the Rocky Mountains, to travel again over the trails, and to the town which still bears my name."

The town of Nordegg, which grew to a population of 3,500 at its peak and produced nine million tonnes of coal over the years, received a death sentence in 1955 when Brazeau Collieries closed the mine. The railways had switched to diesel fuel and coal was no longer needed. The remaining 130 families moved out, the stores were shuttered, and the Nordegg United Church held its last service. The curling rink was taken to Rocky Mountain House and the ice arena moved to Rimbey, fifty kilometres to the east. The station agent continued to dutifully post the weekly arrival and departure times of the train from Rocky until the Canadian National Railways (successor to Canadian Northern) closed the station and lifted the tracks in the 1960s.

Between the 1960s and the 1990s, the Alberta government used Nordegg for a minimum-security prison camp. Former Nordeggers (as they like to call themselves) and their children and grandchildren met once a year to maintain the links forged during the early years of Alberta's history. The Nordegg Historic Heritage Interest Group (now the Nordegg Historical Society) came into being to protect the Brazeau Collieries' mine site and what was left of the original town. The federal government desig-nated Brazeau Collieries as a national historic site, interpretive signs were erected, and a commemorative plaque was scheduled to be dedicated there in August 2005. "The historical landscape reflects the roles of entrepreneurs, labour, and evolving technologies in an industry that played a central role of the West after the First World War," said the accompanying press release. "This land is your link with history," wrote local historian Anne (McMullen) Belliveau. "Here, you can touch eternity." Nordegg would undoubtedly have approved.

Hunting and Painting with Rifle and Brush—1910-59

CARL RUNGIUS FINDS BIG GAME AND ARTISTIC INSPIRATION IN THE MOUNTAINS

Carl Rungius found his destiny as a hunter and painter of North American wildlife after failing to spot a moose during a hunting trip to Maine with his wealthy American uncle in 1894. As a young boy in Germany, inspired by the frontier writings of James Fenimore Cooper, Rungius had dreamed of capturing, on canvas, the fierce battle of two rutting bull moose, but the animals had been hunted to extinction in much of Europe by the middle of the 1800s. The remaining few moose were kept on the private hunting estates of the nobility, so there was no opportunity for Rungius to observe their behaviour, much less hunt or paint them. America seemed to present that opportunity.

If Rungius had seen a moose during his 1894 hunting trip to Maine, and been able to bag it and capture it on canvas, he would have been content to return home to Germany and carry on with his previous routine of working as a house decorator and satisfying his artistic desires by sketching the big cats at the Berlin zoo. As it was, he accepted an invitation from his uncle, a German-born Brooklyn physician named Clemens Fulda, to stay in the United States for another year and try for a moose the following fall. His uncle had a large room in his brownstone mansion that Rungius could use as a painting studio, and there would be lots of opportunity for him to acquaint himself with American big game both as a hunter and as an artist.

Rungius, who had learned to ride a horse and shoot a rifle during two years as a Prussian cavalry officer, was twenty-five when he accepted his uncle's invitation to spend a year in the United States. Born in 1869 in a village near Berlin, where his father served as a Lutheran pastor, he started studying life drawing at the Berlin Art Academy at age eighteen, and surprised his parents—who had insisted, with his future security in mind, that he apprentice as a house painter—when he received a commission from a parishioner to do an oil painting of his father's church. Critical recognition followed when Rungius showed his work at the Greater Berlin International Art Exhibition. But life as a full-time artist didn't seem to be in the cards for him because he had little prospect of making a decent income from his art.

Rungius doesn't seem to have seen a moose in the wild during the year he spent living in the United States courtesy of his uncle's patronage. (He used a New York taxidermist's specimen as a model for his first moose painting.) It is known, however, that he spent some time in Wyoming ranching territory during this period, and that the experience convinced him the American West afforded opportunities for big-game hunting and painting that Europe lacked. By the spring of 1897, he was based permanently in New York, making important business connections with his uncle's help, spending his summers in Wyoming, and contributing illustrations of elk, pronghorn antelope, and mule deer to such American outdoors magazines as *Forest and Stream, Recreation, Everybody's Magazine,* and *Outing.* (His first recorded moose killing was in Wyoming in 1898 and the following year, at age thirty, he bagged his first grizzly.)

His painting went hand in hand with his hunting. Rungius hung the carcasses from tripods made of branches and manipulated them to indicate running, walking, or scratching—actions too quick to record by sketching from life. "Large animals have to be studied in parts," he explained. He would then make detailed pencil drawings from different angles and work these poses into finished canvases when he returned to New York.

In the summer of 1904, Rungius visited the Yukon to hunt and paint Dall sheep, grizzly bear, and caribou. One of his sheep paintings, "Wary Game," subsequently appeared in the New York Zoological Society's *Bulletin* magazine, where it was seen by Jimmy Simpson, the Banff guide and outfitter. (Simpson had joined the Society so he could sell to the Bronx Zoo some of the wildlife that he live-trapped in the Rockies.) "That fellow knows his animals and he knows his sheep," Simpson remarked. He wrote Rungius a letter offering to take him on a bighorn sheep hunt in the Rockies, with Simpson supplying the pack horses and the guiding expertise at no cost to the painter. (In later years, the art-loving Simpson would accept a Rungius painting as a gift every time he loaned his horses and outfit to the painter.) Rungius was initially hesitant. "Another guide looking for another customer," he commented. However, his wife, Louise—an American first cousin whom Rungius had married in 1907—detected a sincere tone in the Simpson letter and urged Rungius to accept the invitation. After exchanging a few letters with Simpson, Rungius agreed to visit the Rockies in August 1910. The CPR, when told about Rungius's growing reputation as a wildlife painter, provided a free pass for his train travel.

Rungius shot and killed a grizzly bear during his trip through the Rockies with Simpson, and the wildlife and landscape of the mountains subsequently became the sustaining focus of his work. Wyoming had opened his eyes to the possibilities available for a hunter and painter of big game, but Rungius found the atmosphere in the Rockies more inspiring. "Wyoming is fairly arid in most places, and the lack of humidity—'atmosphere' to a painter—results in sharp edges, even at a distance, which give objects a photographic appearance," he said. "But in Alberta, with its scenic grandeur and its remarkable wealth of big game species, I have found at last the land which I have been seeking." In the high ranges of the Rockies, the landscape of mountains, glaciers, and lakes excited Rungius as landscape never had before.

Rungius returned to the Rockies in 1911 to hunt and paint bighorn sheep ("doubtless, our finest game animal") in alpine settings, and he continued to make annual summer visits with Louise until 1921, when they built a six-room studio-home in Banff that they named The Paintbox. They then lived in Banff each year between April and October and spent the winter months in New

Carl Rungius: "That fellow knows his animals." (Glenbow Archives NA-3466-52)

York, where Rungius's market was. His paintings fetched between US$1,500 and $3,500 for an 86 x 119-cm canvas. (The equivalent of $15,700 to $36,000 in 2004 American dollars.) His clients were mostly wealthy American hunting enthusiasts who also happened to be Simpson's clients. Rungius also produced a steady body of work for the New York Zoological Society, which commissioned him to paint game animals that the Society felt were in danger of dying out.

Rungius was not the first artist to work in the Rockies. Paul Kane, Henry James Warre, and John Mix Stanley had sketched extensively in the mountains during the 1840s, William Hind had sketched the gold-seeking Overlanders during their trek across the Rockies in 1862, and the CPR brought several painters—including Lucius O'Brien, T. Mower Martin, and John Fraser—into the region from the 1880s onward to produce images for promotional brochures. But none of these CPR-sponsored painters lived in the mountains, and they seldom ventured more than a few kilometres into the bush to find their subjects. Their paintings—as befitted their promotional purpose—depicted enticing scenes of quaint Arcadian splendour. Rungius, on the other hand, was as much at home in the wilds as in the studio, and he ventured deep into the wilderness on horseback to capture a stark, forbidding, and awe-inspiring landscape. More than just background settings for his animal renditions, the mountains competed with the animals for domination of his canvas.

Once settled in Banff as a semi-permanent resident, Rungius became the leading figure in a talented colony of locally based wilderness artists, including Illingworth Kerr, Belmore Browne, Nicholas de Grandmaison, and Peter and Catharine Whyte. They displayed their work at the local CPR hotels, the Banff Springs and the Chateau Lake Louise, and Banff soon became known as one of the few places in Canada where one could see good Western Canadian art. A visiting sportsman, William N. Beach of New York, commented, "Rungius always depicts big game animals in the way the hunters dream about—posed for a perfect shot."

The 1920s brought Rungius critical acclaim—as well as steady sales. Roger Whitman, writing in *Country Life* magazine, described him as "our foremost painter of wild animals. His paintings have gained for him a recognition that each year becomes more fully established." A painting Rungius did of Lake McArthur, a glacially fed tarn located between Lake Louise and Field, British Columbia, won first prize at the prestigious Carnegie International Exhibition, and was reproduced in the *New York Times*. The Calgary Stampede board invited him to show his work at its annual agricultural exhibition, and the CPR purchased some of his paintings for its trail hiking brochures.

Rungius, like many North Americans, struggled through the Depression of the 1930s. He and Louise gave up their Manhattan apartment in 1933 to save money and, for the first time ever, spent part of the winter in Banff, where Carl—at age sixty-four—decided to take up downhill skiing. A badly sprained ankle quickly ended that activity. He then considered spending winters in California, where friends were offering him hospitality. But Rungius still needed his New York connections so, in 1936, after dismissing the fact that he was suffering through what he called "a long dry spell," he and Louise returned to Manhattan. He had been asked to paint a backdrop for a diorama of North American mammals at the American Museum of Natural History, and that job would eventually bring him a paycheque of $3,500.

In 1937, a Berlin city official visited Rungius in Banff and invited him "to return to the fatherland where you belong." Germany, said the official, would welcome Rungius with open arms. "We need people like you. Why, I am sure that (Nazi kingpin Hermann) Goering would give you permission to hunt on one of the imperial preserves." Rungius was not buying, however. "These are my hunting grounds," he said, pointing toward the Rockies. "I will come when your führer can offer me better than these, and greater freedom."

Louise, who suffered from heart problems, died in 1940 at age sixty. Carl had depended on her to look after his business affairs as well as his personal needs, and found being "a one-horse affair" hard to bear. He began using a sleeping bag in his New York studio so he wouldn't have to make the bed. When friends gave him a toaster so he wouldn't have to leave the house to get breakfast, he burned the bread and blew a fuse. "It's not exactly easy," he said. "Reading a newspaper and making toast do not work well together, and it takes too long to get the smoke out of the apartment."

In 1950, when Rungius was eighty-one, he suffered a series of small strokes that he attributed to "too much drink." Friends suggested that he slow down but he always seemed to have commissioned work to finish—orders for paintings that the buyers planned to give as Christmas presents. "I often think how lovely it would be if I could call myself retired and give my full attention to the amusing side of life," he said. "But then, it isn't in the makeup of a painter." He told a *Calgary Herald* reporter the secret of all success was willingness to work. "I have always been a hard worker."

Rungius took his last hunting and sketching trip into the Rockies at age eighty-three (he told the *Herald* that he bagged his last moose, his largest ever, just a year or two previously), and then sold his Banff home, studio, and contents to Eric Harvie, the Calgary art collector and philanthropist. Harvie told Rungius he could live in the home rent-free for the rest of his life. Rungius seemed to be under the impression that Harvie would turn the home into a museum, but this never happened. The house was eventually sold to the federal government and demolished for redevelopment.

Harvie, founder and prime benefactor of what is now Calgary's Glenbow Museum, acquired several of Rungius's major works during the last years of the painter's life. He purchased the contents of Rungius's New York studio in October 1959, a few months before the painter died of a stroke, at age ninety, while working at his easel. To these Harvie added eight Rungius works that he purchased from Jimmy Simpson, and some paintings that he purchased from Rungius's relatives. In 1977, the Glenbow augmented its Rungius collection by acquiring ten paintings from the New York Zoological Society's Gallery of Wild Animals.

At the time of his death, Rungius was widely hailed as a major talent. The *New York Times*, in its obituary, described him as "one of the world's outstanding wildlife painters." After that, Rungius became a forgotten figure for many years, especially in Canada, because private American collectors held much of his work, and little of it was on public display. However, this situation began to change in the 1980s when the Glenbow—which by then had acquired three-quarters of Rungius's work, about 2,400 pieces—mounted the first of three major exhibitions of his work.

Canadian artist Robert Bateman described Rungius as a "brilliant artist," comparing him to John Singer Sargent and Winslow Homer "in his ability to say all that is needed with a minimum of strokes." Douglas Allen, an American artist and critic, called Rungius "America's master portrayer of big game animals and their habitat."

The first Glenbow exhibition, in 1985, revealed Rungius's strengths as a painter of the Rocky Mountain landscape and cowboy subjects. *Calgary Herald* critic Nancy Tousley described his precisely observed paintings of a 1915 Wyoming roundup as "among the most accurate representations of the life of the working cowboy ever produced without a camera."

The second Glenbow exhibition, in 1990, brought praise for Rungius's ability as a printmaker. "His etchings are in a class by themselves," said Donald Crouch, a fine art professor at the University of Illinois. "No one ever did them as well as Rungius."

The third exhibition was presented at the Glenbow in 2000 (the organizers said they wanted to do Rungius again because wildlife art is always a guaranteed crowd-pleaser) and then toured across Canada and the United States. While some critics dismissed the wildlife paintings as "sentimental" and "romanticized" art, made to order for rich clients with conservative tastes, all agreed that Rungius's renditions of the Rocky Mountain landscape were on a par with those painted by J. E. H. MacDonald in the 1920s and Walter Phillips in the 1940s. "Wonderful depictions of the wide-open spaces and mountain passes of the West," critic Sarah Milroy wrote in the *Globe and Mail*. "His ability to convey the particular light of that region is at times quite marvellous." Milroy concluded that while the touring show failed to convince her that Rungius was a great artist, "it certainly makes a convincing case for his place in any social history of the West, or any account of North America's cultural attitudes toward animals in the wild."

Ken Jones: Mountain Guide—
1910-2004

A CANADIAN JOINS THE RANKS OF THE EUROPEAN ALPINE LEADERS

Ken Jones was the first Canadian to earn certification as a mountain guide in the Rockies, and thus the first outsider to be accepted into a closed fraternity that previously consisted only of European mountaineers who had developed their skills in the Swiss Alps. He joined the fraternity in the early 1930s, when the European-born guides were encouraging their own children to go into another line of work because they thought that guiding didn't pay enough.

Jones, who jokingly referred to himself as the first Canadian Swiss guide, was an athletic individual who went into guiding because he couldn't find work in his chosen field of civil engineering. Raised on a homestead near Golden, British Columbia, he earned his engineering degree by correspondence from the University of British Columbia after two years of medical studies at McGill University in Montreal. Before that, at age eighteen, he played amateur hockey for the Kimberley Dynamiters of the Western Senior League and dreamed of a career in the National Hockey League. However, his English-born mother, the former Sarah Jane Huxley of Shropshire, told him that hockey was a "ruffian's game" and insisted he do something more "honourable" with his life. "You're going to your uncle's place in Montreal and you're going to become a doctor," she said.

Jones's uncle, Arthur Huxley, was the Canadian representative for a company in Birmingham, England, that sold pharmaceutical products. Jones stayed at Huxley's Montreal home while attending

McGill, but that arrangement ended when the company closed its Canadian operations and recalled Huxley to England. Jones couldn't afford to rent a place in Montreal so he dropped out of medical school and returned to Golden. The University of British Columbia was offering some degrees by correspondence, but medicine wasn't one of them so Jones switched to civil engineering.

When he started mountain guiding, in his early twenties, Jones used skills he had been developing since he was nine years old. He had done his first skiing going back and forth to elementary school on wooden skis built by the Swedish settlers in his Golden neighbourhood. He had learned to climb while chasing goats with his schoolmates on nearby Willowbank Mountain and Redburn Peak, when he often carried a coiled rope as if he were an experienced mountaineer. "It was just for show—we were imitating the Swiss guides," he said. The pipe-smoking guides, who worked for the Canadian Pacific Railway's resort hotels as escorts for climbers, made their permanent homes in Golden, and Jones became friendly with many of them.

During the early 1930s, while completing his correspondence courses in engineering, Jones spent his winters at Chateau Lake Louise, then a summer hotel, where some of the guides worked in the off-season as caretakers. The guides didn't like doing this hotel maintenance work—it was something of a comedown for them after being the monarchs of the mountains during the summertime—so they were happy to let young Jonesy share the chores. He, for his part, was happy to be accepted into their circle because "they were my mentors and my friends."

Their friendship was sealed after one of the guides, Edward Feuz Jr., shot a moose that had wandered onto the hotel property, and Jones helped him dispose of the carcass in the bush. "The wardens were our friends, and we knew them very well," Jones said. "But somehow I don't think they would have been very understanding about us shooting a moose in the national park."

Jones's first professional mountaineering experience came in 1933, when he was hired as a guide's assistant to pack gear for Katie Gardiner, a British climber who subsequently wrote her name into the record books as the female who achieved the greatest number of first ascents in the Rockies. Packing soon led to full-fledged guid-

ing and, by the mid-1930s, Jones was working as a climbing and skiing guide for two of the foremost backcountry lodges in the
Rockies—Mount Assiniboine Lodge on the British Columbia side of
the Continental Divide, and Skoki Lodge near Lake Louise. At the
same time, he achieved distinction as a competitive skier, defeating
the reigning Alberta amateur cross-country champion in a race at
Lake Louise, and claiming the aggregate title for cross-country,
downhill, and slalom at the Dominion Ski Championships in Banff.

In 1937, Jones finally got a job in the profession for which he had
trained when the Consolidated Mining and Smelter Company
hired him to survey gold mining claims in the Yukon. He worked
there for only three years, though, mainly because the Second
World War had started and "I wanted to fly those fancy planes." He
earned his wings in 1941 but was grounded because of a hearing
problem. He spent the first part of 1944 in the Rockies near Jasper,
teaching mountain warfare and survival to troops bound for
Europe. After his discharge, he returned to guiding at Mount
Assiniboine Lodge and Skoki Lodge. The manager at Skoki, a
German-born baroness named Lizzie Rummel, characterized
Jones as a "real guide" who "takes people out, has them do more
than they ever thought possible, and brings them home laughing
and talking about an early start for tomorrow."

In 1960, Jones moved with his wife, Bridget, to Nanton, eighty-
five kilometres south of Calgary, and they ran a guest ranch there for
the next thirty-five years. The same year, Jones assumed the manager's job at Skoki Lodge ("my eyes always need some mountains to
lean on," he said), taking over from an eccentric operator named
Ray Legace who had made baked beans a staple of every meal
served at the lodge. After disposing of forty-three cases of leftover
beans, Jones improved and varied the menu by adding such items
as flapjacks, roast beef, turkey, and "real vegetables and potatoes."
It wasn't gourmet fare, but it was wholesome. "You don't need seven
types of quiche for a mountain experience," said Jones. "But you do
need something that is pleasant to eat and gives you energy."

Jones continued working at Skoki until 1967, when former Skoki
manager Rummel (who had opened her own lodge at Sunburst
Lake) and Mount Assiniboine Lodge operator, Erling Strom, asked
the British Columbia government to hire a warden for Mount

Assiniboine Provincial Park, and recommended that Jones be given the job. He worked as a warden there until 1974, when he suddenly quit and went back to guiding. "I was just fed up with the park's bureaucracy," he said. "I was gradually going under with the restrictions they put on me."

Jones maintained his association with the Skoki and Mount Assiniboine lodges until he was into his early nineties. When he became too old for mountain guiding, he spent part of each summer and winter doing handyman chores at the lodges, chopping wood, hauling water, and shovelling snow. He also revelled in the role of mountain raconteur, telling stories to the guests about his life as a guide. When he lost his hearing he became an accomplished lip-reader, and the stories continued to flow. Many of them were collected and published in a 1996 book, *Ken Jones Mountain Man*, compiled and edited by outdoors enthusiast Lorne Tetarenko and his daughter Kim. One of the most popular was a story Jones told about betting a friend a forty-ounce bottle of rum that he could catch a cutthroat trout weighing five pounds or more. Jones caught his fish and won his bottle of rum, but only did so by stunning the fish with his rifle before hooking it on to his fishing line. "It takes real talent to catch these beauties," he said with a grin.

Barb Renner, who managed Mount Assiniboine Lodge with her husband, Sepp, said they never knew when to expect Jones, so the door was always kept open for him. "There was a bed with his name on it." In his later years, he went into Assiniboine by helicopter but up to then he didn't think anything of hiking or skiing the thirty-five kilometres from Banff to the lodge. "If he tried to hitchhike on the highway, no one would pick him up," Barb Renner said, "because he had an axe in one hand for clearing brush, and he carried his ice axe in the other."

Jones made his last trips to Assiniboine and Skoki in the spring of 2003, when he was ninety-two. He went into Skoki by snowmobile and joked that if he had taken a week to get into shape, he could have travelled the twenty kilometres from Lake Louise on skis. Eleven months later, on 25 January 2004, he suffered a fatal stroke at his home in Nanton and died the following day at the hospital in High River. "The mountains were Ken's heart and soul," Kim Tetarenko said. "He really was connected to them."

The Emperor's Ice Axe—1925

YUKO MAKI AND HIS JAPANESE COLLEAGUES
CONQUER MOUNT ALBERTA

Most of the major peaks in the Rockies had already been scaled by 1920, but one forbidding summit thwarted all challengers. Mount Alberta, fifth highest in the chain, remained unvanquished long after its taller sisters had been conquered. One reason was its constant susceptibility to rapidly changing weather patterns and falling rock. Another was the fact that Mount Alberta's summit rose above sheer black cliffs that defied all but the most accomplished alpinists. Norman Collie, the British mountaineer who named it in 1898 after Queen Victoria's popular daughter, declared there was a "sublime aloofness, an air of grim inaccessibility about Mount Alberta that was most impressive." (He took pains to explain afterwards that he didn't mean to suggest that the princess herself possessed such alienating characteristics!)

The mountain rises above the headwaters of the Athabasca River in the southwest corner of Jasper National Park. Standing 3,619 metres tall, it is hidden from the nearest highway, the Icefields Parkway, ten kilometres to the east. A visitor has to hike southward along the Athabasca River for about fifty kilometres before the intimidating north face of the black-walled giant comes into view.

An American climber, Howard Palmer, was the first to launch an assault on Mount Alberta. He inspected the mountain from its foot

143

in 1920 and came back four years later to climb it. Bad weather foiled his attempt. "The ancients would have found it an admirable model for the Tower of Babel," Palmer wrote. "It possesses no easy side."

In 1925, a team of Japanese climbers led by Yuko Maki took up the challenge. Maki had become famous throughout Japan in 1921 after completing a daring ascent of Switzerland's Mount Eiger along a previously unclimbed ridge. The story goes that he was travelling by train to Tokyo with a member of Japan's imperial family, Marquis Mori Tatsu Hosokawa, when the nobleman produced a book containing a photograph of Mount Alberta shot by Palmer in 1920. The caption read, "A Formidable Unclimbed Peak of the Range." Hosokawa suggested to Maki that Mount Alberta might become his next target, and the mountaineer readily agreed.

Hosokawa and two Japanese newspapers provided monetary support for the expedition to Alberta. Three Swiss guides joined the six Japanese climbers when they arrived in Jasper, and the party embarked on 11 July 1925 with thirty-nine horses and provisions for twenty-five days. They reached the foot of Mount Alberta on 21 July. A rough natural stairway of crumbling shale took them up one of the black cliffs guarding the summit, after which they resorted to extraordinary measures to reach the top. At one point, they climbed on top of one another to form a human ladder so they could surmount a rock overhang, four metres high. Then they crossed a narrow ridge with a sheer vertical drop on either side by straddling it horse-riding style.

When they reached the summit, after sixteen hours of strenuous climbing, Maki used loose rocks to build a small cairn and solemnly inserted into it an ice axe that Marquis Hosokawa had given him as a farewell gift. In an empty tin can he left a note listing the names of the nine victorious climbers. "We came from Japan so far called by this charming great mountain," Maki wrote.

Over the next twenty-three years, the story of the ice axe atop Mount Alberta assumed legendary dimensions. Jasper residents, listening to stories told by the local horse packers who had accompanied the Japanese expedition, came to believe that the axe had been given to Maki by the Japanese emperor himself, and that it was made of solid silver. It wasn't until July 1948, when American climbers Fred Ayers and John Oberlin made the second ascent of Mount Alberta, that the truth became known. "The axe was not silver but a good Swiss make, weather-beaten and rusty," Oberlin wrote in the *American Alpine Journal*. "However, if the axe were new and shining when placed in the cairn, it must almost have looked like polished silver."

The Americans removed the axe, engraved with Marquis Hosokawa's initials, because they thought it should be safeguarded in a museum somewhere. The wooden handle snapped when they tried to pull it out of the ice, but they took the rest of it anyhow and donated it to the American Alpine Club's office in New York City. There it remained for the next forty-seven years.

While most Canadian mountaineers knew that the axe part recovered by the Americans was made of steel, some persisted in believing that it really was made of silver. This made for a better story. Who could resist the saga of a silver ice axe, personally blessed by the emperor of Japan, being carried to the top of a remote and forbidding Canadian mountain by an intrepid team of loyal mountaineers?

In 1965, a team of five Japanese climbers came to Canada to make a fortieth-anniversary ascent of Mount Alberta. When they reached the cairn built by the 1925 team, they found the bottom part of the broken ice axe. One of the climbers put it in his pack, took it home, and gave it to the Tokyo office of the Japanese Alpine Club.

In 1995, the top part of the axe was repatriated to Canada. Jasper mountaineer Greg Horne was doing some research at the American Alpine Club's New York library and archives when he accidentally discovered the broken axe, identified by a tag, included in a bundle of old ice axes lying under a table. Excited by his find, he briefly considered putting the axe in his bag, sneaking it past the security guard, and bringing it triumphantly home to Canada. Instead, he left it under the table and, when he got home, he told a Jasper historian, Edith Gourley, about his discovery. They wrote a letter to the American Alpine Club requesting the return of the axe for use in a permanent mountaineering display at the Jasper-Yellowhead Museum. The American Alpine Club took a while to respond, but eventually put the axe in the mail.

The bottom part of the axe came back to Canada two years later. When members of the Japanese Alpine Club learned that both parts of the axe still existed, they invited a Canadian delegation to Tokyo for a ceremonial reunification before the axe went back to Canada. The Japanese pulled out all the stops for the 1997 ceremony. Crown Prince Naruhito and Prime Minister Ryutaro Hashimoto were on hand, along with eight hundred members of the Japanese Alpine Club and other dignitaries, to witness Mike Mortimer, president of the Alpine Club of Canada, and Lori Ann Perlin of the Jasper-Yellowhead Museum assemble the fabled ice axe. "It was just unbelievable the way the two pieces matched up," Mortimer told a *Calgary Herald* reporter. "It was as if they had been broken yesterday." The story made the front pages of all the Japanese newspapers, read by an estimated twenty million readers.

The final chapter in the saga of the Mount Alberta ice axe was written in August 2000, on the seventy-fifth anniversary of the historic climb. Three climbers from the Alpine Club of Canada and three from the Japanese Alpine Club joined forces for a joint celebratory ascent of Mount Alberta. They carried the seventy-five-year-old axe in two custom-built museum cases for assembly at the summit. Members of the Japanese media and a Canadian film crew accompanied the climbing party. Bad weather, however, prevented the climbers from venturing beyond the base camp. A cold spring followed by a wet summer had left the mountain in treacherous shape, with masses of hardened snow overhanging on the edges of the precipices. "Although everyone wanted to climb the mountain, it was not worth dying over," base camp manager Greg Horne said. Instead, the mountaineers settled for climbing such modest neighbouring peaks as Little Alberta, Mount Woolley, and Mount Engelhard, and a previously unclimbed ridge of Engelhard that they named Tomadachi (Friendship) Mountain.

Though the 2000 Mount Alberta climb was unsuccessful, the hoopla surrounding it in Jasper mirrored the excitement in Japan for the first axe reunification ceremony. As Calgary climber Dave Dornian wrote in *Gripped* magazine, what could be more romantic than reuniting the halves of a legendary lost ice axe on the summit of a mountain, seventy-five years after the first ascent? "Banners fluttered from every lamppost. Our team was introduced to the public in the town park. There were horses, wardens in Stetsons, and enough flash photographs to raise skin blisters."

A number of ceremonial axe assemblies took place in Jasper, including one at the Jasper-Yellowhead Museum, where the ice axe now has a permanent home. Alpine historian Bob Sandford told the *Edmonton Journal* that the axe would always symbolize the common history and heritage that links the mountaineering communities of Canada, the United States, and Japan. "That which was lost has finally been found, and that which was separated is at last rejoined."

 *Campus in the Clouds—1933*

NED CORBETT AND ELIZABETH STERLING HAYNES PAVE THE WAY
FOR THE BUILDING OF THE BANFF CENTRE

The curtain had lowered on the 1932 Alberta Drama Festival, the prizes had been handed out, and the three adjudicators had adjourned to a room in Lethbridge's Marquis Hotel for brandy and cigars. After agreeing that the theatrical offerings were disappointing, compared to those of previous festivals, the three men discussed possible ways to improve standards. "What this country needs is not a good five-cent cigar," said adjudicator Leonard Brockington, Calgary's city solicitor, after he had quaffed several drams. "What this country needs is an honest-to-God theatrical training centre where the leaders of community theatre could get some fundamental training in the elements of good theatre." "Amen," replied Edmonton adjudicator Edward Annand "Ned" Corbett, community outreach director for the University of Alberta. "And the place to hold it is Banff."

Corbett, a former Presbyterian minister who had "started on the road to Damascus then fell among educators," first approached the Alberta Drama League—organizers of the provincial theatre festival—with a plan for a two-week summer theatre school in Banff. However, the league's executive officers thought the idea premature and said they didn't want to be stuck with the costs of what they called a "venture that was doomed to failure." Corbett refused to let the idea die. He discussed it with his boss, U of A president Robert Charles Wallace, who was more encouraging. However, Wallace noted that the Institute of Pacific Relations was meeting at the Banff Springs Hotel that summer, and he suggested there might be a problem with accommodation. If Corbett could find other accommodations and a place for the participants to meet and perform, Wallace would be prepared to approve an expenditure of one thousand dollars to fund a summer school. The money, Wallace said, would come from a ten-thousand-dollar grant that the Carnegie Corporation of New York had given to the university for development of drama in Alberta.

Corbett called on a powerful ally to bring the idea to fruition. Elizabeth Sterling Haynes, an actress and director who had trained at Toronto's influential Hart House Theatre, was already fostering the growth of community drama in rural Alberta in her role as the University of Alberta's Carnegie-sponsored full-time travelling drama specialist. That, in Corbett's mind, made her the obvious choice to run a theatre program in the Rockies. She readily agreed when Corbett asked her to line up a selection of twelve one-act plays for the participants to study and perform.

Corbett had to use all his guile and charm to persuade the townsfolk of Banff to support the project. "We have thought of going to Jasper," he told school board officials, town council, and service club members. "There is quite a lot of accommodation there." "Oh, no, this won't do at all," they responded. "You have to come to Banff." Corbett admitted later in his memoir, *We Have With Us Tonight*, that Jasper would never have been suitable because "the road from Edmonton was awful. It was also more difficult to get at than Banff, and not as well known then. So Banff it had to be."

The Banff school board agreed to let Corbett use the elementary and high school classrooms, library, and meeting rooms, the only charge being for janitorial service. The local Little Theatre, keen to have the summer school in Banff, offered the use of Bretton Hall, "a rather shaky old theatre just across the bridge and facing the Bow River." It wasn't the most sophisticated facility, but it did have the necessary stage, dressing rooms, curtains, and workshop space.

Availability of accommodation at the Banff Springs Hotel never became an issue. "I was perfectly certain that none of those likely to attend could afford to stay there," Corbett said. Instead, he arranged with local tourist cabin owners to reserve tentative accommodation for forty to fifty participants, and booked additional rooms at the smaller, less expensive hotels. With his basic requirements thus satisfied, Corbett started advertising the first annual "School of the Drama, Banff, August 7 to 25, 1933. Registration Fee, $1. No Tuition Fees." Aside from Haynes, the staff would include Edmonton lawyer Ted Cohen, an experienced stage manager, and his brother Elliott, an accomplished stage technician. Courses were to be given in staging, costuming, play production, and voice.

Corbett and Haynes hoped for perhaps 50 registrants, and were surprised when more than 190 enrolled. One came from as far away as Australia. A few more came from eastern Canada and the United States. Many were rural schoolteachers from Canada's four western provinces. Most were women.

The participants played to an international audience when delegates to the Institute of Pacific Relations' conference took time out to see a program of three one-act plays, including a well-received melodrama by Mary Carolyn Davies entitled *The Slave with Two Faces*. Among what Corbett called "a large and distinguished audience" were visitors from Japan, China, and Australia; two members of the British House of Lords; the Prime Minister of New Zealand, Walter Nash; a vice-president of General Motors; Henry R. Luce, the founder of *Time*, *Fortune*, and *Life* magazines; "and many other noted people whose names I have forgotten."

Aside from the international visitors, Corbett recalled two Canadians—a farm couple from the Lloydminster area of Saskatchewan—who left their mark on the first Banff summer school. The man was about sixty, his wife was about fifty, and they had driven their battered old Model T six hundred kilometres along Alberta roads for their first camping holiday in thirty years. They pitched their tent on the side of Tunnel Mountain near Banff, paid their registration fee, and listened to a few lectures by Haynes and her colleagues. They then stepped forward and offered their services. The man was a skilled carpenter and he was put to work building stage sets. His wife, an accomplished seamstress, helped sew the costumes. "They were a quiet, dignified and extraordinarily handsome couple," Corbett wrote in his memoir, "and were soon popular with students and staff."

The couple, whose last name was Bicknell, had written a one-act play called *Relief*, about life on a Saskatchewan wheat farm during the Depression. They asked director Haynes if she would read and criticize the play for them, and were somewhat taken aback when she became enthusiastic about its possibilities and offered to stage it on the closing night of the summer school. With the authors playing an aging farm couple, the play proved to be such a success that it was later entered in the Saskatchewan Drama Festival and chosen to represent that province at the Dominion Drama Festival in Ottawa in the spring of 1934. The authors won an award for writing one of the best Canadian plays, and received "very high praise" for their acting.

Because of the unexpected success of the first Banff summer school, Corbett was given the go-ahead from U of A president Wallace to repeat the experiment in 1934, with a larger budget and staff. The faculty included Haynes's former Hart House mentor Roy Mitchell, of New York University, and three other Americans who "gave the school its first promise of the international stature it has since achieved." The second year was memorable among other things, said Corbett, for the folk-singing classes offered by Mitchell's wife, Jocelyn Taylor, and her New York University colleague Wally House. "They were both accomplished guitarists and their repertoire of folk songs represented every part of North America and many European countries." Already, the little summer theatre school in the mountains was beginning to take on the trappings of a cosmopolitan centre for the arts.

In the third year, 1935, the theatre school shared facilities and janitorial expenses with painter Alfred Crocker "Ace" Leighton and his Calgary art students, and thus set in motion the juxtaposition of the various artistic disciplines that have been a key feature of the Banff Centre for Continuing Education ever since. Leighton was a talented thirty-four-year-old watercolourist from England who first came to Canada in 1925, when hired by the Canadian Pacific Railway to paint lakes, mountains, and other scenic locales along the railway's main line. He returned in 1927 to work exclusively in the Rockies, which had impressed him during his first visit. He came back to stay in 1929, when invited to become head of what is now the Alberta College of Art and Design in Calgary.

Leighton spent three years developing the college's young art school and then began inviting his colleagues and most promising students to work with him for three weeks in the summer at a dude ranch near Seebe, in the foothills fifty kilometres southeast of Banff. He spent two summers at Seebe, sketching in the mountains with such promising young artists as Stan Perrott, Bernard Middleton, and Marion Nicoll, and then accepted Corbett's invitation to move his classes to Banff.

Leighton taught for only one summer at Banff. He took a leave of absence from the college to recover from health problems caused by overwork, briefly returned to England, and then gave up teaching. But he did continue to paint occasionally in the mountains and left a small body of work that includes some of the finest watercolours ever done of the Canadian Rockies. "In high places he discovered a pale and delicate poetry," wrote Saskatoon art curator and critic Terry Fenton. Leighton, who died in 1965, also left behind a sprawling house that he built on a windswept acreage near Millarville, fifty kilometres south of Calgary, because it had an unobstructed view of five hundred kilometres of the Rocky Mountains. In 1970, Leighton's widow and fellow artist, the former Barbara Harvey of Calgary, turned the house into a public art gallery and museum called the Leighton Art Centre.

Haynes's involvement with the Banff summer program ended shortly after Leighton left for England in 1936. The Carnegie grant had run out and that spelled the end of her job as travelling drama specialist for the U of A. She moved to New Brunswick and ran the drama division of a government summer school for teachers. She later returned to Alberta and remained active in theatre as a director and teacher until deteriorating health slowed her down. She died in 1957.

Corbett's job as head of the Banff summer school also ended in 1936. He moved to Toronto for what he thought would be a temporary assignment as director of the Canadian Association for Adult Education (CAAE), and never returned to Alberta. He remained with the CAAE until his retirement in 1951 at age sixty-four. He died in 1964.

A. C. Leighton painting in the Rockies: "In high places he discovered a pale and delicate poetry." (Glenbow Archives NA-4348-3)

While the original dreamers and artists moved on, the work of the Banff summer school continued. Leighton's place as head of the art division was taken by another English-trained painter, Henry

George Glyde, who was to spend thirty summers in Banff. Vancouver theatre director Sydney Risk, North Carolina playwright Frederick Koch, and Alberta playwrights Gwen Pharis (later, Ringwood) and Elsie Park (later, Gowan) joined the drama division when Haynes left for New Brunswick. Toronto conservatory professor Vigo Kihl added a classical music dimension to the programming by offering a master class in piano. And thirty-five-year-old Donald Cameron took Corbett's place as director of the summer school.

Cameron, who grew up on a farm near Innisfail, Alberta, and studied agriculture in university, had no background in the arts but he was committed to building on the foundation established by Corbett, Haynes, and Leighton. He was, in his own words, "a professional scrounger" who succeeded in raising money where others might have failed. During the height of the Depression, he raised $150,000 (more than 2 million in 2004 dollars) to build a new theatre on Banff's main street when Bretton Hall was demolished to make way for a new National Parks administration building. He also raised money for a temporary dining hall and dormitory for the summer students.

Cameron achieved his greatest success as a "scrounger" in 1945 when he asked Calgary lawyer Eric Harvie for a million dollars to build a permanent administration building for the summer school. Harvie, who was looking for a suitable project to be financed from the estate of former *Calgary Herald* publisher James "Bertie" Woods, wouldn't commit to giving one million dollars. "But I like your story, I like your enthusiasm, and I believe you have something in Banff that could interest me very much," he told Cameron. "You can count on fifty thousand dollars. Let me see what you can do with that."

Cameron commissioned an architect, John Rule, to draw up sketches for a building that would provide a dining room for 300, classrooms and sleeping quarters for at least 150, and would cost up to $100,000. Cameron then persuaded Ottawa officials to grant him the use of a sixteen-hectare site on the side of Tunnel Mountain, immediately above the town, for a nominal leasing fee of one dollar per year. Ottawa also agreed to provide roads, walks, and sewer and water services to the site. Harvie was impressed. So was Mrs. Woods. She agreed to increase the gift from her husband's estate from $50,000 to $100,000.

On an August evening in 1946, Cameron brought a group of students and faculty to the Tunnel Mountain site for a picnic. "This is our campus in the clouds," he said, as a piper played songs evocative of Cameron's Scottish heritage. Playwright Elsie Park Gowan called it the "birth night" of the Banff School. In later years, Cameron would be accused of "empire building" as he continued to "wander up and down the highways and byways of Canada, rattling my little tin cup for contributions." However, as Gowan wrote, "it is well to remember that this fellow's plain talk paid the shot for other people's sonatas. His businessman's solidity built the stage under Titania's fairies."

Cameron, who was appointed to the Canadian Senate in 1955, remained actively associated with the Banff Centre, in various capacities, until the mid-1970s when his age and failing health led to his retirement. At that point, the Centre was on the point of becoming an autonomous, provincially funded, year-round, post-secondary educational facility, offering fine arts courses in the summer and advanced management courses in winter. Cameron died in 1989. The Centre's main administration building is named after him, and the prestigious Donald Cameron Medal is given annually to a Canadian who has made an outstanding contribution to the arts. Recipients of the medal have included writers Timothy Findley and Robertson Davies, architect Douglas Cardinal, and filmmaker Denys Arcand. Every time it is awarded, people are reminded again of the scrounger and builder who transformed the visions of the original Banff dreamers into an internationally acclaimed arts and business institution.

The Champagne Safari—1934

THE WILDERNESS ODYSSEY OF CHARLES BEDAUX

In the winter of 1933, three thousand unemployed Albertans applied for work as cowboys, trail cutters, and movie extras when word got around that a mysterious French millionaire named Charles Eugène Bedaux was going to lead a 2,400-kilometre odyssey from Edmonton through the Rockies to tidewater on the Alaskan Panhandle, and film the entire venture to immortalize his triumph in the wilderness.

Fifty-three of the applicants were eventually hired, at four dollars a day, twice the going rate. They became part of a $250,000 expedition that included Bedaux's American wife, Fern Lombard, her Spanish maid, Josefina, Bedaux's Italian-Swiss mistress, Alberto Bilonha Chiesa, and a Hollywood cinematographer named Floyd Crosby who later achieved fame for his photographic work on such films as *High Noon* and *The Old Man and the Sea*. One hundred and thirty horses and five tractor-tanks packed twenty tonnes of gear, including such luxury items as truffles, French wine, silverware, fur parkas, silk pyjamas, *pâté de foie gras*, caviar, Devonshire cream, French novels suitable for reading aloud, and enough ladies' shoes to fill several leather trunks. The expedition became known as the "champagne safari."

The expedition leader was a forty-eight-year-old Paris-born playboy and tycoon who had fled to New York in 1906 at age nineteen after a brief stint as assistant to a Montmartre pimp who was

Charles Bedaux repairing a rifle: "I enjoy doing things that have not been done before." (Glenbow Archives NA-1040-9)

shot to death. Bedaux worked initially in New York as a sandhog, hauling dirt from beneath the East River for a new subway line. Standing 1.7 metres tall, and weighing just fifty kilograms, Bedaux lasted only a month in the tunnel job before collapsing. He spent the next two years drifting across the United States, teaching French at Berlitz schools, doing piecework in factories, and picking fruit in California. While working as a lab assistant at a St. Louis, Missouri, chemical factory, he convinced his employer to let him experiment with a time and motion study program to analyze industrial efficiency and eliminate unnecessary worker movement on the shop floor. Through that experience he honed a skill for correcting inefficiencies in American industry.

In 1917, while living in Grand Rapids, Michigan, Bedaux acquired American citizenship. At the same time, United States intelligence agents were investigating him as a possible "German agent" because, according to their files, his friends tended to be "low types of persons, apparently enemy-born." He married Fern, the daughter of a Michigan attorney, settled in Cleveland, and began marketing his patented method of making assembly lines more productive. Labour unions didn't like the system because it made the employees work harder with no increase in wages, but the factory bosses did, and it made Bedaux his first million by the time he was thirty-four.

By 1920, Bedaux was back in New York, living in a suite at the Plaza Hotel and being written up in *Forbes Magazine* as the "famed discoverer of the unit of manpower measurement—one of the top five income earners in the United States." He established regional branches of the Charles E. Bedaux Company across the United States, and expanded further into England and Germany. In his spare time, he travelled throughout Europe, the Middle East, and the entire African continent, and hunted game fowl and rabbits in Scotland, France, and Hungary.

In 1926, Bedaux made his first trip to Canada. He travelled by horse and canoe through northern British Columbia and the Yukon, fell in love with the bush country, and vowed to return. "I work hard," the amateur explorer said. "Between work periods I enjoy doing things that have not been done before." He completed the first crossing of the Sahara Desert by passenger automobile in 1929, and then sailed the South Seas "to contemplate the world from afar."

When he returned to Canada in 1932, Bedaux travelled by train from Vancouver to Edmonton, flew by bush plane to Fort St. John, British Columbia, bought sixty-two horses, hired a cook and a few wranglers, and spent forty-five days exploring in the Peace River country. He told the *Edmonton Journal* he planned to be back in 1934 to complete a "fifteen-hundred-mile tractor trip" through wilderness trails from Fort St. John to Telegraph Creek, on the Stikine River in northwestern British Columbia. "As for the reason for the trip, Mr. Bedaux expects to show that it can be done, and that there will be some interesting information gathered regarding the country."

Bedaux announced the details of his 1934 expedition at a press conference in his New York office, on the sixty-third floor of the Chrysler Building, flanked by his wife, Fern, and his mistress, Bilonha Chiesa. Fern tolerated his frequent affairs because she viewed none of the mistresses as a threat to her marriage. She was, said Fern's niece, Betty Hanley, "like a queen with her concubines. One saw them follow her about, keeping respectfully behind."

Bedaux's previous expeditions had received scant coverage in the newspapers so for the 1934 trip he hired a publicist, Austin Carson, to build up press interest. The wranglers, outfitters, and trail cutters would be on horseback, Bedaux said, while he and the rest of the party would travel in five specially built Citroën light trucks with rubber-tired wheels in the front and Caterpillar tractor treads behind. "The Prairies need a northern outlet to the Pacific," he said. "If I succeed, it will open up a vast region which has never been explored." Similar half-track vehicles had been successfully tested in the Gobi and Sahara deserts, and Bedaux considered them ideally suited for the muskeg trails of the Canadian north. His expedition second-in-command would be an Edmonton geologist, Jack Bocock, and the party would also include a Citroën mechanic from Paris, three BC government land surveyors (their employer

Fern Bedaux (L) and her husband's mistress, Alberto Bilonha Chiesa: "Like a queen with her concubines." (Glenbow Archives NA-1040-11)

saw the advantage of letting Bedaux cover their expenses while they did the mapping), a Swiss alpine guide from Jasper, and a radio operator who would send regular wireless dispatches to Bedaux's New York publicist. Thus the stage was set for one of the most bizarre expeditions in the history of modern exploration.

Edmonton's Macdonald Hotel became expedition headquarters during the week before departure. The canvas-topped, nickel-plated Citroëns were paraded around the city for the benefit of bemused Edmontonians, and Bedaux busied himself with a round of champagne banquets and press briefings. "Everyone says that to take a fleet of automobiles through the unmapped Rockies, where there are no roads, can't be done. I say it can. I have done the impossible before." On 6 July the expeditioners attended a farewell champagne breakfast hosted by Edmonton city council, after which the provincial lieutenant-governor, William Walsh, wished them Godspeed.

The Bedaux Sub-Arctic Citroën Expedition, as Bedaux now called it, crawled along dirt roads at an average speed of six kilometres an hour, travelling north from Edmonton to Athabasca and then west toward Fort St. John. Steady rain turned the roads into mud and the vehicles broke down frequently. The wranglers had to winch the vehicles free of the muskeg to clean the tractor treads. The expeditioners camped in tents until they reached the village of Hythe, where they stayed in a hotel with leaky ceilings. Bedaux told the villagers he was "just a nut who likes to do things first" and paid them five dollars apiece ($71 in 2004 dollars) to be part of a filmed bon voyage scene.

When they reached Fort St. John on 17 July, the expeditioners spent six days waiting for the rain to stop so they could travel along a trail cut by an advance team packing drums of gasoline for the Citroëns. This would prove to be the toughest part of the trip for the vehicles. After watching them bog down in the gumbo several times, the Citroën mechanic, Charles Balourdet, suggested the vehicles be abandoned and the rest of the trip completed on horseback. But even though he had bought one hundred packhorses and hired several cowboys in Fort St. John, Bedaux wasn't ready yet to give up on the vehicles. It wasn't until 7 August, when the expedition reached the junction of the Graham and Halfway rivers, about 140 kilometres from Fort St. John and more than 500 kilometres short of

Telegraph Creek, that Bedaux finally decided this was unsuitable country for Citroëns.

Bedaux spent four days devising a spectacular Hollywood ending for the Citroëns. He ran two of the vehicles off a cliff into the Halfway River, and sent a message to New York saying nine of the party narrowly escaped death when the vehicles plunged. He put the third vehicle on a raft and floated it down the river toward a cliff rigged with dynamite. The dynamite failed to detonate and the raft continued on its journey down the river. A Fort St. John garage owner, Bert Bowes, eventually salvaged the Citroën and used it as a work vehicle until the early 1950s. Bowes also recovered the fourth and fifth vehicles, which Bedaux abandoned on the shores of the Halfway. One Citroën, fully restored, is now on display in the Reynolds-Alberta Museum in Wetaskiwin.

Bedaux bought an additional thirty-six packhorses from local Natives to replace the Citroëns. The party then rode into the high Rockies through country that was still a blank space on the map. When they reached the Native village of Whitewater (later Fort Ware and now Kwadacha), in the Rocky Mountain Trench at the confluence of the Fox and Finlay rivers, one of the government geographers, Frank Swannell, named local landmarks after members of the expedition, including the wife, the mistress, and the Hollywood cinematographer. Swannell named the highest peak Mount Bedaux. "It really is a home for the gods," Bedaux said.

The horses grew weak from hoof rot and malnourishment caused by a lack of grazing land, and had to be shot at the rate of two to three daily. On 8 September, Bedaux lightened the load by opening the case of champagne he had been saving for the celebration at journey's end. "It seems incredible," he wrote in his diary, "but it was the first time any of the cowboys had tasted champagne."

Although the advance team, led by BC government geographer Ernest Lamarque, cut and mapped a trail all the way to the final destination at Telegraph Creek, they were unable to get word of this achievement back to Bedaux because the government survey office in Vancouver failed to relay the radio communiqué. When he reached the western boundary of the Rockies on 30 September, still 320 kilometres short of his goal, Bedaux called a halt to the expedition and gave orders to turn back to Whitewater. The weary expeditioners took another month to reach Edmonton, where Bedaux declared the trip a partial success because Lamarque and his advance team had made it to Telegraph Creek. This, Bedaux said, provided proof that a route to Alaska was feasible, and he would be advising the International Highway Commission accordingly.

Bedaux returned to northern British Columbia the following year, journeyed on horseback from Telegraph Creek to Watson Lake in the Yukon, and announced plans to build one road from Edmonton to the Pacific and another from British Columbia to the Yukon. Before the road-building project could get under way, however, Bedaux got caught up in other activities. In 1937, he made headlines when the Duke and Duchess of Windsor accepted his invitation to hold their wedding at his sixteenth-century Renaissance château in the south of France. He organized a tour of German factories for the Windsors and was about to do the same in the United States when union bosses threatened mass demonstrations denouncing the Bedaux industrial efficiency system as a diabolical process designed to turn workers into machines. Bedaux withdrew from the royal tour, which the Duke promptly cancelled, and fled with Fern to Europe.

The unfavourable publicity surrounding the Windsor fiasco marked a turning point for Bedaux. Industries would no longer touch his efficiency system for fear of labour unrest, and the directors of his own company ousted him as president because his name was now bad for business. He switched focus from industry to government and struck deals with the regimes in Turkey and Greece to reorganize their national economies. He also established close business ties with several leading Nazis, including Joachim von Ribbentrop and Fritz Wiedemann.

During the Second World War, Bedaux assumed responsibility for reorganizing the French coal industry for the Nazis, and acted as an intermediary between Berlin and the puppet Vichy French government. "The Germans were the only ones left in Paris to do business with," he would say later. When the United States entered the war after the attack on Pearl Harbor in December 1941, German soldiers arrested Bedaux because of his American citizenship and held him for two weeks in a concentration camp. His influential Nazi friends effected his release and put him in charge of an ambitious German plan to build a railway line and pipeline across the Sahara. He flew to Algiers in October 1942 and was assembling workers and equipment for the construction project when American and British forces invaded North Africa. The Americans arrested Bedaux in early 1943, flew him back to the United States, and held him on suspicion of collaborating with the enemy.

Bedaux was detained at a Miami immigration building. In January 1944, the federal justice department told him he would be charged with treason. He had been asking for sleeping pills to counteract his chronic insomnia and on 14 February he took an overdose of the hoarded pills. Four days later he died. He was fifty-eight. His suicide note said, "I cannot defend my good name now without endangering those I love."

The news media had little sympathy for the Paris-born tycoon. *Newsweek* magazine called him an opportunist and said he committed suicide to avoid a treason trial. Writer Janet Flanner characterized him in *The New Yorker* magazine as a swindler and a Fascist, who duped the Duke of Windsor and was only too happy to collaborate with the Nazis. McKenzie Porter, in a 1956 article for *Maclean's* magazine, took the allegations a step further and suggested that Bedaux could have been a German spy. The 1934 champagne safari, said Porter, could have been a scouting trip aimed at determining if Alaska could be defended successfully from northern BC and the Yukon.

However, Canadian historian Pierre Berton dismissed the notion that Bedaux was engaged in espionage: "If true, the Bedaux expedition must have been the most expensive and cumbersome cover operation ever mounted, and Bedaux himself must go down as one of the most inept spies in history." The real explanation, Berton wrote in his book *My Country: The Remarkable Past*, is likely much more mundane: "Charles Bedaux, *circa* 1934, was exactly what he claimed to be: a rich nut who liked to do the impossible." Bedaux's biographer, Vancouver writer Jim Christy, concluded likewise in his book *The Price of Power: A Biography of Charles Eugène Bedaux*. While Bedaux was enigmatic, Christy wrote, there is no direct evidence linking him to espionage.

The 1934 expedition consolidated Bedaux's place in the history of Canadian exploration, albeit for its extravagance and eccentricity.

While some have written it off as little more than an expensive joyride along wilderness trails previously traversed by Natives, it did provide important data for future road builders. When the Americans realized after Pearl Harbor that the only protection for the entire northwest coast of North America was a single abandoned cannon (converted into a flowerpot!) on the grounds of the territorial courthouse at Juneau, Alaska, they took immediate steps to build a road linking air bases along the northwest staging route. Much of the resulting Alcan Military Highway (today's Alaska Highway) through British Columbia follows the route taken by the Bedaux expeditioners of 1934.

As for the expedition footage shot by cinematographer Crosby and his cameramen, it never received a public screening. Fern kept the twenty cans of nitrate film at the Bedaux château until her death in 1974, when she bequeathed the film to a friend in Paris. Five years later a Montreal filmmaker, George Ungar, read about the expedition in a back issue of *Maclean's* magazine and began work on what he thought might be a five-minute animated film about this strange piece of Canadian history. As Ungar learned more about Bedaux, however, his envisioned film project grew bigger. His decision to turn it into a ninety-four-minute feature documentary came after he tracked down the heirs to the Bedaux estate and acquired the long-lost Crosby footage. "It was like finding some gilded icon from another era," Ungar said. He spent the next ten years scrounging to get funding from various film agencies and arts councils and eventually completed the $500,000 documentary in 1995. Titled *The Champagne Safari*, it contains twenty minutes of the original Crosby footage (including the scene where the Citroëns plunge into the river) and has been aired on regional television networks across Canada and the United States.

Springtime in the Rockies—1937

WILF CARTER FINDS MUSICAL INSPIRATION IN THE MOUNTAINS

His professional name was Montana Slim but it might more appropriately have been Rocky Mountain Slim, because it was in the foothills of the Canadian Rockies that Wilf Carter, a cowboy singer from Nova Scotia, found a home and a coveted western way of life.

The sixth of nine children in a Baptist minister's family, Carter first came to Alberta in August 1923 at age nineteen, on a boxcar carrying farm labourers across the country for twenty-five dollars per person ($284 in 2004 dollars). He baled wheat on a farm near Drumheller, worked at the Calgary Stampede as an outrider for the chuckwagon races, and sang his yodelling songs at house parties, cattle roundups, and square dances around southern Alberta. He had been yodelling since he was a child in Port Hilford, Nova Scotia, when he paid twenty-five cents to see a Chautauqua tent-show performer who called himself The Yodelling Fool. His mother told him he sounded like "a band of coyotes" but young Carter kept practising until he thought he must sound like one of his father's Swiss ancestors.

Carter's first musical break came in 1930 when he landed a steady gig playing guitar and singing on a popular Friday night radio show, *The Old Timers*, broadcast by Calgary station CFCN. Two years later, he was hired by Banff's Brewster Transport to entertain for five dollars a week ($70 in 2004 dollars) the tourists travelling on the company's trail rides through the Rockies. Expecting to be on the trail for only one day at a time, Carter showed up for his first mountain engagement dressed only in shirt and jeans with no overnight bag or change of clothing. However, when he discovered he would have to be on the trail for a week, he quickly made up for his lack of gear by "borrowing" a saddle blanket from his horse and using it to stay warm at night. "Nobody came near me after I had spent the night under a horse blanket," he said afterwards. "I admit the scent from the sweat wasn't too good, but it helped me fall asleep in the mountains and have happy dreams of things to come."

Carter developed in the mountains what he called his "echo" yodel, a "three-in-one" call that few singers could emulate. In the Yoho Valley, just east of Field, British Columbia, he would stand on a bridge and sing to the Takakkaw Falls, trying to perfect the yodel. "It took years to do it," he said. "But it seemed to get better as I hollered into the canyons." Fellow country singer Ian Tyson characterized Carter's yodel as "that high echoed sound that seemed to be bouncing off some Rocky Mountain glacier."

In 1933, Carter met a CPR executive who listened to him sing and invited him to entertain on the railway company's cruise ship *Empress of Britain* during its first voyage to the West Indies. Carter stopped off en route to audition for RCA Records in Montreal, and recorded an original composition about Albert Johnson, the so-called "Mad Trapper" of Rat River, Yukon, who was killed in a 1932 shootout with RCMP officers trying to arrest him for trapline violations. By the time Carter returned from the cruise, RCA had pressed and released the recording, which became a best-seller in Canada. On the flip side of the seventy-eight was an up-tempo Carter tune, "My Swiss Moonlight Lullaby," which he said was the first recording ever to feature the echo yodel.

A 1934 audition with CBS Radio in New York resulted in a daily radio show for Carter, broadcast over a network of 250 stations, featuring him as a performer nicknamed Montana Slim. "Cowboys in my day always had nicknames," Carter explained. A CBS secretary chose the name for him because he was tall and skinny and had once been to Montana. Carter performed on the show for three years, but he missed Alberta and came back in 1937 to live on a cattle ranch just south of Calgary. His new bride, a New York nurse named Bobbie Bryan, came with him.

Carter briefly resumed his career as a trail-ride performer, and said he had difficulty convincing one of the clients—a female schoolteacher from Minnesota—that he was indeed the same Wilf Carter who had recorded "My Swiss Moonlight Lullaby." Carter took her up to the bridge in the Yoho Valley where he had first practised his yodelling, and asked her to wait while he walked down to the base of the falls. "Then, as if on cue, the moon came up over the mountain," he said. "I sang the lullaby and played my guitar. She was finally convinced. She wanted me to write a song about her so I went back and wrote 'My Little Yoho Lady.'"

In 1937, Oklahoma cowboy singer Gene Autry starred in a western movie musical entitled *Springtime in the Rockies*. It was a lightweight effort about a range war and it didn't do well at the box office. But it had a catchy title song, which became a hit for Autry in the United States and did the same for Carter in Canada. The Carter version featured Wilf's trademark yodel.

Carter suffered a back injury in a 1940 car accident that took him away from performing for nine years. But because he had made so many records before the accident, RCA could keep releasing new songs as if he were still active. He returned to touring in 1949, and the following year set an attendance record at Toronto's Canadian National Exhibition, performing for fifty thousand people in one week.

In 1950, another Autry hit, "Blue Canadian Rockies," became a hit for Carter in Canada. By this time, Carter had recorded hundreds of tunes for RCA and was widely hailed as the person who "practically started Canadian country singing." He was constantly on the road, performing at concerts, fairs, and dances, which meant he didn't get to spend much time in the Rockies any more. But he always retained a strong connection with the mountains. When the Calgary Stampede organizers honoured him in 1964 for "thirty-three wonderful years" of musical achievement by presenting him with a bronze statue of a horse and a framed photograph of Mount Assiniboine, Carter said both gifts had very special significance for him. He had often ridden in the mountains with the sculptor

Charlie Beil and had camped "right where that picture was taken."

Carter remained one of country music's most popular entertainers through the 1960s, and he continued to tour steadily through the 1970s and 1980s, when he was well into his seventies. Through much of that time, with his daughters Sheila and Carol performing as backup singers and dancers, Carter toured as "The Family Show With the Folks You Know."

In 1972, RCA Records presented Carter with a plaque for his accumulated record sales. Fellow country singer Tommy Hunter noted that Carter's first hit record, "The Capture of Albert Johnson," had helped save RCA from bankruptcy during the Depression. Carter's other honours included a place in the Songwriters' Hall of Fame in Nashville, and the Martin Guitar Entertainer of the Year for his contributions to Canadian country music. Carter was blasé about the honours. "They can give you all the awards in the world; that isn't what counts," he said. "It's the people. They've given me what I have today."

As he grew older, Carter cut his performances back to twenty a year, but he continued to record and he kept coming back to spend his summers on his ranch near Calgary. "Calgary is my home, and the fans here are the best I've ever met," he said. He liked to saddle up his horse, Blaze, and ride the range to work with cattle.

Carter recorded his last album, *Whatever Happened to all Those Years*, in 1988, when he was eighty-four, and he continued touring for another four years until his deteriorating hearing forced him to retire from the stage. After that, he performed occasionally in nursing homes, and liked telling about a resident who came up to him after one performance: "He said I wasn't a bad singer, but that I wasn't as good as Wilf Carter."

Carter eventually sold his ranch and bought an apartment in Calgary where he spent his summers until his death. He spent his winters in Scottsdale, Arizona. He died in Scottsdale in December 1996, at age ninety-one, two months after being diagnosed with stomach cancer. "He was the sound of Western Canada in the 1930s and 1940s," said Ian Tyson. "You could not overstate his influence."

 *The Royals Pay a Visit—*
1939

JIM BREWSTER ENTERTAINS THE KING AND QUEEN

In the summer of 1939, King George VI, accompanied by Queen Elizabeth, the future Queen Mother, was making the first visit by a reigning British monarch to Canada. Local tour bus magnate Jim Brewster offered to be the chauffeur for their two-day stop in Banff. He could have asked one of his employees to do the driving but Brewster wanted this assignment for himself. He planned to have the royal couple ride in a gleaming red Packard that he bought especially for the occasion. The Queen, however, had other ideas. Her mother-in-law, Queen Mary, had visited Banff in 1901 when she was the Duchess of Cornwall and York, and had often reminisced about her ride in a horse-drawn democrat wagon. Queen Elizabeth now wanted to do the same.

Brewster hunted high and low for a democrat and eventually found one on the Sarcee (now Tsuu T'ina) reserve near Calgary, a dilapidated model that he rented for five dollars. "The springs were sticking up through the seat covers, and the wheels were so loose they wobbled at every turn," he said afterwards. "My mechanics worked on it for a week, but they couldn't do much about it. Finally, we ripped off the upholstery and used two buffalo robes for their majesties to sit on."

"Brewster, do you think this wheel's going to come off?" the Queen asked as the democrat wobbled around the perimeter of the recently opened Banff Springs Hotel golf course. Brewster had the same concern, but he hastened to assure Her Majesty that everything would be all right. "No, ma'am, this buggy's good for a thousand miles." The Queen laughed: "I'm afraid we won't be with you quite that far."

When they continued their tour later that evening, the royal couple decided to ride in Brewster's new car rather than in the creaky old democrat. They took photographs of beaver, moose, and mountain goats, and talked about hunting big game. "I understand you have some wonderful animal heads in your home," the Queen said. Brewster acknowledged that he had some record-winning trophies. "Would you mind if we saw your home?" the Queen asked. "I'd be delighted," Brewster said. He knew his wife, Dell, would also be delighted "even if she didn't know they were coming."

Brewster's wife was sitting alone in their eight-room brick bungalow when the royal couple dropped in. "I may forget a lot of things about the royal visit, but never my wife's face as we walked in the door," he said afterwards. "She was so excited she

Jim Brewster drives King George VI and Queen Elizabeth around the Banff golf course: "Brewster, do you think this wheel's going to come off?" (Glenbow Archives NA-4325-11)

nearly fainted, and her face was white as a sheet. However, it didn't take two minutes before the Queen and she were chatting away like old friends." The royal couple stayed for more than thirty minutes, asking questions about the Native artifacts and other items that the Brewsters had on display in their living room.

For Brewster, the 1939 royal visit was the highlight of a fifty-year career in the Rockies that began in 1892 when he was ten and his brother, Bill, was twelve. The elder sons of an Ontario-born dairy farmer who supplied the Banff Springs Hotel and the local townsfolk with milk, they learned about fishing and hunting in the mountains through their friendship with a Stoney trapper named William Twin. They got their first opportunity to demonstrate their guiding skills when the manager of the Banff Springs asked their father, John Brewster, if he knew someone who could lead a couple of his guests to the best trout fishing lakes in the area. The father suggested his young sons be given the chance and, in the process, he unwittingly chose their future careers. By 1900 the Brewster boys were in business for themselves as "W. & J. Brewster, Experienced Guides and Packers."

The brothers struggled in the beginning because most of the guiding and outfitting work went to Tom Wilson, the first and best-established guide in the Rockies. However, the CPR gave them a needed boost in 1901 when it paid their way to New York to promote Rocky Mountain sport fishing and hunting at a sportsman's show in Madison Square Garden. This brought more tourists to the Rockies and more business for the brothers. The CPR then gave them an additional boost by awarding them its coveted outfitting concession for Banff. With the money from that contract, and some investment capital from two hunting enthusiasts they had met in New York, the brothers were able to expand and diversify. They built a livery stable followed by a general store and small opera house on properties they leased in Banff, and ran a twice-daily stagecoach service between Banff and the nearby coal-mining town of Bankhead (torn down in 1922 following closure of the mine).

The brothers scored a business coup in 1905 when the CPR sold its livery service to them and awarded them the contract to transport hotel guests between the railway station and the Banff

Springs. They also hauled foodstuffs and heating fuel for the hotel and took the guests on sightseeing tours to Lake Minnewanka, Mount Norquay, and other local points of interest. In 1906, Jim Brewster moved temporarily to Vancouver to do some real estate investing with his recently retired father. Bill remained in Banff and expanded the business into ranching and providing livery service for the CPR at Laggan (now Lake Louise) and Field, British Columbia.

Bill, who had a reputation as a womanizer, suddenly left Banff in 1909 when a woman who bore him two sons while married to another man left her husband and demanded that Bill accompany her and the children to New York. Bill complied and Jim returned to take over the operations of Brewster Brothers. The partnership's assets then included, along with the previous acquisitions, a bakery, blacksmith shop, warehouse, and other buildings. Further expansion saw Jim investing in Banff's Mount Royal Hotel and in various Edmonton real estate projects.

By the start of the First World War, on paper Jim was a wealthy man, with a personal net worth of $375,000. He was then in the process of taking Brewster Transport into the automobile era by phasing out the horse-drawn wagons and replacing them with motor vehicles. However, the war was not good for the tourism business. Jim began drinking heavily as his fortunes declined and eventually yielded managerial control of the company to his brother, Bill, who had moved from New York to run a dude ranch in Montana.

With Bill looking after the day-to-day operations, Brewster Transport prospered and expanded during the 1920s, building up a 79-vehicle fleet of touring cars and buses. The success prompted others in the tourism industry to note cynically, "Tourists come to the Rockies for a change and a rest. The CPR takes the change and the Brewsters take the rest." Jim, who retained the positions of vice-president and treasurer, spent his time wheeling and dealing and scouting out new investment opportunities. In 1926, through a tip from a former manager of the Banff Springs Hotel, he secured the concession in Hawaii to provide transport services for the Matson Steamship Hotels on the island of Oahu. Two years later, Brewster Transport received Alberta government permission to provide a bus service between Banff, Calgary, and Edmonton.

The Depression of the 1930s hit Brewster Transport particularly hard because of the decline in world tourism. The company was able to survive for a while with a loan from the CPR, but had to scale back its Hawaiian transport operation and terminate the bus service between Banff and Calgary. Bill resigned from the company in 1933 when his annual salary dropped from $5,000 to $4,000, and he opened a Ford car dealership, repair shop, and service station that proved to be very successful. Jim continued to wheel and deal, despite the mounting financial troubles, and even went so far as to invest in a new ski development at what is now Sunshine Village, eight kilometres west of Banff.

Brewster Transport was in better financial shape by the time the King and Queen visited in May 1939. Although Jim continued to drink heavily (during a typical bender he would check into Calgary's Palliser Hotel with enough liquor to keep him going for several days), he and his business manager, Lou Crosby, managed to bring down company debt, restore the Hawaiian operation to profitability, build the Columbia Icefield Chalet, and establish a bus service from Waterton Lakes through Calgary and Banff to Revelstoke and Vancouver.

Entertaining royal visitors was nothing new for Jim. He had been doing it for more than thirty-five years, and could boast of having played golf with Edward, Prince of Wales (the future King Edward VIII, who abdicated in 1936 and became the Duke of Windsor), and his brother, the Duke of Kent. He also hoped to get in a game with King George VI, but the monarch had injured his hand before arriving in Banff and was unable to play.

The King and Queen impressed Jim. "I've never met a couple who were so gentlemanly and ladylike and democratic as those two. When my wife was presented to their majesties, they both put out their hands to greet her at the same time, just as easy and friendly as you please. If they arrived back tomorrow, it wouldn't be too soon for me." The *Crag & Canyon* newspaper said it was "both logical and fitting" that Jim should have been chosen to escort the royal couple because of his previous associations with royalty and because of his extensive knowledge of the national park's history and development.

After the euphoria of the royal visit, Jim suffered a series of reverses. First came some serious competition from Greyhound Lines of Chicago, which forced Brewster Transport off the road by offering a discount-fare bus service from Banff to Vancouver. Then came the wartime closure of the Banff Springs Hotel and a decree by the federal government that, as a measure to conserve gasoline and rubber, all sightseeing tours by bus or car should be halted. Jim managed to weather these crises but, coupled with his drinking problem, they took their toll on his health. In February 1947, just a few days after celebrating his sixty-fifth birthday, he fell victim to a stroke and died.

Jim bequeathed his shares in Brewster Transport to his wife, Dell, and daughter, Fern, and requested in his will that they keep the business going for as long as it was "reasonably profitable." Business manager Crosby took over as president and general manager, ran the company for another seventeen years, and merged it with a competitor, Rocky Mountain Tours. He died in February 1964 at age seventy-six. A year later, "the largest privately owned sightseeing company in the world" was sold to Greyhound. "After building it up for seventy years it hurts to see it crumble," said Bill Brewster, then eighty-seven. "Jim always said he wanted to create something around him that would last a hundred years."

The home where Jim and Dell entertained the King and Queen eventually passed into the possession of their nephew Joseph Brewster, who sold it in 1980 to a cousin, Gary Charlton. A year later, the house was gone. Charlton had it demolished for redevelopment just as Alberta Culture was about to mail him a notice saying the house would be designated as a heritage site. "The protection of the historical treasure hunters came too late," *Alberta Report* magazine said.

River of No Return—1953

Marilyn Monroe Makes a Mountain Movie

The invention of CinemaScope brought half a dozen Hollywood filmmakers into the Rockies in 1953, all eager to use the new wide-screen technology to create spectacular movies that would lure TV-coddled audiences away from their living rooms. Among them were big-name directors Raoul Walsh, Anthony Mann, and Otto Preminger. Walsh came with Alan Ladd and Shelley Winters to make *Saskatchewan*, an adventure movie about a stoic Mountie who rescues the female survivor of a wagon train attacked by warring Sioux. Mann had James Stewart and Ruth Roman starring in *The Far Country*, a western about a loner cowboy who signs on to lead a female saloon owner's wagon train to the gold-mining camps of the Klondike. Preminger created the biggest buzz of all when he brought Robert Mitchum and Marilyn Monroe to star in *River of No Return*, a western about a homesteader robbed and beaten by a ruthless gambler and then nursed back to health by a beautiful saloon singer.

None of the principals involved in *River of No Return* wanted to be in Alberta that summer. Preminger, born in Vienna, wanted to be back in Europe making his own films. But he had to be in the Rockies because he owed Twentieth Century-Fox one more movie under the terms of his five-year contract with the studio. Mitchum didn't want to work with Preminger because he had come to blows with the director while filming a previous project, *Angel Face*.

Studio head Darryl F. Zanuck, however, insisted on having Mitchum's star power in the movie when he decided that *River of No Return* should be a "big picture" rather than a cheap B western, as originally envisaged. Monroe didn't want to work with Preminger either because of his reputation as a dictatorial sadist who, in the words of Norman Mailer, "was famous for grinding actors' bones in the maw of his legendary rage." Nor, after starring in *Gentlemen Prefer Blondes* and *How to Marry a Millionaire*, did she want to appear again as a stereotypical dumb blonde. She told *Variety* magazine she "blushed to the toes" at the thought of playing a "rear-wiggling cabaret singer." But she, too, was under studio contract and had to do the movie or face suspension.

There were no outward signs of dissension when the trio arrived in Jasper on 26 July 1954. More than two thousand people ("practically the whole population of Jasper," said the *Calgary Herald*) showed up to greet the celebrities as they stepped off the CNR train from Vancouver. Two Mounties in scarlet tunics, Constables J. E. Snider and A. P. Dirk, were on hand to escort the stars to the waiting cars while scores of amateur and professional photographers shot pictures. The stars posed and waved and then made their way to a Jasper motel called Becker's Bungalows where they stayed for the first part of the filming.

The early scenes were shot near Devona Flats, thirty kilometres northeast of Jasper townsite, on the banks of the Snake Indian River. A chartered train ferried the cast and crew back and forth daily. The conductor was a Jasper resident named Bob Sansom, who viewed Monroe—then twenty-seven—as a "rather endearing but tired little girl" because she usually slept in his sleeping bag in the caboose. After ten days at Devona, the team drove by car and truck to the Maligne River, ten kilometres east of Jasper, where they filmed for another five days.

The storyline called for Mitchum, Monroe, and Tommy Rettig, a young actor playing Mitchum's son, to do some of the major scenes on a raft, braving rolling rapids, wild animals, fortune hunters, and war-painted Natives while tracking down the renegade gambler (Rory Calhoun) who had assaulted Mitchum and stolen his rifle and horse. Preminger shot the close-ups for these scenes around Jasper while his assistant director, Paul Helmick, used stunt doubles and dummies to film action and stunt sequences along the Bow River near Banff.

Filming had barely started when Monroe and Preminger stopped talking to one another. Monroe had brought along her acting coach, a German-born elocutionist named Natasha Lytess who annoyed Preminger by passing herself off as Russian and by insisting that Monroe abandon what the director called the "soft, slurred voice that was so much part of the unique image she projected on the screen." Instead, he wrote afterwards in *Preminger: An Autobiography*, Lytess had Monroe enunciating with such ferocity "that her violent lip movements made it impossible to photograph her." Preminger eventually lost patience with Lytess and barred her from the set. Monroe then refused to come out of her dressing room and sent a telegram to Zanuck threatening to quit the movie. Zanuck wired Preminger saying that Monroe was "money in the bank" for Twentieth Century-Fox and that the director should do whatever it took to keep her from quitting. Preminger swallowed his pride and allowed Lytess back on the set. However, he was exultant when Mitchum took charge of the situation, snubbed the acting coach, slapped Monroe on the behind as the cameras rolled, and said, "Now stop that nonsense. Let's play it like human beings. Come on." Monroe was so startled, Preminger said, that she "dropped, at least for the moment, her Lytess mannerisms."

The local newspapers offered no hint of the trouble on the set. In an interview with an *Edmonton Journal* correspondent, Preminger sang the praises of Jasper's Mount Edith Cavell, saying he had "fallen in love with its grace and beauty" and planned to change the script to accommodate shots of the mountain. Monroe, meanwhile, visited a provincial fish hatchery and told a reporter she was impressed to learn that the baby trout became the finest game fish in North America when released into the glacial waters of Maligne Lake.

While Monroe and Preminger filmed and fought on the main set, the second camera unit was having its own problems. Roy Jenson, a Calgary Stampeders' linebacker working as Mitchum's stunt double, had some scary experiences while on a raft running the Bow Falls. In one incident, a rescue boat operator accidentally crowned him with a rock tied to the end of a rope being used to pull him ashore. In another, Jenson had to scramble to save Helen Thurston, who was doubling for Monroe, and Harry Monty, doubling for Rettig, when the raft snagged a rock and tipped over. "I was too busy trying to save our lives, my life, to get scared," Jenson said afterwards to biographer Lee Server, author of *Robert Mitchum: Baby, I Don't Care*. "But I did get scared later on, back in the motel room, remembering what had happened."

Mitchum later appropriated the incident, telling people he and Monroe had been on the overturning raft when it went over the falls. "Coming out, the skiff had hit a rock," he said in a 1991 television interview with the CBS network. "On the way back, I had to plug up the hole with my elbow. We finally made it to shore and I carried Marilyn out." But in fact the stars were permitted to work only on a raft secured to the riverbank. Mitchum's story was pure Hollywood fiction.

There was one mishap that made the local news at the time. On 14 August 1953 the *Albertan* newspaper reported that Monroe had "nearly drowned" when she slipped on a rock in the rushing waters of the Maligne River, and her waist-high rubber wading boots filled with water. The star sprained her left ankle, couldn't stand up, and had to be pulled to safety by Mitchum and a dozen crew members. The following day, the *Calgary Herald* reported that Monroe was back at work "despite a torn ligament" and that her ankle was heavily bandaged. Local photographers took pictures of her posing on crutches next to the motel's "no vacancy" sign. The motel owner's daughter, Susan Becker Davidson, recalled afterwards that the injury "didn't keep Marilyn from smiling."

Monroe's ankle made the news again on 21 August 1953 after the stars and crew moved to Banff. Monroe took a tumble on the set, reinjured the ankle, and had to be confined to bed. "It was never like this in Hollywood," she told the *Albertan* in an interview at her suite in the Banff Springs Hotel. "It seems I'm really living the title of this movie. All these wonderful mountains must be jinxing me." A Hollywood orthopedic surgeon, Robert Rosenfeld, was flown in at the request of Monroe's future husband, retired baseball great Joe DiMaggio, and she spent the rest of her time in Banff with her leg in a cast. Bellhops at the Banff Springs drew lots for the right to push her wheelchair around the hotel.

Marilyn Monroe on crutches outside Becker's Bungalows in Jasper: "All these wonderful mountains must be jinxing me." (Whyte Museum of the Canadian Rockies NA66-1673)

The stars left Alberta at the end of August and *River of No Return* was completed in Los Angeles. Mitchum and Monroe redid some of their rafting scenes on a hydraulic platform in front of a screen shot of the raging river while special effects experts stood to one side throwing buckets of water and shooting metal-tipped arrows into the logs at their feet. Preminger took off for Europe before the final scenes were shot and another director, Jean Negulescu, added the finishing touches to the movie. Preminger later renounced the film and its star with a cruel parting shot: "Directing Marilyn Monroe was like directing Lassie—you needed fourteen takes to get the bark right." Monroe also distanced herself from the movie. "I wouldn't accept it as an assignment today," she said in a 1955 interview with *Variety.* "I think I deserve a better deal than a grade-Z cowboy movie in which the acting finished second to the scenery." While the reviews were lukewarm ("It's a toss-up whether the scenery or the adornment of Marilyn Monroe is the feature of greater attraction," Bosley Crowther wrote in *The New York Times*), the film did reasonably well at the box office, finishing nineteenth among the top grossing pictures of 1954.

Stories of Babylonian decadence in the Rockies abounded locally after the stars left Canada. In one story, Monroe was said to have been kicked out of the Jasper Park Lodge because she "dressed inappropriately" for the dining room. Her handlers said she was evicted because she dressed in the skin-tight jeans that the wardrobe department made for her to wear in the movie. However, other witnesses said it was because Monroe stripped off too many layers of clothing while posing for photographs on a bearskin rug in the main lobby. A bearskin rug also featured prominently in a story about DiMaggio and Monroe, who spent time together in a private cottage near Jasper when she wasn't on call. A succession of cottage owners later came to believe that a ratty old hearth rug passed on from owner to owner was the "rug that Joe and Marilyn slept on."

Doubts about the seriousness of Monroe's ankle injury were voiced after it was learned that she went partying one night in Banff, sans cast or bandages, with her old friend and former roommate actress Shelley Winters. According to Winters's autobiography, *Shelley: Also Known as Shirley*, Monroe went tripping onto the dance floor as Winters cried out, "Watch your step, you're supposed to be crippled." Other writers, however, hinted darkly that the injury was serious enough to precipitate a dependency on barbiturates and painkillers that eventually led to Monroe's death from a drug overdose in August 1962. "Monroe's studio drug habit had begun on the set of *River of No Return*, when she suffered from mild exposure and exhaustion during location filming," biographers Peter Harry Brown and Patte B. Barham wrote in *Marilyn: The Last Take*.

Mitchum's drinking provided additional grist for the rumour mill. Stunt double Jenson recalled that when Monroe was out of commission with her ankle injury Mitchum spent his days and nights in the Banff Springs Hotel bar, drinking gin and telling stories. "He was incredible," Jenson said. "The guy could drink two or three quarts of gin and not even show it. I could go away for a steam bath and a nap and some dinner, and when I came back they would still be there, talking and drinking." After one bender, Mitchum told a *Herald* correspondent that moviemaking was an "ulcer business," rife with fear, intrigue, and indecision. "It's like walking through quicksand," he said. "By the time a movie has gone through the mill, as many as five people with five separate ideas have had a finger in the pie."

The residents of Jasper and Banff remembered Mitchum as being surly and aloof, but had fond memories of Monroe as being sweet, shy, and approachable. Alden Bradley, who was nine in 1953, recalled meeting Monroe while he and two companions were riding their bikes along a mountain highway near Jasper. He remembered being surprised when Monroe asked if she could borrow his bike. "She rode it for about a mile or so, speeding up once in a while and weaving goofily around the road, laughing with us the whole time," he told a *Saturday Night* magazine writer in 2000. "She was so happy, joyous even. She just couldn't get enough of us that day. It seemed like she was really enjoying being out on her own."

When Monroe died in 1962, there was no mention in the Alberta newspapers of the summer she had spent filming in the Rockies. Nor was there any official municipal or national park recognition of her visit. However, that lapse was finally corrected in 1998 when Canadian Pacific Hotels and Parks Canada erected a plaque near the Banff Springs Hotel golf course, jointly commemorating the park's first automobile-accessible campground and the fact that Monroe's dressing-room trailer had been parked in the campground during the 1953 filming in Banff. "We're really commemorating filmmakers in the Rockies as much as Marilyn Monroe," CP Hotels historian Bob Sandford told the *Herald*. "The plaque speaks to the rich cultural and heritage significance of that site."

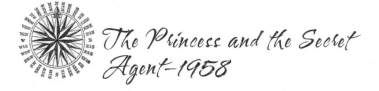

The Princess and the Secret Agent—1958

CONRAD O'BRIEN-FFRENCH ASSUMES A NEW IDENTITY IN THE ROCKIES

To his Rocky Mountain neighbours, Conrad O'Brien-ffrench was a cultured, well-spoken mountain-lodge proprietor who taught art at the Banff School of Fine Arts and loaned his lodge to Princess Margaret when she visited the Rockies in 1958. Behind that courtly façade, however, lay a shadowy figure with an intriguing past. If his autobiography is to be believed, O'Brien-ffrench was a restless adventurer who once worked as a British intelligence officer and may have been the inspiration for Ian Fleming's James Bond.

Just how much of his story is true remains a matter of conjecture. Traditional official secrecy surrounding anything to do with intelligence work meant that O'Brien-ffrench could make his secret-agent claims with impunity. However, it is known, from the parts of his autobiography that can be verified independently, that he established a new life for himself in Western Canada just before the Second World War, and that he made his home there until he moved to Colorado in the early 1970s.

Born in London on 19 November 1893, O'Brien-ffrench spent his early years at a villa in Italy, where he said that his father, Harry, an Australian-born idler of Irish descent, lived the life of a decadent nobleman on inherited money. The family returned to England when O'Brien-ffrench was eight and, when he was fifteen, he attended an agricultural school in Gloucestershire with the intention of becoming a gentleman farmer. In 1910, at age seventeen, he abandoned his agricultural aspirations and moved to Canada in search of adventure.

O'Brien-ffrench joined the Royal North West Mounted Police at a time when any youth who was medically fit would be accepted as a recruit. After training in Regina he was posted to a detachment in the southwestern corner of Saskatchewan, close to the Montana border. There, he broke horses and chased cattle rustlers for a couple of years until his mother, Winnifred, became seriously ill in England. By that time, O'Brien-ffrench had "fallen in love with the West and knew I would return to it later. But in the meantime I was impelled to return to England to be by my mother's side."

O'Brien-ffrench's mother died in 1914, just as the First World War was starting. He became a captain in the Royal Irish Dragoon Guards, which went to Europe as part of the British Expeditionary Force, and he fought in the Battle of Mons, Belgium, in August 1914. He was taken prisoner by the Germans and spent the rest of the war at an internment camp in Burg bei Magdeburg in eastern Germany where a fellow prisoner taught him to speak Russian. O'Brien-ffrench spent much of his time in captivity secretly gathering information from downed Royal Flying Corps pilots about German troop movements, and mailing the information as coded correspondence to a friend working in London at the British War Office.

In 1919, O'Brien-ffrench was hired by the War Office and posted as a military attaché to the British embassy in Stockholm, where his knowledge of Russian allowed him to exchange information with espionage agents operating in the new Soviet Union. From there he moved to Finland and then to India, where he served in 1921–22 as aide-de-camp to the visiting Prince of Wales.

O'Brien-ffrench left the military service in the mid-1920s. He spent the next few years playing polo, wandering around Europe, learning new languages, and studying art. Money doesn't seem to have been a problem for him because he was in no rush to find a new career. In 1931, he married a Swedish woman named Maud, for no other reason than "I was thirty-seven years of age and felt the time had come for marriage." Had he been wiser, he said, "I would have recognized that emotionally I was quite unfit for marriage."

The couple settled in the resort town of Kitzbühel, Austria, where O'Brien-ffrench established a travel agency, Tyrolese Tours, as a front to cover his newly assigned covert activities as a British intelligence operative watching the rise to power of Hitler's National Socialist party. He didn't make much money as a peace-time spy: "I was receiving less pay than a window cleaner." But he did the work because he thought it important. "I saw the Nazi cause as evil, although it had plausible, even most convincing, reasoning."

O'Brien-ffrench spent six years in Kitzbühel, and became acquainted there with the author Ian Fleming, then working as a correspondent for the Reuters news agency. They frequently talked about international politics. While O'Brien-ffrench never revealed that his real mission in Austria was to move in influential circles and keep tabs on Hitler, he suspected that Fleming must have known this, and used that knowledge when he later developed the charac-ter of James Bond, his most famous fictional spy. "I guess my life, with the number of glamorous people with whom I was associated at the time, could have served as his model," O'Brien-ffrench told a Vancouver newspaper reporter in 1970.

O'Brien-ffrench separated from Maud in 1935, shortly after their daughter, Christina, was born. Mother and child moved to Stockholm while O'Brien-ffrench continued his intelligence work in Austria, now posing as a self-styled international playboy "living the life of a dilettante on the continent." He did this until 1938, when Germany annexed Austria and began arresting people sus-pected of being anti-Nazi. O'Brien-ffrench fled to Switzerland, divorced Maud, and began to make plans to move to Canada. "I knew that the Germans had uncovered my activities in Europe and that I was a marked man." He pinpointed Vancouver Island on a map, and decided that was where he would settle.

O'Brien-ffrench bought a small acreage near Duncan, British Columbia, where he hoped he would "shut out the world with its dangers and discords." He renovated a house on the property, hired a man to work as cook and caretaker, and looked forward to "escaping from the cacophony of human minds and the end of civ-ilization as I knew it." However, in 1939 his country called him again to patriotic service.

O'Brien-ffrench spent the first part of the Second World War in Scotland inspecting companies that had applied for export permits to send goods to Allied countries subject to wartime censorship. He spent the last part of the war in Trinidad censoring mail. When he returned to Canada in 1945 he brought with him a new wife, Rosalie, whom he had met and married during a sojourn in Oxford.

The damp climate of Vancouver Island didn't agree with Rosalie so O'Brien-ffrench looked for a place in the Rockies where they might live. He found it eight kilometres east of Banff, a sixty-hectare tract of land that he bought from a coal mining company that was going out of business. He sold his Vancouver Island property, built a cottage, lodge, stables, and paddock on the Banff property, and called it Fairholme Ranch, after a nearby mountain range. He and Rosalie lived in the cottage and rented the lodge to long-term tenants for five hundred dollars a month. They had two sons, named John and Rollo.

From the late 1940s onward, the couple pursued an interest in ontology, the branch of metaphysics (later called attunement) dealing with the nature of being. They divided their time between Banff, where O'Brien-ffrench taught art courses at the School of Fine Arts, and 100 Mile House in the British Columbia Interior, where an ontology teacher named Lord Martin Cecil had founded a spiritual community. They also spent time in Loveland, Colorado, where an ontology master named Uranda had established a communal farm called Sunrise Ranch.

In 1954, when O'Brien-ffrench was sixty, his marriage dissolved. "Tough on me, tougher still on the kids, but Humpty Dumpty had fallen off his dream wall, and that was that," he wrote in his memoir. Rosalie and the children moved to Vancouver while O'Brien-ffrench remained in Banff.

In July 1958, Princess Margaret, Queen Elizabeth II's younger sister, made her stop in Banff. The twenty-seven-year-old princess stayed, not at the Banff Springs Hotel where visiting dignitaries normally stopped, but at the fourteen-room Fairholme Ranch Lodge owned by O'Brien-ffrench. The *Calgary Herald* described O'Brien-ffrench as a retired British army captain who had built the lodge as a "little bit of heaven away from the wartorn world." The newspaper said the federal government would lease the lodge for five days, and that O'Brien-ffrench would vacate it during this period so the princess could have "complete privacy." The *Albertan* added that O'Brien-ffrench would be paid a rumoured $100 a day to stay away from the lodge, but he hotly denied this.

Princess Margaret arrived by train from British Columbia on 26 July 1958. Tour officials said she would be "resting" in Banff after a hectic two-week tour to mark the one-hundredth anniversary of BC's establishment as a British colony. As a result, her official engagements would be limited to a short tour of the School of Fine Arts and a dinner at the Banff Springs hosted by the Alberta government. A mountain in the Fairholme Range would also be named in her honour. As for having "complete privacy" at the lodge, she would be sharing it with a dozen RCMP security officers and sixteen members of the Banff Springs housekeeping staff. With little else to report on, the newspapers focussed on the lodge and its mysterious owner, who was "believed to be in Banff but had skilfully avoided all reporters." In fact, O'Brien-ffrench was staying at the Banff Springs, where he met the princess at a

Conrad O'Brien-ffrench saluting a bear at the Banff nuisance grounds: "A little bit of heaven away from the wartorn world." (Whyte Museum of the Canadian Rockies V439/LC accession 2769)

cocktail reception. She thanked him for a "perfectly lovely visit to Fairholme, which she said had been peaceful, and beautiful, and very comfortable."

Using information gathered from his Banff friends and neighbours, the newspapers put together a detailed and fairly accurate summary of O'Brien-ffrench's life and career, but made no mention of his years spent as a secret agent. Nor did the papers mention that, at the time of Princess Margaret's visit, Fairholme Ranch was up for sale. O'Brien-ffrench had been trying to unload the place for a couple of years, without success.

The extensive news coverage surrounding the princess's visit gave O'Brien-ffrench what amounted to free advertising for his property. Within a month of her departure, he had sold the place to the federal parks department for "the fattest cheque I had ever endorsed." He moved to Vancouver to be close to his sons, buying a two-bedroom home in West Vancouver to which he added an art studio by building on top of the adjoining garage.

O'Brien-ffrench spent fifteen years in West Vancouver, watched his sons grow to manhood, painted in oils and watercolours, taught ontology, and held an exhibition of his paintings that was sponsored by the Ontological Society of Vancouver. He gave one newspaper interview during this period, in February 1970 to the *Lions Gate Times*, in which he talked openly about his life as a British Secret Intelligence Service agent. "Master spy lives in quiet retirement here," the headline said.

In 1973, O'Brien-ffrench sold his West Vancouver home and moved to the Sunrise Ranch in the foothills of the Colorado Rockies just north of Denver, where he started an art program for the commune's residents, contemplated the meaning of life, and wrote his autobiography. It was published in 1979 under the title *Delicate Mission: Autobiography of a Secret Agent*. O'Brien-ffrench died on 23 October 1986, a few weeks short of his ninety-third birthday. His ashes were buried at the Sunrise Ranch, which later opened its gates to the wider world as a spiritual retreat and conference centre.

Back to the Land–1968

Chief Robert Smallboy Creates a Spiritual Foothold in the Wilderness

In the shadow of the Rockies, a wild place of grizzly bears and clear mountain brooks, a group of Alberta Natives decided, in 1968, to travel back in time. In an age when many Native leaders were seeking to adjust to the demands of a modern world, Chief Robert Smallboy led twenty-seven families away from the security of their reserve at Hobbema, eighty kilometres south of Edmonton, to establish a wilderness settlement that would serve as a stepping stone to the past.

Smallboy, the salaried chief of the Ermineskin Cree band, was acting in accordance with his belief that the only way to get away from what he called the "contamination" of the white-oriented world was to abandon the reserve system and rediscover the lives of his ancestors. He had seen the indignities inflicted on his people by the white people and their liquor, especially after 1960, when the federal government gave Natives the right to vote and to bring alcohol on the reserves. Speaking through an interpreter, because he refused to use English, Smallboy told an Edmonton reporter in 1968 that alcohol was destroying the lives of his people: "I've seen an Indian controlled by alcohol, living out of garbage cans, looking for empty bottles. He would empty those, straining them for drinks. That's one reason why I don't drink." He also avoided television: "What the Indian picks up from TV is the bad habits of the white man—how to steal, how to lie, how to murder."

Smallboy decided that for his people to survive without the temptations of the white world they needed clear running water, fenceless forests, abundant game, and a religious sense of harmony with nature. He had lived as a small farmer at Hobbema, struggling to support his late wife, Louise, and six children on the returns from thirteen dairy cows before being elected chief in 1959, "and I had a vision that no family could survive on just a quarter section of land." When his appeals to the federal government to increase the size of the reserve fell upon deaf ears, the 70-year-old chief took his 105-year-old mother, four sons, two daughters, several grandchildren, and 143 followers—about one-third of the band—and settled on provincially controlled Crown land on the Kootenay Plains within the Rocky Mountain front ranges, sixty-five kilometres west of the old coal mining town of Nordegg, adjoining the David Thompson Highway. In choosing that location, Smallboy was following in the spiritual footsteps of Peter Wesley, a Stoney chief also known as Moosekiller, who rebelled in 1892 against a government prohibition on Natives leaving reserves without passes, and who took one hundred followers from Morley to live on their traditional hunting grounds on the Kootenay Plains. The Wesley band continued to camp there illegally until 1947 when the federal government gave them their own Bighorn Reserve on a two-thousand-hectare tract of land west of Nordegg.

Smallboy's breakaway band trucked in a hundred horses and dozens of dogs from Hobbema, parked their vehicles, and pitched their tents. They hunted, fished, farmed, foraged, worshipped the old religion, and danced the old tribal dances. "I will stay here and I will die here," said Smallboy. "That is something I cherish, living in harmony with nature."

A year after settling there, Smallboy told a reporter for *The Native People* that his people were enjoying the traditional way of life. There was plenty of open range for their horses and cattle, and those who were not farming were working as labourers at the nearby Big Horn Dam project. They were still living in canvas tents, because the Alberta government classified them as illegal squatters on provincial land, but they hoped eventually to acquire title and build permanent structures.

By 1970, concessions were being made to white ways. Although the government still considered them to be squatters, it looked the other way when a few of the residents replaced their tents with sturdier log and wood-frame houses. A power plant supplied electricity to two portable classrooms, where an Alberta public school curriculum was being taught along with lessons in Cree. "The way we are living is both Indian and non-Indian," said Smallboy. "The children learn the English way and at the same time try to maintain an Indian way of life. White-oriented education is good for the child; I respect it. But the Indians don't know how to use it." The teacher, a Native woman from Saskatchewan who lived in a construction trailer at the camp, had the only television, and it was supposed to be used strictly for educational purposes. But the camp's spiritual leader, Lazarus Roan, admitted that he occasionally tuned in to *Hockey Night in Canada*: "The only thing I miss on TV is the hockey games."

In 1971, a split developed when Smallboy and twenty-one families left the Kootenay Plains and trekked sixty kilometres north to set up a camp at a more secluded mountain hideaway, along a forestry road midway between the Cardinal and Brazeau rivers, just east of the Jasper National Park boundary. After the clearance work on the Big Horn Dam project was finished, Smallboy had decided that he wanted to move deeper into the wilderness. Six families, led by Joe Mackinaw, stayed at Kootenay Plains and established a less stringent set of rules for the camp, which included eliminating Smallboy's ban on consumption of alcoholic beverages. A further rift in the group occurred during the mid-1970s, when several people left the Smallboy camp and went back to Hobbema to apply for jobs created following the discovery of oil on the reserve. However, if he was disappointed to see his band dwindling to just twenty members, Smallboy didn't show it. His way, he said, "would be a hard choice for some Indians to make."

As it turned out, many of the Natives who left the Smallboy camp to take advantage of the sudden oil wealth at Hobbema later returned to get away from the growing problem of crime, spousal assault, and other violence triggered by widespread drug and alcohol abuse on the reserve. One of them, Fred Roan, said that at age eighteen he had all the money, sex and drugs he needed, but no sense of who he was. When he returned to the camp he stopped drinking and took renewed pride in the community's efforts to rediscover traditional medicines and dances.

While the camp's location, an hour's drive from Robb, the nearest community, was remote enough to keep most unwanted visitors away, it did draw a number of outsiders, including journalists, backpacking hikers, white hunters, New Age spiritualists, and a Hollywood stuntman who came to teach the Natives traditional dances he had used in the movies. Perhaps the most notorious of the visitors was American Indian Movement activist Leonard Peltier who was arrested by Hinton police, acting on a tip, while he was hiding out at the camp in 1976, and extradited to the United States where he was convicted of killing two FBI agents.

Smallboy's efforts to get legal title or a lease for the land were continually frustrated by bureaucratic buck-passing. Ottawa said it was up to Alberta to handle the chief's request because the province administered the land. But Alberta said that Crown land was a federal matter. An opportunity to draw public attention to the case came in 1980 when the white world recognized Smallboy's service to his people by awarding him the Order of Canada. Smallboy said he would accept the appointment so as to seek Governor General Edward Schreyer's support in acquiring land for his people. But he acknowledged that his chances of success were limited: "If I got the land, there would be other tribes or people that would want to make the same request to the provincial government. That's the only reason I haven't got this land."

Smallboy never received title or lease for the land. He was also disappointed in the government's failure to act on other Native requests. Because of this, in November 1980, he took part in one of the largest Native demonstrations that Alberta has ever seen. More than five thousand Natives, representing every band in the province, assembled on the steps of the Legislature to protest what they viewed as the Lougheed government's efforts to keep protection of treaty and aboriginal rights out of the new Canadian constitution. A century of broken treaty promises and unsettled land claims had left Smallboy and the other Native leaders with little hope that such traditional rights as Native control over reserve land and resources would be guaranteed by the constitution.

By the end of 1981, Smallboy's worst fears had been realized. The Trudeau government and nine provinces (excluding Quebec) voted to remove protection of Native rights from the constitutional package. Smallboy and his colleagues then took the battle to London, to launch a series of challenges in the British courts, demanding that the rights of indigenous people be entrenched in the Canadian constitution as they were in the British North America Act. During that trip, Smallboy and the Native delegation took time out to visit the Vatican, where they had an audience with Pope John Paul II. Smallboy told the Pope that the white man had more respect for money than for God.

The British High Court refused to hear the constitutional challenge. Chief Justice Lord Denning declared in January 1982 that jurisdiction involving Natives had passed from Westminster to Ottawa in 1867, the year of Confederation. However, a process of constitutional amendment by Canada's first ministers did eventually result in an affirmation of existing aboriginal and treaty rights and a principle being adopted that such rights are "guaranteed equally" to male and female aboriginal persons.

The affirmation of the treaty rights occurred in 1983 at a time when Smallboy was in failing health after suffering frostbite to his feet while searching for a restaurant on a severely cold winter night in Banff. For a month, he refused treatment. When he finally arrived at hospital in Wetaskiwin, sixty-five kilometres south of Edmonton, gangrene had set in, forcing amputation of one leg. He checked himself out of the hospital when the authorities refused him permission to use the Native healing ritual of burning sweetgrass because it set off a smoke alarm.

Smallboy never fully recovered. He died on 8 July 1984, at age eighty-six, at his home in the Rocky Mountain wilderness. "He was a man of great resolve, but not militant, and his story should be his monument," said historian Grant MacEwan. "He worked for Indian rights and even harder for Indian ideals."

Three years after Smallboy's death, the *Edmonton Journal* reported that his dream of establishing a traditional place in the wilderness for his people was gradually dying. The modern world's encroachments were proving relentless. The camp had a satellite dish to pull in the signals of the outside world, the residents lived in log homes with gas heating and generator-powered electricity, and most drove new cars to town when they went shopping. Oil royalties from Hobbema paid for the new vehicles. "The band has been baptized in oil," said Bob Smallboy, grandson and namesake of the late chief.

By July 2004, the trappings of the modern world were more in evidence at the camp than ever before. Big-screen TVs, video games, and the sounds of rap music were new signs of a world Smallboy and his followers had sought to shun. The one hundred residents were still squatting on Crown land but, after thirty-six years, they had no plans to move. Nor did the government, which had always looked the other way, express any intention of relocating them back to the reserve. "We've been here a long time, and we've buried our old people here, we're not about to be leaving," Chief Wayne Roan told the *Journal*. He was pleased to see that the enthusiasm for traditional ceremonies such as the three-day sun dance still existed, and he was proud to be chief of a place where young people could be free of alcohol and drugs.

Jon Whyte, Mountain Chronicler—1941-92

THE BARD OF THE ROCKIES LEAVES HIS MARK

Jon Whyte was the first native-born bard of the Rockies, a linguistically gifted poet and essayist who produced some of the most radical and innovative poetry to be published in Western Canada during the 1980s, as well as some of the most evocative and provocative columns ever to appear in Banff's weekly *Crag & Canyon* newspaper. He died in early 1992 at age fifty, much too soon for the rest of Canada to fully appreciate his literary gifts.

In his final column for the *Crag*, published on 21 February 1991, Whyte noted accurately that he had helped stimulate a revolution in writing and publishing in what some might have regarded as just another resort town with motels, tour buses, and souvenir shops: "If the quality of information visitors to Banff and its three adjacent national parks now receive is better and more accurate than it was twenty years ago—and I think it is—it is largely because I zealously praised that which was well done while deploring the shoddy, hapless research sometimes passed off because 'it's only a book for tourists.'"

Whyte could never have been accused of shoddy research or dashing off quickie books for tourists. He led by example. He showed that it was possible to live a literary life in small-town Alberta, put mountains on the writing map, and inspire others to do the same. He authored or co-authored half a dozen well-researched and well-written books about the history and culture of the Rockies, while encouraging others to achieve similarly high standards in research and writing. "He gave hope," fellow mountain writer Sid Marty said, "because he came out swinging, elegantly, against the forces of dullness and the pea-brained developmentalists who look at a wild river valley foreseeing nothing but golf courses." Additionally, Whyte wrote and published several well-received volumes of poetry. When he did his last column for the *Crag & Canyon*, he observed that he had written close to one thousand of these weekly newspaper essays that amounted to "a chronicle of this place which is our place."

Whyte made the Rockies his "place" starting in the spring of 1968 when, at age twenty-seven, he came home to Banff, the town where he was born in 1941. His grandfather was a Banff merchant who changed the spelling of his last name to White because the customers constantly misspelled it that way. Jon's father, Dave (Jack) White, retained the White spelling for business purposes after he took over the store. Jon's mother, Barbara Carpenter Whyte, was a teacher who moved in 1956 to Medicine Hat, where Jon completed his secondary schooling. By the time he returned to Banff he had spent nine years at the University of Alberta and Stanford University in California, completing postgraduate degrees in such diverse fields as medieval English and communications.

Initially Whyte planned to stay in Banff just long enough to produce and direct, for his Stanford master's thesis, a documentary film about the pioneering outfitter and guide, Jimmy Simpson. After that, he planned to apply for a teaching job at the University of Alberta. However, when he finished the Simpson film, he stayed on in Banff to continue the work of preserving natural history and culture that had been started by his uncle and aunt, Peter and Catharine Whyte, two landscape painters who spent their adult lives collecting the heritage materials for what would become the Whyte Museum of the Canadian Rockies.

To earn his daily bread, Whyte managed the Banff Book and Art Den, which he claimed—with some justification—was one of the three best bookstores west of Toronto. He became very adept at gently offering unsolicited advice, steering customers away from escapist literature toward more serious work, and he didn't think it at all unusual that the bookstore sold more Dostoevsky and Jorge

Luis Borges than Raymond Chandler or Erle Stanley Gardner. "There's no condescension here because this is a resort area," Whyte said. "Our main customers are not the tourists who go shopping for shirts on Banff Avenue. They're the music and drama students from the Banff School of Fine Arts, and the university students who work at the Banff Springs Hotel."

Whyte was not always the biggest fan of the Banff School of Fine Arts (later renamed the Banff Centre for Continuing Education) because he felt initially that it would bring too many new residents to town and thus magnified the housing crunch in a municipality limited in size by virtue of being located in a national park. Yet he did like the fact that the Centre's four hundred "bright and alert" students enlivened the cultural life of his community. "They're the best readers," he maintained.

By the early 1970s, Whyte was both manager of the Banff Book and Art Den and a partner in Summerthought Press, Banff's first publishing house. When writers Brian Patton and Bart Robinson were nearing completion of a manuscript for the first comprehensive trail guide to the mountain parks, Whyte and bookstore owner Peter Steiner formed Summerthought to publish it. The resulting book, *The Canadian Rockies Trail Guide*, appeared in 1971 and became a runaway bestseller. Thirty years later it was into its seventh edition, with more than 200,000 copies sold.

Using skills he had developed while working on student publications at university, Whyte edited and helped design *Canadian Rockies Trail Guide* and did the same for Summerthought's second publishing venture, *Banff Springs: The Story of a Hotel*, by *Guide* co-author Robinson. At the same time, Whyte pursued his own interest in writing. Summerthought's third publication, *Three*, was a book of poetry by Whyte, Charles Noble, and John Thompson. While selling books and editing the writings of others occupied most of his waking hours, Whyte regarded writing poetry as his primary calling. "Poetry is concerned with the quality of life," he said shortly after a segment of his first published poem, the epic five-part "Homage, Henry Kelsey," appeared in an Edmonton literary quarterly, *White Pelican*, in 1971. "If we're ever going to get the tribal history of this country done, it's going to be by the poets."

Whyte's own contribution to what he called the "tribal history" included books that he wrote or co-wrote about the Natives of the Rockies, the wildlife painter Carl Rungius, Lake Louise, and Lake O'Hara. He said that one of his favourite occupations, when not writing himself, was "encouraging other people to write the books I lack the time to write."

Whyte considered Henry Kelsey to be his spiritual mentor. A Hudson's Bay Company adventurer, believed by many to be the first white man to see and explore the Prairies, Kelsey led an expedition to what is now Saskatchewan in 1690, and later wrote about his experience in prose and poetry. Whyte initially viewed the poetry as doggerel and thought of doing a parody of it. "But, as I reread him, I kept hearing in his poem the genuine." Kelsey was, Whyte decided, an "ancestral voice." Instead of parody Whyte produced a tribute in verse that the Ontario poet Al Purdy hailed as "both epic and a celebration of the west that was."

Whyte began his career as a newspaper columnist at about the same time that he launched his career as a poet, bookseller, editor, and publisher. He wrote initially for the now-defunct *Summit News* in Banff and moved to the *Crag & Canyon* in 1974, when his friend Brian Patton became editor. While writing for a small-town newspaper might have seemed like a step in the wrong direction for a poet of serious purpose, Whyte welcomed the opportunity to expound on any subject that, as Patton said, "might rise to the surface of his highly eclectic mind." That meant the readers had to learn to expect the unexpected. On any given week Whyte could be writing about the changing seasons, his memories of childhood, his fascination with a squirrel that took up residence in Banff's Luxton Museum, or his contempt for the "villainies and injustices" of civic politicians that he felt were "eroding the spirit of the town."

He had the whimsical omnivorousness of the English essayists Laurence Sterne and Charles Lamb, and his interest in nature and the outdoor life paralleled that of Henry David Thoreau, one of Whyte's particular heroes. But Whyte was rarely pleased with his newspaper columns. He estimated that forty-five out of every fifty were just "filling space" and he rejected suggestions that the columns should ever be collected and published in a book. "I don't write them for that purpose," he said. "I put the durable stuff into my books. For a good time, read my poetry."

However, his friend Patton did feel that the columns deserved to be collected and bound. In 1992, a few months after Whyte died of liver cancer at age fifty, Patton republished a selection of the columns in a book titled *Mountain Chronicles*. "They should be available for those who missed them when they were first published," Patton wrote in the introduction. "And for the rest of us, we should read them once more and have them accessible, for they provide an important chronicle of this place. Our place."

The best and most accessible of the columns were charming, nostalgic evocations of the Banff that Whyte had known from birth to age fifteen, when he and three siblings moved to Medicine Hat with their schoolteacher mother. Whyte's writings about that formative period in his life were similar in theme to that of William Kurelek's Prairie childhood paintings. "We cannot go back," Whyte wrote, "but memories can be warm." The horse-riding school across the road from his house had been "a paradise any kid would wish never to leave" and the annual flooding of the outdoor skating rink always brought forth the first intimations of romance: "Skating hand in hand and consummating the affair with a not very secret kiss in the penalty box." (Strange symbolism there.)

Whyte's other columns reflected the love of obscure words and wordplay that also defined some of his poetry and prompted the Canadian novelist Robert Kroetsch to describe him as a "gifted word-buster, a crotchety bamboozler, a high country raconteur who takes readers on a trail ride clean around the world." One such column took readers to a storm-swept ledge where Whyte invited them to play a game of making up definitions for Alberta place names while waiting for the storm to pass. Didsbury, suggested Whyte, could be defined as an illicit relationship between an older woman and a younger man: "They're always seen near cheap Bowness motels but, if you're mixed up in *didsbury*, that's what you have to do." Kananaskis could be another word for being aggressively amorous: "He is nice enough in the bar, but when he gets you alone in the car he is so *kananaskis*."

A third type of Whyte column was the kind he wrote with what fellow Alberta writer Myrna Kostash called "real dash and withering indignation—to remind his readers that we live in circles of commitment to one another and all living things, and that the language of commerce and self-interest impoverishes our speech if it holds a monopoly." These were the columns in which Whyte rebuked the local tourism bureau, national park administration, Banff Advisory Council, and Chamber of Commerce for trying to lure too many people into an already crowded area, especially during those times of the year when the tourists were scarce and the residents should be able to relax, get to know one another, and "saunter, amble and otherwise enjoy the very reasons we choose to live here." His suggestion that the tourism promoters "should dry up and blow away like a tumbleweed" didn't endear him with the Banff business crowd, but it was entirely in keeping with the beliefs of this self-styled contrarian that he should complain that his town, his community, and his beloved Bow River Valley were being slowly destroyed by the "constantly gathering forces of darkness."

While Whyte's newspaper columns entertained and sometimes exasperated the townsfolk of Banff, his poetry brought him to the attention of the wider reading world. When the first part of "The Fells of Brightness," a long ("six thousand verses and growing") poem about the Rockies was published in 1981, Robert Kroetsch hailed it as "a poem on its way to greatness" and the poet Eli Mandel predicted that the finished work would be seen as a "creation of genuine power." In 1983, Whyte received the first Stephan G. Stephansson poetry award from the Writers Guild of Alberta for the complete book-length version of his homage to Henry Kelsey. By the mid-1980s, Mandel was calling him "one of the two outstanding radical innovators in Canadian poetry" (the other being Ontario poet Christopher Dewdney).

Whyte made a career switch in 1980 when he accepted an appointment as heritage collection curator at the Whyte Museum of the Rockies, a historical museum, art gallery, and library founded two decades earlier by his aunt and uncle, Catharine and Peter Whyte. While the job was paid employment it was also a labour of love because it allowed Jon to catalogue and document the materials that his aunt and uncle had collected over a lifetime. It also allowed him to continue writing. His daily routine now consisted of "showering during the sportscast, followed by an array of museum jobs for six or seven hours, and two or three hours of being an author."

Jon Whyte in 1986: "If we're ever going to get the tribal history of this country done, it's going to be by the poets."
(Whyte Museum of the Canadian Rockies photograph by Craig Richards, V692/PA133E-81)

Notwithstanding the demands of the museum job, Whyte actually became more prolific as a writer through the 1980s and into the 1990s. He also found the time to co-found and later serve as president of the Writers Guild of Alberta, as well as being active in such organizations as the Alberta Museums Association, the Canadian Parks and Wilderness Society, the Alpine Club of Canada, and the Banff International Festival of Mountain Films. At the time of his death in January 1992, Whyte was working on the third and fourth volumes of his projected five-part poetic series on the Rockies, and had taken what he had planned would be a two-year break from writing his *Crag & Canyon* column to complete a social history of the town of Banff.

Whyte received the liver cancer diagnosis in the summer of 1991 and told a newspaper interviewer a few months later that the medical prognosis was "guardedly optimistic." When he died, on 6 January 1992, his friends remembered him as a dedicated keeper of the spirit of Canada and our country's consummate mountain poet. "He died too young, he deserved more time," Myrna Kostash wrote in the foreword to a collection of Whyte's poetry, *Jon Whyte: Mind Over Mountains*, published eight years after his death. "He was hauled away in the middle of a thought, a passion, a meal, and we will never know what it was he was about to tell us, show us, summon us to . . . He would have made an extraordinary old man."

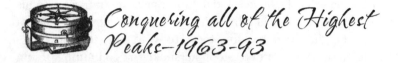

Conquering all of the Highest Peaks—1963-93

DON FOREST MAKES UP FOR LOST TIME

Don Forest didn't take up mountain climbing until he was forty-three, and then he started setting records with a vengeance. In 1979, after sixteen years in the mountains, he became the first climber to, as he put it, "knock off" all fifty-four peaks, eleven thousand feet (3,350 metres) and higher in the Canadian Rockies. (Eleven thousand is an arbitrary benchmark set by the alpine fraternity to separate the mountains from the molehills.) At age seventy-one, when others of his generation were golfing in Arizona, he became the oldest climber to reach the top of Canada's highest mountain, Mount Logan in the Yukon. Two years later, he became the first climber to scale all eighteen of the eleven-thousand-foot peaks in British Columbia's Interior Ranges. "They say that life begins at forty," he said. "For me, life began at forty-three."

It began in 1963 when Forest's oldest children, twins Kathy and Ken, decided to take up mountain climbing at age sixteen. Forest, wiry and physically fit, didn't want to sit at the bottom of the hill, drinking hot chocolate, waiting to drive the kids home. He wanted to go up rock faces too. He bought himself a pair of climbing boots and started accompanying the children on outings organized by the Alpine Club of Canada.

His first "eleven-thousander," Mount Temple in the Bow River Valley, made for a nerve-wracking experience. Forest was struck

201

with something called "sewing machine legs"—a nervous condition, well known to climbers, where the legs shake uncontrollably like a Singer gone berserk. Over time, Forest conquered his nervousness, but not his apprehension. He discovered that you climbed at a mountain's sufferance, and only got back down if the mountain allowed you.

Forest and his two children had spent a lot of time in the outdoors before they started climbing together. A lumberman's son from Hanna, Alberta, he learned to hunt ducks and rabbits with his father as a child and, when his children were old enough to carry a gun, he taught them to hunt too. His wife, the former Peggy Dalton, enjoyed the outdoors too, but she didn't go hunting or join the rest of the family when they took up climbing. Instead, she worked out at the gym and looked forward to going to dances with Forest when he came back from the mountains.

Dancing had brought the couple together in the first instance. This was during the Second World War when Forest was a radio mechanic at the Royal Canadian Air Force bombing and gunnery school in Lethbridge. Peggy, who worked at Eaton's, was one of the young women who attended the YMCA dances and volunteered to dance with lonely servicemen. "You were only supposed to dance with them once," she said. "But that didn't happen."

They settled in Edmonton after their marriage in December 1945. Forest took advantage of government funding for veterans to attend university and earn his electrical engineering degree. During the Great Depression, when the lumber industry failed and his father switched to farming and tried to make a living on a quarter section north of Prince Albert, Saskatchewan, there had been barely enough money in the household coffers to let Forest finish high school. However, the post-war government grants allowed him to parlay an interest in things electrical into a professional career. He worked at Alberta's provincial telephone company for three years, and then joined an Edmonton firm of consulting engineers.

In 1961, Forest moved to Calgary to open a second office for the Edmonton firm, Hilliker and Bishop. It was, he said, a good move for the family. All of his children were drawn to what he called "the mountains in our back yard." Younger daughters

Susan and Sylvia joined the rest of the family on the cliffs as soon as they were old enough to scramble.

In 1966, Forest learned the rudiments of skiing so that he and the family could enjoy the mountains even more. Daughter Kathy, who worked at Lake Louise as a ski instructor, taught him a few basic moves, and he learned the rest by trial and error. He laughingly characterized his cumbersome style as "mostly survival," but he was pleased that he could now explore mountain valleys as well as climbing to the tops of the highest ridges.

Forest said he liked mountaineering because of the sense of freedom it gave him: "Whenever you take out a licence to go game-bird hunting or fishing, they give you a book of 1,001 things you can't do. And you have to pay for it. When you go mountaineering, there are no rules. The only ones are those you impose on yourself for your own preservation." Asked about the dangers involved, Forest compared climbing with driving: "You can drive dangerously or safely, and you can climb dangerously or safely. I think I climb safely." Indeed, during his thirty-five years in the mountains, Forest suffered nothing more serious than a cracked tibia, some bumps to the head, and a couple of dislocated fingers.

During the summer of 1970, Forest climbed five major peaks in the Rockies accompanied by Glen Boles, an accomplished Calgary climber he had met three years previously. Over the next nine years, they pursued a common goal of tackling all the eleven-thousanders in the Rockies, encouraging, bolstering, and pushing one another to try again after every failed attempt. When Forest finally conquered his last eleven-thousander, Lunette Peak, on 19 August 1979, Boles was on hand to record the event in his diary: "We all shook hands, then gave Don an affectionate hug, for we were as happy as he was. He had just mastered number fifty-four."

Boles and Forest did much of their climbing with three other friends, Lyn Michaud, Mike Simpson, and Gordon Scruggs, and collectively they became known as the Grizzly Group. The friends had various explanations for the origin of the name. Boles and Simpson recalled that it stemmed from a close encounter the group had in the mountains with a bear. Forest maintained that it came from the fact that they all looked "grizzled" whenever they returned from a week-long mountain trip. Either way, the name became synonymous with the camaraderie developed among five friends who climbed together for thirty years. Whenever the Grizzlies were on the trail, the snakebite (a mixture of overproof rum and triple sec) flowed freely while Forest recited the poems of Robert Service. He found it soothing while venturing into the wilderness to quote the words of the Yukon bard who wrote about the "unharnessed big land" with the "silence that bludgeons you dumb."

During the early 1980s, while looking for other goals in the mountains, Forest added canoeing and backcountry horseback trips to the list of things he liked to do in the outdoors. In 1986, he climbed in the Himalayas for the first time, scaling peaks 6,000 metres and higher, and the following year he took on the challenge of becoming the first to climb all eighteen of the eleven-thousanders in British Columbia's Interior Ranges. He was now sixty-seven and showing no signs of slowing down.

In June 1991, with one BC eleven-thousander still left to go, Forest decided to take time out and tackle Canada's highest mountain, 5,959-metre Mount Logan in the Yukon. He had gone as high as six thousand metres in the Himalayas, and felt he was still strong enough to attain the same altitude. It wasn't an easy climb for him; he had to take massive amounts of antibiotics to deal with a urinary tract infection suffered on the way up. However, on 6 June he celebrated his seventy-first birthday on the mountain, and a few days later he became the oldest person in history to reach the Logan summit. His one-word comment in his journal: "Exhausted."

Forest climbed his last BC eleven-thousander, Mount Sir John Abbot, in May 1993, and once again his friend Glen Boles was on hand to document the occasion: "We followed the ridge on rock and loose snow, then slithered up through frost feathers to gain Don's remaining prize. And he was happy." Forest was even happier when he learned that his youngest daughter, Sylvia, had just earned her own place in mountaineering history as a member of the first all-female team to climb Mount Logan.

With his major climbing achievements behind him, Forest began taking more backcountry horse trips with daughters Kathy and Sylvia, both national park wardens, and scaled back his summit attempts from thirty to twelve peaks a year. He said it wasn't a matter of slowing down—he still had the stamina of a forty year old—it was more that he had already reached the remotest peaks and conquered the most difficult of them. With close to five hundred ascents to his credit, he had nothing left to prove. "I've climbed so many of them, I don't need to climb them any more." He had even named one of them, albeit unofficially. He gave the name Outlaw Peak to a small mountain in Kananaskis Country because he mistakenly thought that a neighbouring mountain, Banded Peak, was called "Bandit" Peak.

Forest continued climbing until he was seventy-nine, when a severe case of shingles left him without the strength to go up rock faces any more. However, he continued to ski in the mountains, and was cross-country skiing with daughter Kathy in the foothills southwest of Calgary on 27 November 2003—"doing what he loved best," as the death notice said—when he succumbed to a heart attack at age eighty-three. Kathy spoke for his friends in the mountaineering community when she wrote in a published memoir of her father, *Don Forest: Quest for the Summits,* that he would be remembered as a bold and talented climber whose "devil-may-care attitude carried him to the top of the greatest summits in Canada."

A side from the historians and biographers mentioned specifically in the text, I would like to thank the following authors for
writing the books that supported my storytelling in *Romancing the
Rockies: Mountaineers, Missionaries, Marilyn, and More*:

Janice Sanford Beck for *No Ordinary Woman: The Story of Mary
Schäffer Warren*; Anne (McMullen) Belliveau for *Small Moments
in Time: The Story of Alberta's Big West Country*; Barbara Belyea
for *A Year Inland: The Journal of a Hudson's Bay Company
Winterer*; Pierre Berton for *The National Dream: The Great
Railway, 1871–1881* and for *The Last Spike: The Great Railway
1881–1885*; Lawrence J. Burpee for *The Journal of Anthony
Hendry (sic), 1754–56*; Kathy Calvert for *Don Forest: Quest for the
Summits*; Jim Christy for *The Price of Power: A Biography of
Charles Eugène Bedaux*; Peter Erasmus and Henry Thompson for
Buffalo Days and Nights; Esther Fraser for *Wheeler* and for *The
Canadian Rockies: Early Travels and Explorations*; Harold Fryer
for *Alberta: The Pioneer Years*; Bruce Haig for *Following Historic
Trails: James Hector Explorer*; Carole Harmon and Bart Robinson
for *Byron Harmon: Mountain Photographer*; E. J. Hart for *The
Place of Bows* and for *The Battle for Banff: Exploring the Heritage
of the Banff–Bow Valley*; Athelstan George Harvey for *Douglas of
the Fir: A Biography of David Douglas, Botanist*; Paul Kane for
*Wanderings of an Artist among the Indians of North America from
Canada to Vancouver's Island and Oregon through the Hudson's
Bay Company's Territory and Back Again*; W. John Koch for
Martin Nordegg: The Uncommon Immigrant; David Leighton for
Artists, Builders and Dreamers: Fifty Years at the Banff School;
Grant MacEwan for *Fifty Mighty Men* and for *Métis Makers of
History*; James G. MacGregor for *Behold the Shining Mountains:
The Travels of Anthony Henday, 1754–55* and for *Peter Fidler:
Canada's Forgotten Explorer, 1769–1822*; Ann Lindsay Mitchell
and Syd House for *David Douglas: Explorer and Botanist*; Jack
Nisbet for *Sources of the River: Tracking David Thompson Across
Western North America*; James Ernest Nix for *Mission Among the
Buffalo: The Labours of the Reverends George M. and John C.
McDougall in the Canadian Northwest, 1860–1876*; Joseph L.

Peyser for *Jacques Legardeur de Saint-Pierre, Officer, Gentleman, Entrepreneur*; R. W. Sandford for *At the Top: 100 Years of Guiding in Canada*; Mary T. S. Schäffer for *Old Indian Trails of the Canadian Rockies*; Chic Scott for *Pushing the Limits: The Story of Canadian Mountaineering*; James K. Smith for *The Canadians: David Thompson*; Chief John Snow for *These Mountains Are Our Sacred Places*; Irene Spry for *The Palliser Expedition: An Account of John Palliser's British North American Expedition 1857–60*; Jon Whyte for *Indians in the Rockies* and (with co-author E. J. Hart) *Carl Rungius: Painter of the Western Wilderness*.

About Fifth House

Fifth House Publishers, a Fitzhenry & Whiteside company, is a proudly western-Canadian press. Our publishing specialty is non-fiction as we believe that every community must possess a positive understanding of its worth and place if it is to remain vital and progressive. Fifth House is committed to "bringing the West to the rest" by publishing approximately twenty books a year about the land and people who make this region unique. Our books are selected for their quality, saleability, and contribution to the understanding of western-Canadian (and Canadian) history, culture, and environment.

Look for the following books by Brian Brennan at your local bookstore:

Alberta Originals:
Stories of Albertans Who Made a Difference

Building a Province: 60 Alberta Lives

Scoundrels and Scallywags: Characters from Alberta's Past

Boondoggles, Bonanzas, and Other Alberta Stories